T. L. MAHRT

withstanding the Enemy

A CONTRACT FOR LIFE

I dedicate this book to my daddy;
the beauty of the yellow flowers you would pick from the fields
of greener grass will always brighten my days even years away;
I will always love you more.

Sunflowers

With their heads high,
They look to the sky,
Standing tall to pray,
As the Lord blesses them with more rays,
They're beautiful in every way,
Perfect with yellow flowers,
Moves slowly every hour,
They are a symbol of God,
As they praise him in every way,
I thank God for one more day.

Prologue

SHIT, THAT STINGS. The smell of alcohol penetrates my nostrils as I lift the soaked gauze from my already swelling cheekbone. *Man, he got me good this time,* I think as I assess the damage caused by his iron fist. The half-inch cut stretches along the thin layer of my cheek and my left eye is already swelling shut with a bluish-purple ring.

Damn, there goes my freedom. I know Rick will be locking me in the penthouse until all evidence of his abuse has disappeared. Disappointment fills my heart and I turn my attention away from the mirror—no longer able to look at myself.

I go over the events that caused me to be trapped in this damned prison again. Like I always do when I am alone and bruised.

At the tender age of sixteen, I ran away from my last foster home thinking I knew what monsters looked like: a fat belly under a filthy dishwater-gray wife-beater covered with the stench of cheap cigarettes; a man who was a drunk with wandering hands. I ran before that asshole had a chance to get to me, like he did with some of the other foster girls. Before I ran, I overheard a few of the girls talking about Rick Stevens, saying that he had a reputation of hiring young women and didn't care about their age as long as they were willing to work. They also claimed he provided accommodations along with decent pay.

Knowing he was my only real option, I made up my mind and set out to find him. I realize now that I didn't have a clue about real monsters back then. Even my youth, spent in the poorest of neighborhoods in New York City — where terror flooded the streets — pales in comparison to what being with Rick has been like.

Seven years … but it feels like a lifetime ago.

Rick's building is one of New York's finest skyscrapers with an abundance of floors (twenty to be exact), filled with guards buzzing around — all of whom are completely ignorant to my desperation.

The famous nightclub, which is the highlight of the building, is aptly named Club Envy and it takes up the first three floors of the building. I think Club Ugly is a more fitting name, with all the egotistical males flashing around their money and acting like chauvinistic pigs. All while women circle them like vultures starving for their next meal ticket. *I hate having to go to that place.*

Once, in an attempt to sneak away from the club, I was caught by one of the guards, named Chance. When he stopped me, he said he didn't want to report to Rick what I was doing, so I should return the way I came. He is definitely one of the friendlier guards — the words tall, dark, and handsome also come to mind when thinking of him…

I shake my head and turn my attention back to the black and blue eye staring at me in the mirror. I reach for the concealer in hopes of covering up the mess on my face, but my hand clumsily bumps into something and my eyes dart to the floor just as the concealer hits the hard marble and blows up in a puff of dust.

Shit, now how am I going to cover this? I think as I lean down to clean up the mess.

"Ms. Emma Andrews." A familiar voice sends a vibration of fear down my spine, stopping me immediately.

Chapter One

EMMA

AS HE LEANS closer his long finger traces my cheek down to my chin. He tips my head and his eyes lock onto my mouth —

A blunt force of impact jars me to an immediate stop. I inhale as the freezing water from my glass drenches me.

"Shit, that's cold," I swear. *Damn, I must have been daydreaming again. Did I just run into a wall?*

As I blink to clear my mind, the solid frame of a man's back covered by a black T-shirt comes into focus. My hands fly to cover my face, causing me to drop the glass. I jump as the glass shatters at my bare feet. The remaining liquid splatters my toes, sending a chill up my spine.

Two tree-trunk arms fold around my waist and I am briskly swept up. A faceless man carries me four or five powerful strides before coming to an abrupt stop. With my hands still blocking my vision, my senses heighten, causing the smell of clean linen to waft around me. His solid chest vibrates as his unfamiliar voice tickles my ear.

"Are you all right?"

My chest rises and falls as I labor to control my breathing. It isn't fear that has my body reacting — I know fear all too well. This is something I'm not familiar with. I can feel the energy between us — it's powerful and dangerous like fear, but I am not afraid. This is something else entirely. As my body reacts to this new energy, it grows hotter — feverish even.

The energy intensifies as our bodies merge and he sets me down. My feet land on the icy marble floor, cooling the growing heat of my body. I hear a raspy grumble as the faceless man clears his throat and let's go of me. The warmth of his body dissipates with his release.

"Miss, are you all right?"

Cowardly, I nod my head while still hiding my flushed face in my palms.

Two firm yet gentle hands encircle my wrists, tugging to show my face. I squeeze my eyes tightly shut, desperately wishing I could disappear.

A chuckle echoes in the hallway — of what I assume to be the foyer, judging from the direction he carried me. I open my eyes to the black T-shirt, this time focusing on the hard lines of his chest. He towers over me and a pulsing sensation sizzles through the air like lightning, licking my bare skin. I stumble backward as I try to look up at him.

"Ummm," I manage to mumble and quickly look away.

My eyes dart to the staircase in the foyer which leads to the second floor — my bedroom. The one place I can always run to. Taking another step back, I bump into an unforgivingly hard statue and lose my balance. I tumble toward the floor.

"Easy, I got you." He catches me effortlessly. "Your name's not Grace, is it?" He laughs as he steadies me on my feet.

"Umm, sorry … I…" My chest tightens.

"Hey, easy…" His tone reminds me of someone who is trying to calm a wild animal.

His voice eases my nerves and builds confidence within me. My eyes search for his, needing to see the kindness and tranquility I hear in his voice — something I haven't seen for some time.

His blue-green eyes suck me into their depths, as if dragging me into the ocean with no hope of escaping. I have an overwhelming sense that the man who possesses these magnificent eyes will turn my world inside out…

There it is — fear — kicking off my fight-or-flight reaction. As if in slow motion, I twist out of his arms and bolt for the staircase. Taking two steps at a time, which is impressive with my short stature, I clear it in record time. I scurry around the corner in the direction of my safe haven without so much as a glance over my shoulder.

Slamming the door to my room, I quickly duck under the covers. I close my eyes again, welcoming the darkness. I try desperately to think of anything else but the man I just ran into. Maybe I can drift back to the daydream that was abruptly interrupted.

Okay, where was I, on a beach, with a sexy man, someone to take me away...

A man like him...

Ahhhhhh! My mind races with thoughts of the man with the captivating eyes. I need a distraction.

I pull myself unwillingly out of bed and walk over to the walk-in closet. The realization that I am still wearing my loungewear hits me as I look back at my reflection. Rick will be expecting me in a timely manner for lunch. Lunch with him is the last thing I want to do today, but it's one of his rules: I must always eat with him.

I grab a pair of jeans, a V-neck T-shirt, and a bra and panty set. I know Rick will probably not be thrilled with my choice of outfit, but wearing his ridiculous dresses with the skyscraper heels isn't what I am feeling at the moment.

In my bathroom, I prepare the shower. As I begin to undress, I close my eyes to avoid my reflection in the mirrors. But not even closing my eyes can hide the scars that remain. The scars Rick has given me are deeper than the surface; they are engraved in my soul.

I quickly jump into the shower, trying to take my mind off of Rick. My eyes widen as the freezing water wets my skin. I rub my arms to get rid of the goosebumps.

Grabbing the shampoo, I begin to lather up my hair. I've been blessed with my mother's thick blond waves.

Mom...

I close my eyes and try to enjoy the feeling of the water as it eases the aches and pains of my muscles.

—

The depth of his ocean eyes comes to my mind again and sends a shiver down my spine. What was it about that man? Why is he affecting me in this way?

I shrug, trying to shake him from my mind. *Maybe I imagined him?* It wouldn't be the first time I twisted reality with one of the latest novels I was reading. I rinse the suds from my hair and watch them disappear down the drain. I am always getting in trouble for daydreaming. Rick hates when I escape to my own mind.

Yep, I'm sure I made him up.

ONCE DRESSED, I make my way to the vanity to figure out what to do with my hair. Grabbing the comb, I start working at my ends. A knock echoes through my bedroom, startling me. I take a quick breath and say a silent prayer that it isn't Rick.

"Who is it?"

"Ms. Andrews?" answers the British accent I know so well.

"Come in, Brutus."

You'd think someone named Brutus would be a large man, but this Brutus is quite the opposite. He's in his late seventies, not much taller than me, and can't weigh more than 120 pounds. His white hair and sucked in cheeks make him look frail — not the type of man one pictures a Brutus to be. He walks in and stands in the middle of my bedroom.

Brutus's accent always has me wondering if it is real or not. I mean, isn't it super cliché having a British butler? Maybe they train all butlers in butler academy (that's a real thing, right?) to sound British? I laugh at my own joke — someone has to.

"Please, Brutus, call me by my first name. Just to remind you, it's Emma." I wiggle one of my eyebrows.

The older man's soft blue eyes twinkle as he meets my gaze.

"Yes, Ms. Andrews, I know. I just don't want to get into a habit and slip up in front of the Master. You know how he gets about things of that nature. Everything must be formal."

—

8

"Okay," I answer with a playful pout. "You're right, Rick gets a little butt-hurt when we try to have fun."

"Ms. Andrews! Please watch your language. If Master were to hear you…" He shakes his head.

I lower my eyes. "I'm sorry, Brutus."

"I just don't want you to be swearing." He walks over to me and pats my head like a child. "Well then, it's a good thing the Master will not be home to accompany you for lunch today."

A sudden lightness washes over me. Brutus eyes me and continues, "Especially with the outfit you picked to wear. He would not have approved." He spins on his heel and heads in the direction of my door.

I follow him. "Brutus?"

He stops, turns, and faces me. "Yes, can I get something for you?"

The sweet old man is always looking out for me. He reminds me of a grandpa; that is, what I imagine a grandfather would be like since I never had one.

"Oh, no. I was just wondering, who was here earlier this morning?"

"Who are you referring to?"

"You know, the man that was in the foyer?"

"No, I don't believe anyone was here this morning—"

"The man in the foyer; he was wearing a black T-shirt…"

"I'm sorry, Ms. Andrews. No one was here."

"Are you sure, because I could swear—"

"No swearing, and yes, I'm sure. I would have had to let him in."

"Oh … yeah."

"Is there anything else, Ms. Andrews?"

I smile broadly. "Thank you, Brutus. No, I don't believe so."

"Very well, good day." With that, he turns sharply on his heel and exits.

I make my way back to the vanity. *See. You made him up, Emma. The man with the ocean eyes is a figment of your overactive*

9

imagination. Rick has finally succeeded in making you lose your mind. Mr. Ocean Eyes never existed – did I just give him a nickname? I really am losing it.

I sit down and let out a heavy sigh as a chime on my phone notifies me of an incoming text message. *What does he want now?* I think, knowing that it is Rick before I even pick it up and slide it open. I hold back an eye roll as I read the text.

I will see you at supper. Text me before leaving the penthouse.

I begin my response, already knowing what he wants me to say.

Okay, I will miss you. See you then.

I set my phone back down. I won't be missing him at all.

Chapter Two

EMMA

I HEAR THE sounds of pans banging and a low baritone voice reverberating through the doors as I near them. I pick up my step and walk through the swinging doors into the kitchen.

The kitchen, I imagine, is every chef's dream. Rick purchased only high-quality commercial equipment and the best pots and pans, which hang above the island. I find Rick's chef, Ms. May, on the opposite side of the island with her back to me. She sets a pot in the already piled-high sink. Her curvy hips swing as she sings in Italian, a language foreign to me, but one that sounds so romantic.

I stroll to the island that is set between us and quietly pull out a seat. Watching Ms. May at her craft has always been mesmerizing to me. Across the island, a large pot is on one of the many burners and my mouth is already watering from the aroma.

"Oh dear heaven, child!" a wide-eyed Ms. May yells as she notices me.

I let out a light chuckle. "I'm sorry."

"Honey, you are going to turn me gray, scaring me like that." Her once copper-red hair now glitters gray and is pulled back into the usual neat French braid.

"I think it's too late for that; it's already gray." I laugh.

"Okay, missy, now you are going to sing and dance with me for that remark."

"Oh, no I'm *NOT!*"

"*OH, YES YOU ARE!*" she says playfully.

She makes her way around the island and reaches for my arm, pulling me out of my seat. I know I have no way of stopping this.

She spins me, upping the tempo. We twist and turn about the room, causing my lungs to feel as if they are about to burst, and laughter spills from my lips.

In mid-spin, I see someone standing in the doorway. My heart jumps and I halt, immediately thinking it's Rick. I slowly turn to see who it is.

I let out my breath when my eyes land on Chance's large frame filling the doorway. He raises his hands up in the air, as if to surrender. He is wearing a sexy half smile.

Red hot heat rushes to my face when my eyes meet his.

"Please, ladies, don't stop on my account."

"Oh, you big tease, you just about scared the life right out of her," Ms. May says as she saunters back to her original position. "Plus, pretty boy, I don't give free shows," she teases.

I look at Chance and he winks at me before returning his attention to Ms. May.

He walks past me and takes a seat at the island. In a low, sultry voice he says, "Name your price and I will double it for dinner and the show."

Ms. May waves him off dismissively.

"Come on, honey," Ms. May points at me, "have a seat and let this old mama teach you a thing about men." I obey and take a seat. "First, all men think with their stomachs — and this one has the nose of a bloodhound." She waves her cream-covered spatula toward Chance. "He can smell food a mile away."

"Two miles away," Chance says, wiggling his dark eyebrows at her.

"See, I can't cook anything without this stray walking in here." A smile deepens her laugh lines as she points her spatula back at Chance.

12

"Now, Ms. May, I'm at least your favorite stray," Chance says smoothly.

The bantering between them leaves me thinking that this isn't a rare occasion. Chance must visit her often—though it is my first time seeing him here.

"I will let you think you're my favorite today, but as for my price for a show, you can't handle the price of this old lady."

He sighs heavily and leans back. He lifts his arm and positions it on the back of my chair. Turning his gaze, he locks eyes with me. I feel as if an earthquake roars through my body, causing my hands to shake. The playfulness that sparks in his eyes now resembles longing.

Longing for who, me?

"Well, Ms. May, then it's a good thing I have this beautiful woman sitting beside me."

In the few interactions I've had with Chance, he's always been a bit on the flirty side, but this statement is beyond that. My stomach tightens and I immediately avert my eyes and focus on my hands in my lap.

Ms. May giggles.

"Like I was saying, the way to a *GOOD* man's heart," Ms. May emphasizes the good part, "is through his stomach." She turns her eyes to me. "You better start paying attention, sweetheart, and start learning to cook."

We all laugh, and I am grateful to her for lightening the mood. It is hard not to enjoy time with Ms. May. She has a way about her—an easy and carefree way of living that I admire. Secretly, I wish I was more like her.

Ms. May sets the plates in front of us.

"Bon appétit," she says with a little bow.

The aroma reaches my nose and causes my mouth to water. I hadn't even realized that I was famished until the large helping of creamy chicken alfredo was set before me.

I look up at Ms. May. "Are you going to join us?"

"Go ahead and start. I will save myself a plate. I need to start cleaning up and getting dinner prepared."

I turn to Chance to see he is already digging in.

—

13

"So good … as always … it is … my favorite," he says with his mouth full. I chuckle and pick up my fork, nibbling slowly. I want to savor my meal. As I think about my childhood and remember the days with nothing more than the food I found in the dumpster, I feel blessed by the full range of flavors that are set before me now. I take my first bite and let out an unintentional moan that I immediately regret. A loud clink brings me back to the kitchen and my eyes dart in Chance's direction. His eyes, and mine, move quickly to the fork he dropped on the floor. I hear a tsk-tsk coming from Ms. May.

I look back to Chance. His eyes are glued to his plate as if the whole thing could disappear if he looks away. He shifts uncomfortably in his seat and I put my hand on his left forearm.

"Are you okay?"

He clears his throat. "Yeah."

I sense his discomfort, so I sharply move my hand and shoot Ms. May a puzzled look. She chuckles.

"Eat, child," she says, waving for me to continue.

What is happening? I wonder as I return to my food.

Chance quickly gets up from his seat with his plate, walks to the sink, and rinses it off, readying it for the dishwasher.

He turns to Ms. May. "Thank you for the amazing meal. Hopefully, I will be able to join you ladies again soon." He smiles and looks at me.

I expect to see annoyance in his eyes, which is Rick's usual reaction, but I don't; instead, I see an intensity in his warm brown eyes. The depth is as powerful as Ocean Eyes', but the warmth is not as intimidating. I watch him as he turns and walks out the kitchen door. I release a breath I hadn't realized I was holding.

What the hell was that?!

I get up to clear my plate. "It was amazing, Ms. May."

"As payment you can help me clean up and decide what to make for dinner."

"You know that's my specialty." I chuckle as I walk to my post behind the sink.

She moves to the cupboard and pulls out her tattered cookbook, hugging it to her thick middle like a long-lost friend. She looks up at me. "Oh, and remind me to teach you how to cook that particular meal sometime. You're going to need it." She sways her curvaceous hips and starts humming something low and seductive.

I ignore her and turn my attention to the stack of dirty dishes piled high in the stainless-steel sink. The events from lunch roll around my head and I try to make sense of it. Mindlessly, I begin loading the dishes in the green tray and then slide the first batch into the dishwasher.

Ms. May leans her hip on the counter, blocking me from grabbing another tray.

"Honey, what do you know about men?" she asks frankly, and I feel a flush of warmth to my cheeks. "From what I just witnessed; I have a feeling you don't know much."

I look away from her and begin rinsing off the rest of the pots and pans.

"What do you want me to do with the leftovers on the stove?" I ask, changing the subject.

She lets out a heavy sigh. "Just leave it. I will take care of it." She goes back to her questioning. "Didn't your mother teach you anything about men?"

The thought of my mother sends a stabbing pain to my chest. "No, I was fourteen when she died. I was in and out of foster homes before coming here." I suck in my bottom lip, pulling it between my teeth and biting down.

"Yes, sorry. You were so young. No wonder you're clueless."

I watch as the water ripples down the pan and washes away all the debris. I wish I could wash away all the dirt from my soul, wash away all the painful memories that haunt me.

She begins to portion out the leftovers, somehow sensing my discomfort. From the corner of my eye, I see her exaggerate her hip swaying again, making me roll my eyes. I know her well and I brace myself for the full spectrum of the conversation; she isn't going to stop.

"Where to begin to make sure you are properly educated, dear. Do you know about the birds and the bees?"

"Yes, of course, I'm twenty-three, for heaven's sake!" I snap at her.

"I just wanted to be sure." She shines her mischievous smile at me. I think she enjoys making me squirm. "I sense that you don't want to have this conversation. So I will just tell you one thing and I want you to think about it hard." She starts stacking the containers into the fridge. Leaving one out, she grabs a marker and writes her name on it. She takes her time, intentionally building up the suspense and theatrics.

Good old Ms. May and her drama…

"If a man is interested," she finally continues, "he will try to find ways to be around you. He will treat you good, too."

I think of how Rick is hot and cold to me, buying me things one minute and then in the next, beating me. I need to change the topic—quickly. "Ms. May, how long have you worked here?"

She helps me put the last tray into the dishwasher and lets out a sigh. "That's a long story. I can give you a shortened version of it, though."

She pulls the lever down, closes the lid, and starts the dishwasher. She turns back to me as we both lean our backs against the counter. "I was friends with Rick's mother. We were extremely close. When she got sick, she asked me to watch over him. He was so young then. After she died, Rick's father started drinking heavily and would take it out on him. I didn't like his father much and I had to protect Rick from him many times." She pulls away from the counter. "Rick has kept me employed, though, and honestly, he is very good to me." She turns, staring down at me.

"Rick is *NOT* a bad man, but he is not a *GOOD* man either. He is lost at times," she says, sniffing and dabbing at the corners of her eyes.

I cross my arms and hug myself as I imagine a little boy curled in the corner of a dark room, crying for his mom—something I know all too well. Ms. May's last words, "He is lost at times," causes a sharp stabbing pain in my gut. *Rick's father was a monster.*

I look at Ms. May as her soft gray eyes return to their usual light, bright spirit.

"Chance sure is a good-looking fella—and charming, too. He would be in trouble if I were a few years younger." Her laugh lightens the mood.

My own laugh echoes and I grab the dish towel hanging off my shoulder. I wring it with my hands as my mind wanders to just how handsome Chance is. I quickly dispose of the rag in the dirty bin under the sink.

"Thanks for lunch, Ms. May. I have to get going to the library."

"But we haven't talked about what to do for supper." Her bottom lip turns out as she playfully teases.

"Sorry, but I really need to get going. I'm hoping Ms. Gale has some volunteer work for me. Plus, you know all my favorite dishes anyways."

She gives me a knowing look and raises her arms at me as she lets out a chuckle.

"Okay, if you must go…" She dismisses me with a wave of her hand and turns back to the cookbook as I walk out.

Chapter Three

CHANCE

THE ELEVATOR DOORS squeak shut. I lean my back against the cold mirrored wall as the iron box roars to life and slowly descends. I whistle Ms. May's little tune and the image of Emma laughing and dancing replays for the hundredth time.

God, she is gorgeous with a smile.

Thinking how—if she were mine—it would be my daily goal to see that beautiful smile. *If only she were mine.* The elevator pulls to a stop on the fourteenth floor. I step out and head in the direction of my apartment. Having been up for nearly twenty-four hours, I can feel the exhaustion starting to hit me hard. I pull the keys out of my pocket just as my phone jumps to life. It's Rick.

"Hello."

"Mr. Fletcher, I will be home around four p.m. You are to meet with me at my office no later than five p.m. I need to go over a few changes."

"Yes, sir, I will be—"

Click. Rick hangs up. *What an ass.*

I walk into my dorm-size apartment and throw my phone and keys on the overly crowded table which is covered with research papers and to-go boxes.

I look down at my watch; I have three hours to get some sleep before meeting up with Rick. Stripping my clothes off and gathering them up, I toss them in the bin in the corner. I drag my feet the last few steps in the opposite direction to my bed.

I lie down and stretch out. In only my boxer briefs, the coolness of the sheets against my body eases my nerves. I let out a deep breath and close my eyes. Emma's sweet smile floods my consciousness. *How can she be with Rick?* She seems so innocent.

Emma's moan echoes in my ears causing my body to kick up a few degrees.

Shit, so much for sleep…

EMMA

I SCAN MY room to make sure I didn't forget anything. "Okay — books, check — gym bag, check — "

All right, ready!

Satisfied I have everything, I grab my phone and type out a text to Rick.

Going to the library, then pool.

Not expecting a response, I shove the phone in my back pocket just as it chimes.

Stay in the building, back to penthouse by 5:00 pm. Ready for supper at 6:00, no later. We will be going over some changes around here. I can't have you being late. Then three dots appear showing he is typing. *Have a nice swim.*

I almost drop my phone. I grip on to it tightly, rereading the last line. Rick never responds, let alone: *Have a nice swim.*

What do I say? Is he testing me? And what changes is he talking about? Most of the time I know what he wants to hear, but when Rick is unpredictable, it's a scary thing and it's happening more often lately.

I decide to not respond and pray it was the right decision as I put my phone back and pick up my gym bag.

The elevator opens and I step in, thinking of what book I

want to get lost in this time. I light up the number seven button to head to the small library as my mind drifts to my conversation with Ms. May. What was she hinting at between me and Chance? I jump as the elevator signals a stop that brings me back to reality.

I step into the private hallway, where shades of purple color the walls and extra-large burgundy chairs sit on either side of the elevator door. A hundred-year-old golden chandelier hangs low in the middle of the room. I admire its beautiful grace as I make my way down the hall.

I open the door to the public passageway, which is decorated in a more modern, sleek design with glass windows that show an unbelievable view of the hustle of New York City. I look out to the hazy streets, and the memories of living on those streets haunt me.

I shake my head to clear my thoughts, and feeling more focused, I turn in the direction of the library. The library is the smallest of the businesses on this floor and is privately owned—the other shops include a coffee shop, bakery, and pizza shop—but the library is tucked away in the farthest corner, as if it is being isolated from the world.

Once I reach the library, the smell of old books overtakes me immediately. I enter and a feeling of safety washes over me. Books have that effect on me. I didn't have a lot of books growing up, but the few I did have were great treasures and sources of comfort to me.

I look around the disorganized library to see books thrown askew across the shelves and papers sitting disheveled along the desk. *Oh, Ms. Gale.* I roll my eyes.

"Hello, Ms. Gale?" I shout, though I know you are supposed to whisper in a library.

"Yes, dear, I'm in the A's—you know—the biographies." Her frail voice echoes against the walls.

"Okay," I answer. "Be there in a minute."

I walk behind the desk in the center of the room and set my books in the return pile so I can check them in later. I lay my bag under the desk and make my way to Ms. Gale.

I find the little, fragile old woman standing on a ladder, trying to reach a book on the top shelf. She is stretched as far as she can go.

"Oh, dear me, I must be shrinking in my old age."

"Here, let me help you so you don't fall."

Ms. Gale chuckles as she climbs down slowly. "Well, you can try, but you're not much taller than me, dear." She steps off the ladder and moves aside.

I laugh. "No, I'm not, but if I fall, I won't break like you. Plus, I am tough and can handle it."

She shakes her head. "Yes, sometimes too tough, I'm afraid."

I ignore her and continue up the ladder. "Now, what book do you want down?" I ask when I reach the top.

"*The Diary of a Young Girl.* The one by Anne Frank," she says with a sparkle in her eyes and pointing at the book on her tippy-toes. "Oh, how I love that one."

I turn back to the books and reach up—also having to go onto my toes. I stretch as far as I can. "I … I … GOT IT!"

"Yaayy." Ms. Gale jumps up and down before ripping it out of my hand when I step off the ladder. I shake my head and laugh as I follow her back to the desk. Ms. Gale sits down in front of the register and gleams up at me.

"Child, the history I have with this book…" She pauses. "I lost the first one I owned years ago. I thought I would never see it again. Then, one day, someone donated a stack of books, and sure enough, there it was. You see here." She points to her initials on the edge of the spine. "It made its way back to me." She fans her fingers over the worn cover. "My husband bought this book for me as a wedding gift. That's when I discovered the love of reading…" She trails off and I notice her eyes are glistening.

I watch as her eyes haze—she is clearly lost in her memories. The last time I interrupted her when she was like this, she acted as if she didn't know where she was and who I was. Ms. Gale is at the beginning stages of dementia and her health leaves the library's future in limbo. As she gets lost in her mind, I feel another sense of urgency to convince Rick to let me work here.

I decide to leave Ms. Gale to her memories and walk over to the return pile to help her get caught up. There are two piles, with eight to ten books in each stack. I pick up the first pile and walk over to the computer—fully equipped with a system that dates back to the early nineties. One by one, I go through the pile, logging in the books. I notice most of the books are the ones I borrowed, but I also see a few books on the early wars which are not mine. I also spot a book about poetry that immediately sparks my curiosity.

I look them all up in the dinosaur-aged system. There is no information associated with them. *Of course! Ms. Gale probably just hands them out.*

God only knows who has books out that will likely never get returned. As her dementia progresses, she clearly isn't even checking books in or out, and I can't keep up with it all within the little time I am allowed to help.

I walk over to the second pile just as Ms. Gale comes back to reality. "Oh, thank you, dear. You didn't have to," she says in a barely audible whisper.

I turn to her. "Anytime. Plus, most of these books are the ones I borrowed anyway. I might as well put them away for you."

In a dreamy hen click, she says, "Maybe, but this week there was a young gentleman. He was quite dashing and had the dreamiest eyes. Reminded me of my Hank, when we first met. Oh, how handsome he was…"

I wait for her to elaborate, but she falls silent and I know she has gone into her mind again.

I continue to log in books, almost on autopilot, as my own mind drifts to a pair of my own dreamy eyes—Ocean Eyes. Those haunting eyes can easily suck you into another world.

I blink a few times and chuckle. It's like I'm a kid with an imaginary friend … named Ocean Eyes…

Maybe I should pick a different genre to read this week. Clearly those romance novels are causing my imagination to run wild again.

I laugh at myself and get back to work.

Chapter Four

EMMA

AFTER SPENDING FORTY-five minutes at the library, I leave with my next book tucked under my arm and my gym bag over my shoulder.

I make my way back to the private elevator that is inconveniently across the far side of the building, thinking that if Rick would just give me access to the stairs, I could walk down the few floors to the pool instead of always waiting for the slow elevator.

As I enter and press the button for my floor, the door makes a slight moan when it shuts, and I instantly remember being in the kitchen with Chance. He probably thinks I am so childish, moaning over my lunch. If I explained to him my background, would he understand?

AFTER MY SWIM, I sit down on one of the benches, still feeling the high of endorphins. I begin drying off as I admire the all-too-revealing peach bikini that Rick would never let me wear in public. There is something about the striped suit that I enjoy and a surge of mischief sparks deep inside. *What would Chance think if he saw it?*

The main entrance doors suddenly fly open and Brutus rushes in my direction. I feel my breath stop.

The old man reaches me, and I hear him huffing for air. "Ms. Andrews —"

"Emma," I tease, trying to ease my own panic.

"Ms. Andrews, you're needed back at the penthouse right away."

"Okay." My mind races. "Do I have time to change?"

He looks me up and down. "Best if you do, but you must hurry."

CHANCE

THE PILES OF papers lay scattered across the table — *a puzzle with missing pieces.* I scan them again, trying to make sense of it all. "Just report back" was The Lieutenant's one and only command. But I can't help but try to piece it all together myself. It is in my blood to try to solve the puzzle. For fifteen years I was in the military and it was my job to take down the bad guys. Much like this job, I was always undercover. But after my last high-risk assignment — I shake my head as my nightmares cloud my subconscious. Yeah, I needed a change of pace. *Just report back; don't get swallowed up; don't drown in the memories —*

The alarm sounds on my military watch, signaling it is time to leave. An uneasy feeling washes over me, and I stand knowing this uneasiness has nothing to do with the monsters storming my head.

STANDING AT THE main entrance to the second floor of the penthouse, I hear the door handle rattle. An elderly man dressed in what appears to be a butler's uniform steps out to greet me.

"Mr. Fletcher, we have been expecting you."

I extend my hand. "We haven't had the pleasure of meeting —"

He looks down at my hand with no interest in shaking it

---

before interrupting me. "We have not met, although I have heard a great deal about you from Ms. May." I drop my hand. "I must say, Mr. Fletcher, I do not approve of you sneaking around. But unfortunately, I have no say when it comes to who Ms. May entertains in the kitchen."

In a sharp turn, the old man steps into the foyer. I quickly follow him and shut the door behind me. I fall a few steps behind as I take in my surroundings. Though I am accustomed to the third floor of the penthouse — the kitchen — I haven't had an opportunity to explore the top two levels of the penthouse. At least not since I did an override on the card system allowing me access to the full penthouse.

Shit, maybe that's what this meeting is about. Does Rick know I did an override on the key system?

I am led into a generously sized foyer with grand stairs lining both sides. An ornate chandelier hangs low and is the main focal point of the room. It casts a warm glow, making the gold flakes in the black marble floor flicker.

At the next door on the right, the butler stops and slips into the doorway, shutting the door and leaving me behind.

I am too impatient to wait, so I follow the old man to find him talking to Rick — who is sitting behind an oversized antique wooden desk. The desk is placed in front of floor-to-ceiling shelves that are stacked with books.

"Master, Mr. Fletcher is here for your meeting," the older man says.

Rick, who is in his mid-forties, clearly takes great pride in his appearance, I think as I notice his strong build and sharp clothing. He simply stares at the older man with cold emotionless eyes.

"Brutus, is Andy Marshall here yet?" Rick finally demands.

Brutus takes a step back. "No, he is not here yet."

Brutus visibly shrinks and curls his shoulders. His demeanor is quite different than when he was speaking with me. Since taking this assignment, what I've found most intriguing is the inner dynamics of Rick's household. Watching

---

the interaction between Brutus and Rick causes a few more puzzle pieces to fall into place. *But I don't see Lenny,* I think. He is Rick's assistant and constant companion. They are always together so it is odd to see Rick alone.

Rick waves Brutus off. "I want to speak with Mr. Fletcher first. Do go get Emma; tell her it is urgent that I see her. She will be at the pool."

"Yes, Master," he says with a bow before disappearing through the doors.

"You wanted to see me?" I finally speak.

"I'm sure you have noticed the extra men I have hired. I will be demoting some of the guards we currently have. New guards will be placed in their positions."

"Yes, sir. I have noticed the extra bodies on guard. If I may ask, why?"

"Yes, you may. There has been a compromise in our security operations. And until I find the rat in the building, only a select few are to be trusted. Stakes are high right now. I am putting a team together—guards I trust. These select few will be working closely alongside me."

What is he hiding? What does he not want people to know?

"Sir, what is it that you need from me?" Adrenaline surges through my body.

Rick spins in his chair, stands, and rounds the desk. He straightens his back to meet the five inches I have on him.

"Well, as for the select few, I want you as one of them."

He relaxes a bit and walks around me. As if to size me up.

"I also want James Burns, Dean Hopper, Brett East, and Andy Marshall as my select few. I know you are associated with a few of these men. Does that work for you?"

His question is more of a statement as he appears to be gauging my reaction. *Do I finally have his trust?*

I stand erect, holding my position. "Yes, sir."

"You will each begin specific job training which is essential to protecting the future of this company. Can you handle such responsibility?"

I nod my head to acknowledge him.

"In fact, the two most important positions will be yours and Mr. Andy Marshall's."

There's that name again. At one point or another I've worked with all the men except him. In fact, I know all of them well. But I've never heard of Andy Marshall before.

Rick walks back to his desk and takes a seat. "Mark Nash will now be in command of the security department, taking over your position. He will already be briefed with the details."

Now there is a name I know, *Mark Nash*. He is one of Rick's new goons, and worthless, if you ask me.

"What is my new position, sir?"

Rick shuffles through a stack of papers on his desk. "I have a few things to check before going into further details. Go ahead and have a seat for a minute." He gestures to the chair.

I take a seat and begin studying the room. To my left are more bookshelves filled with volumes that appear to be centuries old. I wonder if Rick has them for decoration or if he actually reads them. I hear the door open and close behind me announcing someone's arrival.

"Thank you, Brutus. You are dismissed," Rick says before I have time to turn around.

I hear Brutus close the door behind him and I turn to see Emma standing in the doorway, wide-eyed. I follow Rick as he stands to greet Emma. I watch him round the corner of his desk, quicken his advance on her, and he backhands her across the face. The slap vibrates through the room with enough force to knock her to the floor, halting me in my tracks. Emma curls up on her side as if expecting another blow.

My fists ball with so much volition my knuckles go white. I dig my fingers hard into my hands to control my impulses as images of different ways to hurt Rick flood my mind. *I could kill him in a split second...* My training kicks in, and I relax my fists and evaluate the situation.

Instantly, I notice the Taser in his hand and the smugness on his face. *This was a test, a fucking test ... but why...?* I conjure a blank expression on my face, removing all emotion and tension from my body.

"Ah," he says, walking over to me with a nasty gleam in his eyes and a smirk on his lips.

He shoves the Taser into the pocket of his slacks and places his filthy hand on my shoulder. "I know I can trust you. You are now part of the select group," he says as he walks back to his desk.

My eyes land on Emma, who is still unmoving. In that moment, I make a silent promise to her. *You will be free of this asshole, even if it is the last thing I do.*

"Emma, leave now and go to your room," Rick demands.

She quickly picks herself up and rushes out of the room.

He glances at me for a brief moment. "Your assignment is different than the others and is critically important." He pauses for some reaction, but I give him none so he presses on. "I heard that you've been paying Ms. May visits from time to time and you have even eaten meals with *MY* Emma. Typically, this is an act I would have disciplinary action for; however, it seems that you have Ms. May impressed." He sits straighter in his chair. "Do understand that *NOTHING* goes on in this building that I don't know about ... and Emma is mine to control...

"I have purchased the library for Emma. She will be busy with the renovations. I'm concerned for her safety. You will be assigned to ensure her safety at all times. I will be sending you an email with her schedule and what I will be expecting of you. Do you understand what I am asking of you?"

"Yes, sir. When am I expected to start my new assignment?" I say rather robotically.

"Bright and early tomorrow morning. You are to report to the kitchen no later than eight a.m. I will be meeting with Mr. Marshall in thirty minutes. We are going over the final details. For now, you will report to him for further details and training. He is strategizing a meeting for all the men to meet sometime this week."

Rick stands and makes his way to me, then extends his hand out. I rise to my feet to meet his hand and shake it firmly. *He wants me to protect Emma... But how will I protect Emma from him...?*

He stares into my eyes. "Don't fuck with me and screw this up. I only give you one chance to do this right."

He drops my hand. "You may go."

Chapter Five

EMMA

DARKNESS SURROUNDS ME as I cover my throbbing face with the pillow—drowning out the rest of the world. *What did I do this time?*

I pull myself up in bed and grab my journal. Poetry has always been my way out; a way to let my emotions free—without consequence.

I finger the worn tatters of the black leather spine of the journal. I open the beloved book and flip to a clean canvas. *A canvas—this is my art.* I close my eyes to absorb my emotion, using the power of words to paint the picture. The words swim in a sea of dark thick blues. Opening my eyes, I let my ballpoint pen scribble...

> *My thoughts spin inside me,*
> *Buzzing all around like a bee;*
> *Growing as high as a tree,*
> *Making me want to flee.*
> *Instantly, I go down to my knee,*
> *Saying a little plea;*
> *These thoughts whispered in my ear,*
> *I pray they will all disappear.*
> *Feeling the dark grow near;*

It is all too unclear
just how severe
I'm falling.
Falling, falling.
Covering my face, sobbing;
My little heart, I'm guarding;
In the dark, I'm starving;
Hugging my knees, I'm breaking;
This life, I'm wasting;
For light, I'm craving.
Craving, craving.
To God, I'm praying;
The light for my saving;
These thoughts to disappear;
That day would be dear;
To start a new year,
With bright new starts,
And big, open hearts.
To feel free,
I wish that were me!

A booming knock echoes through my room and I bolt upright, flipping my journal closed.

"One minute," I say, in a rush to shove my journal into my nightstand and straighten the bed covers.

Rick barges in without warning. "I was being polite with the first knock, don't make me wait. Be ready for supper by seven o'clock; Brutus will escort you to the dining room," he says, standing inches from my face.

He lifts his hand to my cheek, and I flinch as fear runs cold through my veins. He briefly hesitates. "I hate leaving marks on your beautiful face." He rubs his fingers surprisingly gently across the tender spot.

I avoid making eye contact with him but he lifts my chin. His dominating personality commands my full attention. Our eyes meet. "You know I love you and everything I do is to protect you, don't you?" Uncertainty shadows his face as he questions me.

"Of course I know you love me. You provide for me," I say in a shaky voice, my chest squeezing. My stomach flips as bile rises in my throat. I stare directly into his cold green eyes and let out the statement I know he is waiting for. "Thank you, Rick."

His eyes warm and I fear what is to come next.

He brushes my cheek, again and looks down my neck, stopping at the top of my shirt. His eyes flame brighter, and he grips my nape, applying force to tilt my head. Squeezing my eyes shut, I ball my fists. His lips brush mine. And he pulls away briefly before he crashes down onto my mouth— devouring hungrily. My lips stiffen to a straight line, hard and unwelcoming. He breaks away and places his hands on each side of my face. "My sweet, sweet Emma," he says in a raspy voice.

I open my eyes, not recognizing his voice.

"*YOU'RE MINE!* All mine, sweet girl," he says, kissing the top of my head.

He turns sharply and walks out of the room, leaving me stunned.

He never loses control...

Chapter Six

EMMA

"MASTER, MS. ANDREWS is here to join you," Brutus announces my arrival.

Rick is at the head of the large oak table. He looks up at me and begins to rise but stumbles with his chair in a nervous gesture.

He quickly regains his composure. "Thank you, Brutus. I can take her from here."

He walks around the table and extends his arm for me to take. Again, an act out of the ordinary for him. He leads me to the table. Stopping by my chair, he looks me over with a sultry smile which causes my stomach to tighten. He hooks a finger in the top strap of my black halter dress, just above my collarbone, and runs it down the strap, causing a chill to erupt across my skin.

His eyes run the length of me, stopping just above my knees where my dress ends. A groan rumbles low in his chest when his eyes land on my black heels. I start to rethink my decision to wear this dress the minute he reaches around my hips and pulls me against him. I place my hands on his chest and create space between us. He leans in to kiss me and I turn my head, landing his lips on my cheek.

He quickly releases me and steps back, clearing his throat. "One day, Emma, you will desire me the way I desire you," he says, pulling out my chair loudly. "I will be patiently waiting for that day. I will tell you this only once: *Do not* push me away tonight. Do you understand?" he says firmly as he pushes me in.

"Yes, sir, I understand. I won't do it again."

"Please call me Rick," he quickly corrects.

Brutus walks in carrying a tray of salad and drinks. He seems to sense the tension in the room and quietly busies himself by setting the drinks and salads down in front of us and quickly leaving the room without a word.

Rick nods his head for me to begin and I pick at the salad. *What the hell is he up to?* He is so hot and cold. I can usually gauge his mood, but with how fast he is changing it, my nerves are on alert.

I jump as Brutus reappears from the corner of the room, picking up the salad plates as we finish. He adds a bottle of wine to the table and Rick waves dismissively at him and takes over filling our glasses. Rick holds out his glass to make a toast and I pick up mine.

He smiles. "To us and to the future of our love." We clink our globes together, and I bring mine to my lips and play the role.

The wine curls in my mouth and rolls over my tongue. The taste of sweet peaches blooms in my mouth and I realize this is one of my favorite Moscato's. "The wine is very lovely. Thank you."

He reaches his hand over and embraces mine. "I know it's one of your favorites and I wanted to do something special for you tonight." He picks up my hand and guides it to his lips. His lips brush over my knuckles. I study him. He is dressed in a gray suit with a white shirt—a few buttons undone at the top where a tuft of black chest hair peeks out.

Brutus acknowledges his presence with a cough, which gives me the perfect moment to free my hand. "Master, your dinner has arrived," he says as he sets the plates down and removes the silver domes.

My eyes light up to see Ms. May's famous spaghetti. I look up at Rick as excitement bubbles and I bounce in my chair.

Rick tucks a strand of my hair back. "You're beautiful when you smile. I wish to see more of that in the future."

"Thank you! I love spaghetti..." I look down at his plate also covered in the delicious meal. "I thought you didn't like — "

"I like it. it. It is more of the memory I have with the meal that I don't like. Tonight, we will be changing my memory and creating a new one."

My mind fumbles to absorb Rick's confession. Never before has he talked about his past. *Why now?* I don't know how to respond to this side of him. I search his face to read his emotions. *Is that pain?* Quickly, his expression reverts back to steel, hiding any emotion I might have thought I saw. A vision of Rick as a little boy pops into my mind.

"Love, eat," he commands.

My eyes roll to the back of my head with the first bite. It is delicious. I lean my head back in pure enjoyment — but I am purposeful not to moan again. When I open my eyes, Rick is staring intensely at me. I quickly grab my napkin as heat burns my cheeks. "Sorry."

He shakes his head and chuckles. "No, it just amazes me how you act with food. I love watching you eat."

"Oh, uhh, I told you — "

"Yes, I know how you were brought up with no food on the table and I don't care to discuss it tonight." The humor fades from his eyes and in its place, I see anguish. *Does it pain Rick to hear about my childhood?* As quickly as before, the emotion disappears.

"Umm... It's just Ms. May has been helping me work on my table manners and I was hoping I improved for you."

He slams his fork down, making me jump. "Ms. May does *NOT* have the right to change anything about you without my order. This is not something I want to change. Do you understand?" he says with a deep growl.

"Yes, sir ... Rick, I understand."

"Now, please eat. I have somewhere for us to be in a half hour," he says, his tone softening again.

I pick up my fork and we eat in silence.

Chapter Seven

EMMA

WE FINISH UP dinner just as Brutus walks in to clear our plates.

"We are going out for a walk," Rick informs me.

"Okay, thanks again for the wonderful supper."

"You're welcome, but the night is not over yet."

He stands and pulls out my chair. He reaches around for my hand to help me up and brings my hand to his lips and kisses it again. Unwavering warmth expands my chest and I feel my cheeks glow. I hiss. His eyes dilate and he seizes my reaction by pulling me to his chest and kissing a path up my arm.

What the HELL, Emma!

"How I love seeing you blush." Rick lands another kiss, higher up my arm. "It makes me want to see just how deep red I can make your cheeks."

My cheeks flame and I feel a spark of arousal burn within me.

Why is my body deceiving me?

My brain is telling me to pull away from him, but something has me frozen—fear?

Yeah, FEAR. I'm truly fearful of any other emotion associated with Rick. Yes, it's fear.

He tongues across my collarbone, sending the foreign

burning feeling into my stomach. He tilts my head to the side to have better access to my neck, which causes my heart to skip a beat.

My nipples tighten and I hiss out another breath. *Shit ... Stop...* I will my body to listen.

Bang!

I jump and wrap my arms around myself.

"Damn it, Brutus. What the hell are you doing?" Rick snaps.

I look over to Brutus, who stands with a mess of shattered dishes all around him. "I'm sorry, Master, I'm sorry. I will have this cleaned up right away."

"Yes, you will, and you are lucky that I don't take it out of your pay." Rick turns and pulls me toward the door to leave.

"Yes, Master," Brutus calls out.

I turn my head to see Brutus picking up the broken pieces. He meets my gaze and winks. Hiding my smile, I wink back at him.

Thank you, Brutus!

THE DOORS OF the public elevator open wide and Rick clasps my hand and guides me toward the library. As we round the corner, my eyes widen in surprise.

"NO WAY!"

In shock, I meet his green eyes. "Surprise!"

I let go of his arm and bolt to the library's front entrance.

The biggest red bow I have ever seen covers the doors. I pick the card off the bow and open it:

> *To my sweetest Emma,*
> *This is for you, my love.*
> *Rick*

"You're giving me the library?" I ask in disbelief.

"Yes, love. It's all yours!"

"I don't know what to say." I reach up and kiss him on the cheek. Heat grows in my face and I look to my feet, shocked at my own actions. "Thank you, Rick," I whisper.

I look up again and his smile brightens his tan face and his eyes grow warmer. "There's more inside."

I chuckle as I finger the oversized bow. "How do we get in?" I ask, looking for the handle.

Rick's low laughter bounces off the tiled walls. "Well, we cut it," he says as he pulls out a pair of gold scissors from his suit jacket and hands them to me.

"The honor is all yours, love."

Leave it to Rick to have gold scissors, I think as I hold back an eye roll. I take the scissors from him and examine the bow for the best point to cut but Rick interrupts me.

"Here. If you cut it on the side of the bow it will all fall in one piece," he says and points to the left of the bow.

I snip the giant thing and watch it as it curls its way to the floor. I hear the jingle of keys and turn my attention back toward Rick. He holds the keys out for me to unlock the door.

"It's all yours," he repeats.

"Thank you, Rick. I don't know if you understand what this means to me."

He steps aside. "Just unlock it. I want to get to the best part."

My breath catches in my chest as I turn the key. Fear punches me in the gut. *What if this is a sick game he is playing?* I exhale as the key turns and the doors open. The smell of old, dusty books greets me, and I feel an overwhelming sense of security.

My escape.

Rick starts flipping on the lights one by one. I walk to the desk in awe. *This is all mine now.* It doesn't look any different from when I left it earlier, but it feels different. I run my hand across the counter, my mind already pounding with ideas of what I want to do with it.

"Do you love it?" Rick asks, bringing me back to reality.

I look up at him from across the counter. "Yes, oh yes, I do.

I have so much I have been wanting to do with this place—update the system, bring more books in, paint the walls... Wait—" I stop in mid-sentence. "What about Ms. Gale? Oh God, is she okay?"

Rick grabs my hand and pats it. "I bought it years ago from her husband when she started showing signs of dementia. Her husband and I made a deal. She was to continue to run the library until she was unable to. When he died, her son and I sat down to come up with the same agreement. About two weeks ago, her son came to me and informed me that she was going to be placed into a care home." He leans down and kisses my cheek. "You will be given an unlimited budget to make this your dream come true."

"*REALLLY?* You would do that for me?" I spin around with a giggle.

Rick wraps me in his arms, and my cheeks glow. "Yes! My love, I would a hundred times over to hear that giggle of yours."

It's hard to imagine Rick having a compassionate side and it is causing my mind to play tricks on me. Ms. May's conversation rolls into my consciousness.

Maybe Rick is just a scared little boy looking for someone to love him?

His hands shake as he reaches for my left hand; he is searching my face for something, and confusion clouds my mind.

"Rick, are you okay?"

The minute the words slip out my mouth, fear sets in. I never dared to ask him that before but with his unpredictable behavior...

His eyes meet mine. "I'm not a good man, Emma. But I want to be a good man for you. Please be patient with me."

My mind numbs and all words escape me. *What is he talking about?*

"Please, Emma." He hesitates before reaching for his back pocket and goes down on one knee. "Please marry me?" He opens a black velvet box containing an enormous round solitaire diamond set in a thin gold band.

My mouth drops open and an overwhelming sense of nausea hits me. I dive into his eyes and an unfamiliar flash of emotions flickers to life.

NO! But not only NO, HELL NO! I want to scream. *He just backhanded you, throw that in his face along with that* HELL NO! Why would I ever want to marry this man? This man has caused me so much pain. But I remain frozen, unable to respond.

Rick stands back up. "I will never let another have you. I love you more than anyone else can. And from our past, I know I can't force you to love me. But I promise I will let you take your time in wanting me. You will see just how good we can be together."

Just how good we can be together? I can't BE with him.

He picks up my left hand and places the ring on my finger. He pulls it to his lips and kisses it. "I am willing to give you time to desire me. But I am not willing to take no for an answer. Remember, Emma, I only have so much patience in me."

OH, HOLY HELL! How am I going to survive this?

I nod my head.

"Good." His face comes alive. "Now let's go celebrate."

CHANCE

I ROLL MY shoulders in an attempt to ease the tension as I walk into the club—which is my last choice of somewhere to go since I don't like large crowds—but I need a distraction. I need to block the image of Emma curled up on the floor. And after ignoring James the first three times he called, I finally gave in.

Fuck, let it go before you do something stupid—like take Rick out.

I immediately spot James at the bar with three women surrounding him. I instantly recognize one of the girls from the coffee shop. *Damn, I wish I could remember her name now.* I should remember it with the dozen times she wrote it and her number on my coffee cup.

As I make my way over to the group, I begin assessing my surroundings—a habit that carried over from my training in the military. James is wearing dark denim pants and a steel gray button-up shirt—much like how I am dressed for the night. The woman to the right of James has short black hair sitting just above her shoulders with a dark purple dress hugging her slender body. The woman to her right and directly in front of James is tall and built like a supermodel with a black skin-tight, see-through dress with a neon pink bra and panty set. Her long, curly brown hair reaches all the way to the middle of her back. She is obviously digging on James and by the look of it, she is every bit his type with the way he is leaning into her.

The last woman is the one I recognize from the coffee shop. She is shorter than the others and her curves are barely covered by a tight midnight dress. Out of the three women she is more my type, other than her hair color. She has the long hair that I like to wrap around my wrist, but the color is an odd shade of pink.

Her steely blue eyes glance over to me as I stroll up. I give her a smile before James breaks out of the circle and stretches to throw his arm over my shoulders. He slaps my chest and gives the ladies his full attention. "See, what did I say? I knew I could get him out tonight. Am I the man or what?"

"Yeah, okay, whatever makes you feel better about yourself," I laugh and shrug him off.

I look for a bartender and wave him down. "What will it be? I got this round."

His lip curves. "Hell yeah, man! I will take a Bud Light. And these beautiful ladies have been drinking vodka-cranberries." He winks at the ladies. "By the way, this is Jenny, Stephanie, and I think you know Bridget. She works at the coffee shop."

"Hello, ladies. I hope you are enjoying your night hanging around this guy…" I say, pointing in James's direction.

Jenny, the one digging on James, says, "Oh, he is a charmer." She gives him a flirty giggle.

46

James walks around the group and slides his arm over her shoulders, tucking her into his side. Just then the bartender asks for our order and breaks the awkwardness.

I quickly rattle off our order and watch as the bartender starts to prepare our drinks. I feel Bridget come to stand closer to me. I steal a look over at James, who nods his head eagerly.

I did tell myself I needed a distraction tonight...

"So, Bridget, you come to the club much?" I meet her eyes.

She leans closer and I feel her breast press against my chest as she slides her hand up. She flutters her fake eyelashes and makes her intentions evident.

"I came to see you."

Her directness is not a turn-on for me, but I take the bait anyway and turn on full male pursuer. *I need a distraction,* I remind myself. I cover her tiny hand with mine and give her my award-winning smile. "Well, it's a good thing I'm here."

She practically buckles at the knees. And the thrill of the chase dissipates with the knowledge that this isn't even going to be a challenge.

Bridget and I quickly find ourselves in a private little cream-colored booth on the upper balcony.

I watch as the different-colored lights dance, creating a hypnotic atmosphere. Bridget pushes into my arm as she closes any gap between us. "Would you like to dance?" She runs her hand up my leg.

I look down as she glides her fingers in circular motions. I clear my throat. "No, I'm not much of a dancer."

I feel as if I have a pit in my stomach that grows with every circular motion of her fingers. I close my eyes to stop the spinning in my head. Emma's warm smile floods into my mind's eye.

"Maybe, if you want, we could leave..." Bridget brings me back to the loud club as her fingers glide dangerously higher.

My manhood having its own mind—hardens. *Damn.* It's been longer than I care to admit since I've had a woman in my bed. But it isn't the woman next to me that I picture underneath me. No, that isn't the odd shade of pink hair I see lying across

---

my pillow... *Only Emma's golden blond...*

I shake my head. "How about I get you another drink?"

I look up, but my eyes don't focus on Bridget. They lock with the one person I do want my lips on—*Emma.*

Our eyes remain locked for what feels like an eternity.

Bridget nudges me, breaking the connection. "Chance!"

I pull away from her. "I'm sorry, I can't do this."

I don't give her time to respond and I get up to leave.

Nearing the exit, I hear the music come to a stop.

"Ladies and gentlemen, we have a big announcement for you tonight," the DJ rings out, stopping me in my tracks.

My gut hits the floor. I know—for whatever reason—I am not going to like this. Frozen in place, I silently hope I am wrong.

"I want to give a shout-out to my man Rick and congratulate him on his engagement to Emma Andrews. Put those drinks up and cheer the happy couple!" he echoes.

FUCK! I ball my hands in fists.

Time to purchase a punching bag and gear.

EMMA

MY INSIDES HEAT with Chance's penetrating stare and everything around disappears from sight. The liquid flame licks my skin. *Ohhh.* It feels as if he is touching me, sending my nerve endings into overdrive as a ripple vibrates through me.

In an instant it's gone. A lingering roll of smoke spirals around me.

Chance.

Rick invades my consciousness with a nudge as he guides me to the VIP section of the balcony. I quickly sit and look back to where Chance is sitting.

I watch as Chance stands. At this distance it's hard to make out his expression, so I focus my attention on the woman he is

—

48

sitting with. With her eyes wide, she reaches for Chance's arm. He quickly turns and makes a hasty advance toward the staircase that leads down to the dance floor.

What was that all about? And who is she? My chest heavies.

I scan the dance floor for Chance's broad frame just as I hear the music stop, leaving a humming in my ears nearly deafening me. All I can make out from the DJ's announcement are the words... Rick ... engagement ... and my name. *Why did he have to tell everyone?* My stomach clenches and my cheeks heat. I hate being the center of attention. It's so embarrassing.

What was that look all about? Thinking about Chance's eyes locked with mine causes a wave to ricochet through me. *Did I affect Chance the same? Did I see desire? Emma, you're doing it again; your imagination is wild.*

Clearly Ms. May is right about one thing—I don't have a clue when it comes to men.

Rick snaps his fingers. "Love, what would you like to drink? I am ordering a round for the whole club."

I focus on his broad smile—he is handsome with his honey-colored skin, defined features, and green eyes peering down at me.

"Umm ... I will take a white wine, please."

I watch as people congratulate him on his way to the bar and it takes everything in my power not to roll my eyes as the scene plays out. My hatred for this club burns deep in my veins and I begin craving the serenity of my room.

I FIND RICK at the bar, people surrounding him like a mob, handing him shot after shot. As I approach, he starts waving people off and picks up our drinks from the bar and we make our way back to the VIP section.

"We are only staying for one drink," he says, handing me my wine. "I still have a few things I want to talk to you about." He holds out his glass for us to make a toast. "To our future, my love!"

I take a sip and he turns to face me as he places his hands around my waist—pulling me toward him. Surprising me, I part my lips. His mouth lands hard on mine and he drives his tongue into my mouth.

I lose myself within the kiss, burning out the roller coaster of emotions. A stab of need crashes to my center in waves. I moan into his mouth as pure hot lava washes over me and I deepen the kiss, wanting to drown in it. My skin pulses, and I wake to my body's reaction, quickly pulling away from him.

I hear a roar of people cheering us on.

Rick moves away from me and picks up my hand. "Sweet love! I have been waiting for that," he says, kissing my knuckles.

Uneasiness curls in my stomach and I pull my hand from his. "Excuse me. I have to use the ladies' room," I say and walk away without waiting for a response.

I slap my hand to my forehead. *What in the hell are you thinking?* You promised yourself to never, and I mean *NEVER*, kiss that asshole. It was the only thing you had control over.

I feel a sliver of, what?—passion—burrow deep into my heart. "You're an idiot!" I reprimand myself quietly. "This is Rick; you're thinking of … *RICK*. How can you have any kind of feelings for him?"

A knock on the bathroom door causes me to turn and I see Rick walking in. I feel my body and mind at war.

"You've been gone for a long time, my love."

He stops only a foot in front of me, too close. I can feel my body heat radiating off of him. And a flush builds in my cheeks.

I look to his solid chest and lie. "Yes, I'm sorry. I don't think supper is setting well with my stomach. Please forgive me for rushing off."

"Then let's get you home."

Chapter Eight

CHANCE

BANG! BANG! BANG!

The muscles in my shoulders twitch as I jab another blow to the punching bag. Sweat drips down my face and my mind races. Rick sent his email this morning with all the responsibilities of my new position and all the rules Emma must follow. The control he has over her is maddening. But what is even worse is that she's going to marry him.

Fuck. Thank God for this bag.

Bang! Bang! Bang!

I picture Rick's fucking face and land a hard kick. *Bang!*

I roll my shoulders and play over my new routine. Every morning I report to Andy Marshall for training. Rick wants to ensure I am properly trained to ensure Emma's safety. If Rick knew my training, he would know that I am probably more qualified than this mysterious Andy fellow.

Grabbing my towel, I wipe my forehead and gather my gym bag.

Time to finally meet Andy Marshall.

EMMA

MY EYES FLICKER as I roll over in my bed. My mind is foggy, but I am trying to concentrate on anything but Rick.

Anything. Ocean Eyes comes into my mind and I smile. *No man could be that perfect, Emma. It's all a dream. Those Ocean Eyes aren't real!*

My mind spins back to all that has happened in the last twenty-four hours. Slowly, it starts flashing a slide show: the hit to the face, the library, Rick's proposal, Chance, the kiss.

The kiss...

The proposal... I look down at the huge rock on my finger. *OH SHIT, that really did happen!*

I squeeze my eyes tight, blocking out reality and letting my mind spin.

I hear a roaring of waves echo in my ears—piercing through the blackness. A fog rolls through the corners of my subconscious, casting a shadowy silhouette of a muscular frame. I watch the shadowed man turn to face me and my imagination builds, as I am expecting to be greeted with Ocean Eyes, but no. Chance's chocolate eyes blaze to life as he stares into my soul.

A knock on the door rips me back from the shadows and I lose the vision of Chance's warmth.

Like always, I say a little prayer that it's not Rick. Especially after last night's events. Another knock—louder this time.

"Come in," I holler at the door reluctantly. I stand and start making the bed.

"You can come in," I say as I smooth out the last of the wrinkles.

No answer. Odd. Maybe Brutus didn't hear me. I walk around the bed to the door.

Opening it, I don't see anyone standing on the other side. Instead, there is a large arrangement of roses just outside the door. The roses are different shades of purple, ranging in hues of soft pinkish purples to the deepest rich plum. I gasp at their beauty. There has to be at least a hundred of them, if not more.

Stepping into the hallway, I wonder how I am going to get them into my room. Footsteps echo down the hallway and I turn to see Brutus hurrying in my direction.

"Why, Ms. Andrews! These are just lovely." His face lights up.

I greet him with a smile as he walks around admiring them. "Yes, they are!"

"How do you suppose we should get them into your room?" he asks.

"I was just thinking about that. They look heavy and I don't want to drop them."

"I have an idea. Don't you fret — oh, here is a card," he says, handing it to me.

I take it from his hand and he nudges me back into my room.

"Now, go get ready and let me handle this."

I chuckle. "Okay, okay."

He shuts the door in my face, and I look down at the dark purple envelope in my hand. My name is written in golden ink with the most beautiful penmanship. *Do you really want to open it?* I think, assuming they are from Rick. I'm not sure I can handle any more from him.

I turn the envelope and tear it open. I pull out a piece of lavender card stock with a note written in the matching penmanship.

To my beautiful enchantress,
  From the moment I laid my eyes on you,
  I've fallen.
  Your sorcery has deep magnetism,
  Making you irresistible to me.
  For it is you, I have fallen in love with;
  I will wait for you till my last breath, that is the spell I'm under.
                                                                    -Rick

My heart skips a beat. It's beautifully written. I never knew Rick was capable of such poetic beauty. It stirs something foreign inside me. I throw the card down. He is a monster and I need to remember that.

And I know just the way to do that.

———

I storm into the bathroom, mad at myself for even authenticating feelings for him. I turn on my shower and let the water warm up. I take my clothes off with shaky hands as I mentally prepare myself for what I am about to do. With all my clothes in a pile at my feet, I think, *You can do it — remember what a monster he is.*

I turn to face the mirror with my eyes closed. *Come on, Emma, you can't forget… One… Two… Three…*

I open my eyes to see my full reflection. My hands fly to my mouth to silence my cry. A tear slides down my cheek as I examine my torso. Running a hand across the scars, I can feel the crack of his whip as it tears open my skin. *I remember it,* I think as the shadowed form of a man haunts my nightmares. *It was Rick, it had to be Rick,* I think as I hear the shattering crack of the whip through my head. Don't forget. *He is the monster — the shadow.*

My mind races as I continue to run my hands down my torso. *I — I can't feel the scars.* The skin under my fingers feels smooth as silk, as if the scars weren't there. I frantically look down to my stomach. *I see them — bright red and raised.*

My hands tremble as I glide them over each side of my hips. I force myself to look down at the larger scars lying horizontally across each hip.

Why can't I feel them?

My right thumb rubs across my birthmark on my upper thigh. Inside the heart-shaped mark is a scar that mimics my own heart — broken with no hope of repair.

He is the monster, I think as I hop into the steaming spray of the shower.

I GRAB A towel and dry off. The library is going to be a great distraction, I think as I wrap the towel around me and make my way over to the vanity — thankful the mirrors are steamed over.

Absentmindedly, I open the bathroom door and walk toward the closet when I hear voices in my room, causing me to freeze mid-step.

"Oh, Ms. Andrews, I thought you were already dressed," Brutus announces his presence from behind me. I quickly turn around and hug my towel tighter to my naked body.

My eyes lock with Chance's. Instantaneously, my heart dips low into my belly. I stand frozen, watching his eyes run down the length of my body, causing heat to catch like wildfire and spread over my chest. I follow the path of his eyes — a slow lazy path down my body. My nipples tighten as he lingers for a moment. His eyes flame as if he can see right through my towel. The wildfire causes my sex to throb. I feel needy and my eyes heat with passion. I take a sharp inhale.

Brutus breaks the connection. "Ms. Andrews, we will leave immediately," he says, grabbing Chance by the arm and pulling him toward the door. After Brutus pushes Chance out first, he turns, trying to explain.

"I'm sorry again. We were trying to get your flowers into your room." His voice carries around the door as he makes his exit.

In that moment, I notice the large arrangement setting awkwardly in the middle of my bedroom.

"Okay... Umm ... Just give me a minute to get dressed."

I hurry to the closet and slip on my jeans, bra, and another one of my V-neck shirts. I run my fingers through my hair and walk back into my room to see Brutus standing there waiting for me.

"Ms. Andrews, I am bloody sorry. I should have waited for you."

I look up at him in shock; I have never heard anything of that nature out of him before.

I clear my throat. "No worries, you just caught me off guard." I smile at him in hope of easing his discomfort.

"Very good." He claps his hands together. "I have good news; Master will be gone all day today. He wanted me to inform you that Mr. Fletcher will be your escort for the remainder of the day," he says, a little too upbeat for the old man's usual tone.

That is when I know he is up to something. I eye him questioningly. "What is this all about?"

"I can promise you, Ms. Andrews, I'm not hiding anything from you." His thin lips form a broad smile and color stains his pale skin.

"Well, okay, I guess," I reply cautiously.

"Thank you! I was also asked to give you this. Mr. Fletcher will explain the rest. He will be waiting in the living room." He hands me a white envelope addressed to me.

"Oh, thanks." I reach for the envelope as he turns and picks up the flowers like they weigh nothing, moving them to the corner beside my bed.

My eyes widen and I call out just as Brutus walks out the door. "Wait! Brutus—"

He peeks around the corner with a guilty look and winks before he ducks back out.

Dumbfounded by the old man, I wonder what the hell just happened. I look down at the envelope now in my hand. I find myself yet again opening another envelope. However, this one is not a beautifully written poem, but it is from Rick. This letter reflects Rick's other side and sharply explains that Chance will be my personal bodyguard. It also includes a list of what he expects me to do today in the form of a minute-by-minute outline.

I toss it aside and irritation bubbles inside me.

CHANCE

I PUSH UP against the coolness of the floor to ceiling window in the living room outside of Emma's room. I welcome the chill to cool the fire that was set by the vision of Emma—in a towel—nearly naked.

Shit, she's fucking sexy!

The outside world blurs as my mind keeps replaying Emma with her long, wet hair sticking to her skin. I wanted to tug on the thin blue towel that matched perfectly with the icy blue of her eyes. That's all it would take—one little tug. And the towel would pool around her feet as it hit the floor. *Fuck!* Just thinking about her naked has me hard.

The towel was the only thing concealing what looks to be perfect curves. And I want to unwrap her like a gift—slowly cherishing those fucking curves. A need to hold her kicks my body heat up another notch. My dick jumps at the thought.

"Mr. Fletcher, Ms. Andrews will be ready in about ten minutes, if you will remain here and wait," Brutus says, startling me from my fantasy.

I remain facing the window in fear I will give him a heart attack with the size of my erection. I clear my throat. "Thank you, Brutus. I will wait here."

"In the meantime, do you need anything?"

I mentally chuckle. *Nope, nothing you could help me with, buddy.*

"I'm fine. Do you still need a hand with the flowers?" I ask, controlling all thoughts and turning toward him.

"Oh no, Mr. Fletcher. Thank you but I already handled it," Brutus says with a bow and leaves the room.

Since when did his attitude toward me change? Just yesterday he was rude and unwelcoming when he let me into the penthouse and now he is overly friendly. *What changed?*

I turn back to the window, again paying no attention to the busy New York life that is unfolding before me. Instead, I let my mind run free, for just a moment—knowing that in my mind is the only place I can have Emma.

I replay her blush spreading over her soft pale skin. It is an image that will haunt me. How badly I wanted to kiss the downward path it made on her skin.

Lord help me.

I let out a breath—I thought this assignment was going to be easy. I shift on my feet to ease the tightening in my groin; I am again hard for her. Damn, I'm going to have to go jack off

---

57

before this shit gives me blue balls.

Yep, she is going to be the death of me.

"Okay, Chance, you can do this!" I say to the window, attempting to give myself a pep talk.

"What ... do what?" I hear over my shoulder.

Time to put on my poker face. I turn to see Emma walking into the room with a blush already coloring her cheeks.

"I didn't say anything." *LIAR!*

"Oh, I thought I heard you say something," she says as she joins me by the window. Her blush is even more profound the closer she gets.

I distract myself from the dangerous path my mind is wandering. "So, did you get your honey-do list?"

"How ... did you know — ?"

"Rick told me."

"Oh, yes. But can we eat breakfast first? I'm starving!" She stares out the window.

"Of course we can. Ms. May is gone for the day, so we will have to eat out. Where do you want to go?" I ask awkwardly. *Just us — one-on-one.*

I look down at her when she doesn't respond. "Emma, do you know where you want to eat?" I ask again as she continues to stare out the window.

"Oh, umm, yes, you *REALLY* do want to know what I want ... sorry. I'm just not used to that, I guess... Rick never asks me where I want to go, he tells me where I am going," she says with a nervous laugh.

My disgust for Rick is starting to build into a seething hatred, and I patiently wait for her answer as I watch her wring her hands in front of her as she contemplates.

"Well, I guess, how about the coffee shop? If that's okay?"

"That sounds great!" I wink at her in hopes of easing her tension.

Her face lights up and her icy blues sparkle. My chest tightens.

"Really! Thank you! Rick never wants to eat there. And they have blueberry muffins that are to die for." She grabs my arm and starts pulling me to the door.

"Whoa! Hold on a minute." I dig in my heels as a fire burns inside me seeing the lighthearted Emma come to life.

"Are you missing anything before we leave? You don't have a bag or anything? Rick made it sound like we are on a timed schedule today."

"Shit." Her left hand flies to her mouth and her eyes widen, making the huge rock on her finger stand out. "Sorry, I mean, yes, thank you."

I grab her left wrist without thinking and pull her closer to me to examine the oversized rock. She rips her hand back quickly and covers it.

You fucking dumbass!

"I'm sorry—"

"I will go get my things," she says as she leaves the room quickly.

Chapter Nine

EMMA

A FOG OF emotions twist my gut as I practically run to my room and yank off the ring—not wanting it there in the first place. I throw it in the nightstand and slam it shut. *I hate it!* I hug myself as my stomach flips. *I don't want to marry that monster.* And that damn ring is proof of this prison that I have no hope of escaping. I sigh heavily, thinking of the ungodly sized rock in the drawer.

How am I going to withstand a lifetime of Rick?

I grab my bag and slide it onto my shoulder. *Breathe, Emma!* I tell myself, attempting to control my thundering heart. *It's not Rick you have to face, it's Chance… Chance…*

As I walk back into the living room, my eyes land on Chance on the sofa. Magazine in hand, he seems absorbed in whatever article he is reading. I slow my pace and look at him. The combination of awkwardness and excitement twists into a fireball that sits in my gut. He is leaning back in a reclined position; his faded gray T-shirt stretches perfectly across the hard lines of his chest, causing my mouth to water. I run my eyes down his body. His shirt is tucked slightly into the front of his jeans, which hug his hips and stretch down his long thick thighs.

"Ready to go?" he says, causing me to jump.

"Yes," I answer, not trusting my voice with more than a one-word response.

Our eyes meet and I see a flash of fire before he breaks the connection and places the magazine down on the side table.

Did he just catch me checking him out?

He repositions himself and combs his chestnut hair off his forehead. A few strands fall back, and my fingers ache to comb them back into place.

Slowly, he stands from his seated position. He towers over me and I realize we are standing very close together. My eyes land on his chest and I take a sharp breath as he grabs my forearm gently and moves me, creating space between us. My arm burns from his touch and I force myself to focus on my breathing.

He makes a throaty sound. "Okay, to the coffee shop," he says hesitantly — almost sounding guarded.

On autopilot, I turn and follow him.

BOLD AROMAS ASSAULT my senses the minute we round the corner to the coffee shop. I inhale and a sense of pure joy sparks within me. The buzz of the little shop causes all five of my senses to go into overdrive.

I peer around, watching everyone hustle to get their morning fix before they are off to work.

We get into line to order and I look up at the menu that hangs behind the register, causing my stomach to growl at the thought of food.

"What can I get you?" A woman's voice rings with disdain.

"Do you recommend a macchiato over a cappuccino?" I ask without looking away from the menu.

"Cappuccino," she says curtly.

Chance pushes his body against mine and wraps his arms around my waist, pulling me tighter. I feel his body heat penetrate me to my core, warming me from the inside out. He whispers, "Play along. I will owe you big."

Confused, I look at the barista, instantly recognizing her as the woman who was sitting in the booth with Chance at the club. Her steely eyes drill me with enough force that I can feel

---

it. Her eyes narrow as she eyes me, then Chance, then back to me. A sense of overwhelming self-importance swells in my chest.

Without even thinking, I turn my head to the side and kiss his cheek—staking my claim. His arms tighten around me, magnifying the electricity of a humming wave of heat. It vibrates intensely where our bodies mold together perfectly.

"French vanilla latte with a blueberry muffin for her, and I will take a tall black with a ham and cheese omelet," Chance says as he kisses me right below the ear, in the tender spot between my neck and my cheek. As goosebumps ricochet all the way to my toes, he releases me and grabs his wallet to pay. The minute his body separates from mine a wave of longing permeates my body.

Chance picks up my hand and guides me to a table by the window. Once I am seated, I watch him as he walks back to the counter to retrieve our order.

It's not hard to understand what that barista sees in him— he possesses a sexy strength that is hard to ignore. I watch his powerful muscles flex with every movement he makes on his way back to our table. I imagine just how it would feel to be wrapped around that powerful strength. *If only he really wanted me in that way...*

Chance sets the tray down on the table and takes a seat. He reaches out for my left hand and brings it to his lips. As he kisses it, I lock my eyes with his, watching them dance as they deepen with emotion—*is that desire?* He lands a kiss on my bare ring finger and I inhale sharply as a sizzle flows up my arm and everything blurs around me.

A loud crashing sound knocks me back to reality and I abruptly pull my hand back. I spot the barista kneeling down on the floor picking up scattered dishes as she wipes what I assume are tears from her face.

Anger evaporates the intense sensation I am feeling. I look back to Chance and watch as he picks up his fork, acting indifferent.

"Do you mind explaining to me what the hell just happened?" I ask, feeling irritated by his coolness.

He shrugs his shoulders. "Not really, but I owe you one," he says, still eating his omelet.

"Yes, you do. Did you see what you ... what WE did to that poor girl?"

His expression softens—taking me aback. "I wanted to get it across this time that I am not into her. I didn't want to hurt her," he says with concern in his voice.

"Sorry, I just thought you were trying—"

"I *am nothing* like Rick..." he snaps and takes a bite.

CHANCE

I CAN'T TAKE my eyes off her. I watch as Emma moves around the reception desk contemplating her vision of the library with her notebook in hand. *Shit, she is even sexier when she's brainstorming.*

She walks back to the desk and flops down into the chair beside me as she throws her notebook down. She lets out a deep breath.

Yep, she is fucking sexy.

I hold in my burning need to wrap her up in my arms. If I were to close my eyes, I could still smell the lavender scent of her hair and the feel of her body pressing against mine. I give her a questioning look as stress deepens the lines on her beautiful face. "What are you thinking about?"

"I've dreamt about overhauling this library for years. I just thought it would come naturally to me, but now I don't know where to start. And with the deadline Rick's given me—not to mention that I have to report every detail back to him for *HIS* final approval..."

"How can I help?"

Her beautiful smile reaches her crystal blue eyes. "You would help me?"

"Well, yeah. If Rick has me babysitting you, I might as well pitch in," I tease her. "Plus, I do owe you…" *I would do anything to see that beautiful smile…*

She blushes and, fighting the urge to kiss her, I shove my hands into my pockets.

"So, what is first on your list?" I ask her.

Her saucer-shaped eyes look down at her notebook. She picks it up and stands. She paces as she grabs the pencil that is holding her hair back. Her long blond locks spill down her back, causing my dick to jump in a split second. *Well, fuck me.* Just when I was thinking she couldn't be any sexier, she does something like that. I want to take her hair and intertwine it around my wrists, tilting her head back so I can have better access to her sexy as hell mouth. Damn, it should be illegal for her be so sexy and completely clueless to it. *She's going to wreck me.*

"Chance," she says, interrupting my thoughts.

"Umm… Yeah." I shake my head.

"I want to start with the reception area first. It needs an updated computer system, then inventory everything … that will take the longest," she says, setting the notebook down.

She smiles and her eyes brighten. I watch her roll up her sleeves as I await her instructions.

The reception desk is a large rectangle with a computer system on the right side and swing doors on each side. Faded oak drawers line the inside all around. She digs silently through the contents, going down to her knees as she sorts. She stops suddenly and looks up at me, blinking for a second.

"Oh my gosh, I'm sorry, I'm not used to someone helping me, let alone waiting for me to tell them what to do." She laughs lightly.

I drop to my knees and pick up her chin, making her meet my eyes.

"It's fine, just tell me where I can help you."

The second her bright eyes bore into mine, I lose all sense.

Unable to fight it any longer, I tip her chin a little higher and angle her head to have full access to her lips. I lean closer and my eyes find their target. I hear her hiss.

I have never wanted anything more than to kiss her pink pouty lips. I feel drawn to her lips. Her hand comes to my chest.

"Stop," she says just above a whisper.

My vision blurs as she stands and runs in the opposite direction. I blink several times to clear my vision. I look over the desk watching her as she darts into the bathroom.

Shit, I fucked that up!

Chapter Ten

EMMA

THE COLD TILES seep through my clothes as I bury my head in between my knees and hug them to my chest. *I wish I could run away.* My mind races. The look on his face burns deep into my consciousness. His need was so intense it was palpable. *Does Chance know what he is doing to me?*

No, Emma!

My heart fills with dark longing. I remember the feeling of his hand on my chin—soft yet exhilarating. Never has a man's touch vibrated to my core like that. It took everything in me to stop what was about to happen. God knows how badly I wanted him to kiss me.

Okay, Emma, you are going to act normal. It didn't happen, I tell myself. *He doesn't really want me. Why would he? Just look at him, he is gorgeous. He could get any woman he wants. Maybe Rick is testing me? Now, that makes more sense. Damn it; I'm such an idiot.*

You're nothing special! I remind myself and square my shoulders. I may not be anything special, but I'm not going to let him make a fool of me either. I set out in search of him.

I find him sitting in a chair at the desk. My cheeks are burning by the time I reach him. I plant my hands on the desk, feeling the reassurance of the solid wood between us. Before losing my nerve, I square my shoulders again. "I'm not taking your shit. I know what you are trying to do here. Did Rick put you up to this to see what I would do?" My hands are shaking. "Well, you can just … just go to hell and tell Rick 'the prick' that I passed."

His chestnut eyes look up at me, expressionless. *How did he do that?* Anger pools inside my chest. *How can he show no emotion whatsoever…?*

I raise my voice, matching my temper. "Just leave! I don't need you here!"

He slowly stands up, completely unresponsive to my outburst. And an ice-cold chill runs down my spine.

I stumble back, but he reaches for my hand, stopping me from my retreat. He pulls me, bringing me back to the counter. I prepare myself for his fist as I instinctively raise my free hand to protect my face. In a split second, he releases me and backs away. The tension in his body is visible as his knuckles turn white.

"I will *NEVER* hit you. I am *NOT* like fucking Rick!" he says in a dark, slow tone.

Is he mad at me?

My hand drops back to the counter. I search for his truth; flames burn in his eyes and I force myself to look away.

"I can't leave you. It is my job to stay with you at all times," he continues in a soft, gentle tone, causing my heart to beat faster. I meet his blazing eyes.

"Now, what can I help you with, so we can get started?"

In a moment his whole demeanor changes back and I slowly turn my attention to the reception desk and start pulling wires to the computer system.

What does he want from me?

"Emma, I am here to help. It's killing me to just sit here and watch," he says, bringing me back to reality.

I turn toward him as my frustration bubbles. *He just wants to help…*

"Umm, well … I'm trying to get the computer system out so I can make room for the new system. That is, if Rick approves the new system." I pause to tug on another cord. "I haven't shown it to him, yet." I tug another cord out.

"That's where I can help. I can send Rick an email about the system you need while you get it all unplugged for me to move it." He smiles as he pulls out his phone. "So let me see the computer system you want."

I point to my notebook beside him. "I have my list here, but Rick may get mad that it is not coming from me. He asked me to go over all the details with him," I say, embarrassment warming my cheeks.

Chance continues typing. "This is also in my job description. I am to ask for anything that you should need." He leans over to pick up my notebook.

"Oh, okay..."

After a few minutes, I hear him over my shoulder.

"Wow! These are really good."

"What are you talking about?" I ask as I pull the last of the wires and untuck myself from the tight space. I stretch out and dust myself off. He doesn't respond, so I look over his shoulder to see what he is talking about. He flips a page of my notebook.

My thoughts immediately go to the quickly written poems and doodles and I hurry to retrieve my notebook out of his hands. Closing the few feet between us, I reach over his shoulder. "Hey, give me that. That's not for anyone to see."

"OOH it's not, is it?" He pulls it out of my reach as he stands. "If you can grab it, it's yours." He holds the notebook open and continues flipping through the pages above my head.

"Chance!" I try to jump for it with no luck. "Chance, please."

He glances down with laughter in his eyes. "Okay, okay, here, but I was just saying, these are very good."

I quickly nab my notebook and bring it to my chest. "Thank you." I look down.

His phone chimes. "That was quick," he says as he pulls his phone out of his pocket.

"Is it from Rick? What did he say?"

"Well, he said: 'Whatever she wants, get it for her.'"

"Really?"

"Yes, that's what he said."

―

"Then out with the old!" I say as I bounce on my heels.

"If you're done, I will remove the old one and then you can shop your little heart out," he says, sounding almost scornful.

CHANCE

A STRONG CHLORINE odor fills the air and whips around me as I follow Emma to the high-top table, where she deposits her backpack onto the chair.

I watch her nervously turn halfway, averting her eyes from me.

"I will be fine here alone. I swim all the time without anyone watching over me. So ... so ... you can go now."

I notice her strongly grip on to her backpack. Her eyes dart to the locker room doors.

"You know I can't just leave. My orders are to stay with you at all times." I shrug my shoulders in an attempt to ease her discomfort. "I have work emails that I need to send, so I'll just hang out here." I pull out a chair and sit.

I'm not going anywhere. I'd miss my own funeral to see Emma in a bikini...

Her blue eyes blaze in frustration and her bottom lip curls up. "I just don't understand, why now, after swimming here for two years? Now, he wants someone by my side at all times?" She crosses her arms, causing her cleavage to push up.

I feel my shaft stand to attention, making it difficult for me not to look down and give them my full, undivided attention. I focus on her pouty expression, thinking it's a safer choice. And the thought of pulling on her bottom lip with my teeth hits me hard. *Shit, even her pout is sexy as hell.*

"Rick was very clear that I am not to leave you alone. I'm here to ensure your safety."

"Then he should guard me from himself," she says sarcastically before letting out a sigh. "Fine, but you have to look away until I get into the water—"

"Okay, I hate to see anything I haven't seen before." I laugh.

She huffs. "I didn't think about you being here and I brought my favorite swimming suit and it's skimpy and I don't want you to see..." she says quickly, and her cheeks grow rosy red.

I hold up my hands in surrender. "Okay ... okay, Emma! I won't look."

"You promise?" Relief floods her face and she sucks in her lip—biting it nervously—the same lip I was just envisioning myself biting.

"Yes, I promise! I won't look."

She picks up her bag and heads to the locker room to change.

Concentrating on my phone, I open my emails. I see one from The Lieutenant and know he is looking for an update on Rick. Deciding to avoid responding, I toss my phone down. I haven't explained to him my new position with Emma, and I am not in a hurry to either.

The doors of the locker room swing open and Emma emerges in a sky-blue towel. She walks to the edge of the pool with her towel wrapped tightly around her. Her beautiful face blushes as she avoids looking in my direction. *She has no idea just how breathtaking she is.*

She sits down at the edge of the pool with her back to me and dips her legs into the water. I study her braided hair, which reaches almost to her waist, and the thin tiny peach strap of her swimming suit tied behind her neck.

I picture myself untying the thin strap and letting it fall down her back, sliding it down her shoulders to bare her full breasts.

God help me.

"Don't look," she says in a low, barely audible whisper.

I close my eyes. "My eyes are closed."

In my mind, I envision her unwrapping her towel. *She said skimpy ... how skimpy?* My imagination reels with the possibilities.

The sound of water splashing bounces off the walls and I open my eyes. They dart immediately to the rippling of the water as her head breaks the glassy surface coming up for air.

I watch as she swims graceful laps and I am mesmerized to see her look so free.

On her fifth lap, she stops at the opposite end of the pool and hugs the side. The water ripples around her, doing nothing to conceal the perfect curves of her body. I stiffen in my seat. *Perfect.*

I force myself to look away as my shaft hardens. *Control yourself...* I pick up my phone, deciding to focus on the dreaded email. I begin typing my reply to update on the new job change, the whole time thinking about the beautiful woman in the pool making me stumble over my text.

The sound of water dripping onto the floor causes me to look up. Emma is lifting herself out of the water using the ladder. As if in slow motion, she rises step-by-step. The water glistens down her pale, silky skin and I follow her body. Her little string bikini is no longer imaginary as it comes into view. Her arms move up the ladder's handle, revealing just how skimpy it is.

Goddamn. My dick hardens to full attention.

She takes another step and the beautiful curves of her hips come into view—a matching bottom with a little bow holding it all together. How little effort it would take to untie. *Just one little tug...*

Her full, shapely legs lift from the water, making me shift in my seat. Just the sight of her turns me on and I adjust the evidence of just how much. I feel like an inexperienced high schooler, unable to control my libido.

I look up at her beautiful face. She is oblivious to what she is doing. Her earlier demand for me to close my eyes is clearly not on her mind right now. *And fuck me, I will seize the opportunity.*

Just about the time she reaches her towel, realization hits her face. She jets for her towel and quickly covers herself.

"Ugggh..." She shies in frustration. "I wasn't thinking. Did you see me?"

I look back to my phone. "Hmm—what? I'm working on an email," I lie, not wanting to make her more uncomfortable.

"Don't lie! I felt you looking at me," she says, sounding irritated.

I stand up and walk over to her, watching as she shrinks the closer I get. Facing her, I say, "Yes, I was. You're beautiful, Emma! Why are you ashamed of your body?"

She hugs her towel tighter and I can feel her withdrawing. I want to show her what I see. Cautiously, I raise my hands to her shoulders where her towel wraps around her. I hook my fingers on each side and run them to the middle where her hands grip the towel. Pausing for a second, I take my time—trying not to scare her. I lightly pull the towel open and her hands shake, but she does not stop me; instead, she averts her eyes.

I pause. "Why are you scared of me looking at your body?"

She doesn't answer, so I try again. "Emma, what are you so afraid of? I have told you that I would never hurt you. You can tell me to stop and I will."

It feels like an eternity passes before she speaks. "I have marks on my body from things Rick has done to me."

BOOM! It feels as if she just dropped a bomb. *Fucking Rick...*

"I won't go further but I didn't see any marks on your body. If you'd let me, I would like to see these marks..."

Her eyes tell me that she won't resist me, and she nods her head slightly. I pull open the towel. *Control yourself, Chance.* I fight the urge to pounce on her beautiful body. *Fuck, she is the most beautiful thing I have ever seen!*

I take a deep breath and look over her flawless curves. "Emma, your skin's flawless."

This time, it's she who opens the towel for a better look. I shake my head. "Nothing."

Her eyes fill with tears and she drops the towel, letting it fall to her feet. I can't take my eyes off her face, wanting desperately to wipe away her tears as they stream down.

"*LOOK!*" she says angrily.

I snap my focus back to her body, trying to see anything that could resemble a scar. I scan her flat stomach to the top of her hip. All while dreaming of kissing that smooth, silky perfection.

I force myself to focus. I look to her right hip, just under the little bow of her suit, and see a dark purple mark. Stepping closer, I slide my finger under the bow for a better look. She gasps as I move the bow down, revealing a heart-shaped birthmark. *Sexiest fucking thing I have seen.*

Regrettably, I move the bow back in place and take a step back, finding air again as I inhale, not even realizing I had been holding my breath.

Our eyes meet. "I'm sorry, Emma. That is the only thing I see, and to me it looks like a birthmark."

She doubles over, picks up her towel, and wraps it around like a security blanket. "That's *NOT IT!*" she snaps and runs back to the locker room.

Chapter Eleven

EMMA

I WIPE MY tear-streaked face with the back of my hand. *Why … Why couldn't he see the scars?* My gut roils as nausea rises and I cover my mouth with a shaking hand. I face the corner of the locker room, avoiding my reflection.

Breathe, Emma. My mind echoes with Chance's words. *Emma, your skin's flawless. How could that be?* I have seen them. I remember the pain. *Your skin's flawless…*

I inhale and prepare myself to face the mirror again. *Look at them, Emma. Make sure you're not crazy…*

I close my eyes. *See yourself through Chance's eyes.*

I feel like a coward and the nausea boils to disgust — disgust with myself. *You must!*

I stare directly into the icy blue eyes staring back at me through the mirror. "See yourself through Chance's eyes."

I watch my hands shake in the mirror. No, not my hands — this woman in the mirror is a stranger, a shell of someone that I no longer know. I watch as this stranger tugs on the towel and then releases it. My eyes follow the path as the towel drops to the floor in a pool of blue around this woman's feet. I run judgmental eyes up the pale curves of her legs, seeing only soft, smooth skin.

My emotions burn within me as I continue to scan for something, anything, that resembles a scar, but I see none. A fiery rage flames to life, as I look down to my skin and I see nothing.

"I don't understand! I remember, I remember the pain..." My voice quivers.

I lock eyes with the stranger in the mirror. *I believe you... I know it happened... I believe you...*

I WALK OUT of the locker room expecting to see Chance waiting for me in the pool area, but he isn't there. *I must have scared him off.* I turn and start walking toward the main entrance. *Okay, I guess I'm by myself.*

"Hold up," Chance says from behind me, startling me.

I briskly turn around to find him jogging to catch up.

"I thought you left when I didn't see you. I was just going to head back to the penthouse."

"I was in the men's locker room. You took a while in there..." he says as his eyes darken.

I look away. *Please don't ask... please don't ask.* I look away and pray he doesn't want to continue our last conversation.

His eyes flame. "You should be more patient," he teases.

I breathe out. "Or maybe you should stick to me like glue. Then I wouldn't lose you," I tease back.

He bumps me with his hip, almost knocking me over. "Geez..." I laugh lightheartedly.

"You said I should stick to you like glue." He winks.

My heart flutters. *God, he is handsome,* I think as we walk through the doors.

Chance's cell starts ringing as we step into the private elevator.

"Hello," he answers. "Yes, sir... Yes, I understand..." He hangs up the phone. "Change of plans, Emma," he says as he pushes the button for the fourteenth floor.

My chest squeezes.

"That was Rick. He won't be coming home tonight and expects me to stay in the guest room. I need to grab a change of clothes for the night."

We are going to his place...

Memories flood my mind the second the elevator doors open on the fourteenth floor. The hallway is still the same dark colorless gray that I remember, and my heart thumps loudly in my ears as I watch Chance pull out his keys and turn the lock to my old apartment.

Is all my stuff still here? Is Rick playing a game with me?

My hands shake and I feel light-headed. Rick took all my belongings away when he moved me into the penthouse, dismissing it all as garbage. *But it was mine and it was all I had!*

"This … this is your place?" I gasp unintentionally.

"Yes," he says, swinging the door open and walking in.

I peek in, remembering the space with all my belongings in it. Blinking a few times, I clear my mind — *it's all gone.*

"Sorry it's a bit of a mess. I don't usually have anyone over. I just have to grab a few things," he says as he walks to the table and picks up some files and sets them in a crate under the table.

"You can come in. I promise there is nothing hiding that will bite you."

"*Hiding,*" I repeat.

Flashes of living in foster homes and having to hide anything sentimental — in fear of it being stolen — come crashing down on me. *Shit, how did I forget?*

I run to his bed, which is set against the far wall, and grab the corner. I start shoving at the impossibly heavy object, trying to get to the place where I'd hidden my belongings.

I feel a tap on my shoulder. "I've never had a woman want to move my bed…" He chuckles. "What are you doing?"

"I … I … USED to…" I say, breathing heavily.

Suddenly, the bed moves with ease, as Chance glides it effortlessly. I climb onto the bed and lie on my stomach, squeezing between the bed and the wall to reach for the brick that is wedged into the opening of my hiding space.

"Emma, what are you doing?"

"I used to live here," I say, reaching the brick.

My fingers grip it and I try to wiggle it from its place — but it won't budge. "Ugh."

I feel the bed shift again as Chance lies down next to me.

"Can I help you with something?"

"No," I say, moving away.

His weight shifts and I feel his body heat as he moves closer. I hear the sound of the brick drop to the floor.

Without even thinking, I jump over to reach inside, trying to reunite with my beloved items. My hand feels around and bumps the solid box. I grab it and pull my hand back, exposing the old wooden box which is not much bigger than a deck of cards. I let out a squeal of joy.

In a heartbeat, two strong arms enclose my waist—encircling me.

"Sweetheart, you are playing with fire right now and if you don't want to get burned, it would be best if you get off of me." His breath tickles my left ear.

I realize then that I'd jumped over Chance during my eagerness to find my missing treasures and landed chest to chest with him. I gasp and his body heat warms my skin. *Oh shit!*

My nipples stand at attention against his hard chest. With each ragged breath he takes, they ache with need. The image of his thumbs rubbing against them floods my head. *Oh my...*

I look at his face; his eyes are squeezed tight as if he is in pain. *Am I hurting him?*

I shift and an electrifying desire courses to my center. I bite my lip, trying desperately to hold back a moan. The overwhelming feeling that I am made to be in this space—in his arms—causes my body to tremble.

"Umm ... I'm sorry ... I..."

He lightens his hold and slides his arms down my back in a light caress. A charge of energy soothes my trembling and replaces it with a vibrating need. His long fingers wrap around my waist, nearly completely encircling it as he lifts me up. A spark of heat jolts my sex, causing it to swell in arousal. *Oh GOD!*

"Emma," he growls. "I am trying my damnedest to be a gentleman, but you are not helping me out here."

I instantly position myself and lift off of him, feeling his own arousal against my thigh. *Does he want me?*

He opens his eyes, avoiding looking at me, and quickly stands before making his way to the bathroom. I sit back on the bed and fold myself onto my lap—hugging my wooden box to my chest.

I open the box slowly and pull out the golden comb that was my mother's. The painful memory of my dying mother rattles in my head. *Mom...* I set it down on my knee and pull out my dad's pocketknife. I run my thumb across his name. *How can one little kid lose both parents so early − ?*

"So that was what you were after." Chance's voice makes me jump.

I look up at him as he exits the bathroom. "Are you okay? Did I hurt you?"

His eyes flicker with heat. "No, how can you hurt me?"

I feel my cheeks flush. "I just thought … well, how you reacted … I thought I hurt you somehow."

"*OH*… Emma, haven't you ever been with a man?" He stops abruptly.

His eyes divert from mine and I watch as he balls his fist. His face flashes with … *hatred?* Did I see that right? Or was it disgust? Does it disgust him that I am damaged? Does he realize what Rick has done to me?

I watch as his face turns gray with realization and my heart throbs deep in my chest. *Yes, he does, but how could he know about my stolen innocence? Did Rick tell him...? It's my secret! It's my pain − pain I locked away years ago. Pain I promised myself to never relive.*

My vision blurs and I force tears away before bringing my focus back to the pocketknife. *Let it go, Emma, push the pain away, like you always do … to survive...* I rub the hard metal of the knife and the image of the man who once held it comes to mind. *My daddy*, a man—the last man—I felt protected by. A man who I know would have laid his own life down to save mine. A man—who died… His knife has always been representative of my sad life. The safety and protection a knife can bring is overshadowed by the cold, hard metal that feels lifeless and unwanted.

Chance drops to his knees in front of me. "What is it about the knife that makes it so important to you?"

"It was my dad's, and Rick has rules about staff not being allowed any weapons and if they find any they are confiscated. So I hid it." I rub the knife between my forefinger and thumb, mimicking the way my dad used to.

"And the hair comb?"

I feel my lips curve up with the memory of it in my mother's hair. "It's my mom's. She wore it on her wedding day and every year on their anniversary." I run my thumb over the rhinestones. "Now that I found them, I don't know what I am going to do with them. I can't take them back to the penthouse," I say as grief fills my chest.

"What if you leave them here? I will hold onto them for you," he says, walking over to the safe which he uses as a nightstand. He pulls it open with a key. "I can put them in here—till you are ready for them."

"You would do that for me?"

"Yes, it's obvious they mean a lot to you." He reaches out his hand for the box.

Chapter Twelve

CHANCE

MR. FLETCHER,

I expect you to make yourself at home in the guest room. I will be gone overnight several times in the next few months. Make a list of what you need, and I will arrange for Brutus to acquire it for you.

-Rick

I toss the note back onto the midnight-blue covers of the oversized bed. *Leave it to Rick and his demands,* I think as I set my bag down. I walk around the four-poster bed. The room resembles much of the rest of the penthouse with the Victorian décor, the only difference being the color theme of midnight blues and creams.

I make my way to the floral loveseat that is set directly in line with the door on the opposite side. *This room is three times the size of my apartment,* I think as I head in the direction of one of the two closed doors.

There, I find a bathroom and an empty walk-in closet. *This is one of the nicest places I've ever stayed while on assignment...* My mind flashes to memories of sleeping up against the dustiest hut walls, just before my men and I overtook some of the biggest drug cartel operations.

A knock echoes off the walls, shaking me back to reality. "Come in."

"Mr. Fletcher, supper is ready. Ms. Andrews is waiting in the living room," Brutus says before stepping back into the hallway.

EMMA SITS CURLED under a blanket on the couch. Her cheeks are flushed, and she has a book in her hand. *She is the most beautiful thing I have ever seen.*

"So, what are we eating tonight?" I ask her and look down at her book, wondering what she's reading that is making her look so flushed.

"Hi. I'm ready," she says, not looking at me. She stands and starts in the direction of the kitchen. And I turn to let her lead the way.

"So … what are you reading? And what's for supper?"

"I hope you don't mind pizza. Rick never lets us eat simpler food. And I like to make it easy on Brutus when he cooks." She guides me down the staircase and we walk through a doorway just left of the landing. We enter the back side of the kitchen.

"This must be the employees' staircase," I say and make a mental note of how she is avoiding my question about her book.

"Yes, I like using the stairs in the penthouse over the elevator," she says as we round the island.

We take our seats and I eye the meat lover's pizza covered with black olives. My stomach growls.

"It's my favorite pizza," I say.

"Really? No way, it's mine, too!" She looks at me with her eyes wide.

"Yes, really!" I pick up my piece of pizza and hold it up to her. "Cheers."

She meets my pizza with hers and giggles. "Cheers," she says before taking a bite.

After a few bites, I look up at her and my pulse quickens. "You didn't answer me about what book you are reading."

A blush colors her pale skin. "It's just a silly romance."

"I should read it. Is it good?"

"Umm, I don't think you'd like it." She locks her focus on her plate. "Do … do you read romance?"

"No, but maybe I will like this one. Is it good?"

I watch her glance around the room—looking anywhere but at me. "Yes, it's good … there is a lot of … umm, suspense." She pauses. "What do you like to read?"

"I like old war books; that is, when I have time to read."

Her eyes light up. "Did you borrow a book from the library recently?"

"No. Why do you ask?"

"Hmm, someone borrowed some from the library and Ms. Gale didn't have a name on the account. I was just curious." She adds, "You should have seen how Ms. Gale described this mystery man—all handsome and everything. It was cute."

"You think I fit that description … handsome?" I tease.

"Yes," she answers flatly. "Ugh, I mean NO … or I—" she fumbles.

Her quick answer surprises me but her blush tells me that it surprises her more.

"Well, thank you!" I say, sitting a bit higher in my chair. *Lord, I want to kiss her.*

She clears her throat. "What I meant—"

"I'm not letting you take it back now. You will hurt my ego." I look over to her signature blush. "Do you want another slice?"

"Yes, please," she says shyly, holding out her plate.

"Do you know how beautiful you are when you blush?" I ask, unable to stop myself.

Her icy blue eyes dull. "Yes, I have been told," she whispers.

I reach out and grab her hand. "Hey, I'm sorry. I didn't mean to upset you. It's just that I do find you very beautiful and your blushing is—"

"Is it breaking the rules if I go upstairs now or am I only allowed so many feet away from you?" She turns to hide, but I can hear the sorrow in her voice. She sniffs and wipes tears away from her beautiful face—tears that I put there.

I don't deserve her.

"You can go," I say quietly, letting go of her hand before she turns and leaves.

No longer hungry, I stand to clean up the mess — racking my brain wondering where I went wrong. What did I say? I just said she was beautiful. Is that what upset her? But she is beautiful and so much more.

If she were mine … she would never doubt how much I love her… If she were only mine…

"If you are done, Mr. Fletcher, you may leave. I can finish up from here," Brutus says, walking into the kitchen and around the island to take over cleaning up.

"Thanks, Brutus." I turn toward the back stairs and stop in mid-stride. "Hey, the first time you met me you were … different… What's changed?" I ask curiously.

He stops as he rinses off a plate and looks up. "Well, if I'm frank with you, Ms. Andrews fancies you," he says before returning to his task. "And I did my own homework on you — extensive homework, you might say. Your past assignments are rather — *impressive*," he says, giving me a salute with his soap-covered hand. "Thank you for your service, *brother*."

Ms. Andrews fancies you. The sound of Brutus's voice rolls over in my head. What does that mean? *Fancies* — could Emma have feelings for me, as I do for her?

Then Brutus's voice rings out again, only a different word — *brother*. A realization dawns on me; only a fellow Marine would be so bold. And that also accounts for his ability to get information on my past assignments… Brutus was a Marine, too.

I salute him back. "And thank you as well — *brother*."

"It goes without saying but your secret is safe with me."

"Thank you," I say respectfully.

"Don't hurt her," he adds sternly.

"As I assured her: I am not Rick."

MY HEART STARTS beating harder in my chest after

calling out to Emma and receiving no response. After several scans of the rooms on the second floor of the penthouse, I find myself standing in the middle of her bedroom, yet again.

"Emma."

No response. *Fuck ... if something happens to her...*

"Emma." I hear a sound from the bathroom.

I knock—no answer. *Fuck it!* I can't fight the overwhelming need to know she is safe. I turn the handle and the smell of lavender hits my nose as I swing the door open. The sound of water echoes and I turn to follow.

"Emma," I call out again as I walk around the corner.

My eyes land on her lying in the jetted tub with earbuds. I inhale with the relief of knowing she is safe.

Okay, she's fine ... now leave.

I beg myself to turn away but feel completely powerless. Her golden hair is piled on top of her head, causing ringlets to cascade over her pink face as she lies there, eyes closed. The steam swirls from the bubbly surface, camouflaging what lies beneath.

Damn, fucking leave, Chance, I tell myself just as her lips part and she lets out a moan. My heart beats faster in my chest.

My feet feel like blocks of concrete as my body wages war against my mind. The water ripples with every movement she makes, ineffectively disguising her hands as she slowly cups her breast. And I watch the bubbles covering her skin lift as she squeezes her luscious mound gently, letting out a soft moan.

My body's own needs react to her sounds of passion as my hands ache to replace hers, to feel her nipples rub against my palm as I cup her entire breast in my hand. My dick hardens painfully against the restraint of my zipper.

She releases her breast and the tiny bubbles chase her hands like a second skin as she makes her way down.

She drops her knee to the side of the tub, and I lock onto her face, knowing what she is about to do. The moment vibrates across her face as she radiates a glow of pleasure, letting out a deeper, lower, moan.

Out NOW!

I turn to leave before my need completely overtakes my senses. I quicken my steps in a hasty exit. *No, fuck! You will scare her. Leave.*

Just as I reach the bathroom doorway, her soft moans echo louder but this time my name follows that roaring need.

I hiss with the sucker punch to the gut and I use everything I have to run out of her room, knowing I will scare her with the momentum of my desire — *hell, I'm scaring myself.* Never before have I wanted a woman as badly as I do Emma. I feel my insides burn like an inferno and she is throwing the fuel.

I dart to my bathroom and turn the shower on ice cold. Only taking the time to slip off my shoes, I jump in with all my clothes on to extinguish my flame for her. A few seconds pass before my mind begins to clear.

I make another mental note to add extra clothes to the list for Brutus to pick up.

Chapter Thirteen

CHANCE

SITTING IN THE living room in my only other change of clothes, I flip through the magazine, but I cannot focus on the pages with the image of Emma coming into my mind every few seconds.

From the corner of my eye, I see her enter the room. I try to control my emotions, or should I say my libido, by not looking at her.

"Do you have any books here for me to read besides these boring ass magazines?" I ask, trying to look as if I were really studying the pages in front of me.

"Yes, there are some in the studies," she says quietly.

I finally look over at her and put the magazine back on the end table. "Okay, where are they?"

"There is one on the floor above the kitchen where Rick's main office is, but it's usually locked. There is a smaller study on this floor just down the opposite hall from our rooms. I can take you."

"Please, I don't want to get lost," I tease.

She stands up. "It's this way." She smiles shyly but still avoids my eyes.

I follow her as she walks toward the study. As the image of her in the bathroom drifts again to my consciousness, I remember that she was wearing earbuds.

"Do you like to listen to music?"

She pauses. "I like music but mostly if I'm not reading. I listen to audiobooks."

"You mean you listen to a book and read another one at the same time?"

She chuckles. "No, it's the same book. I like to switch between reading and then listening. I like how it busies my mind. Listening allows me to do other stuff that I need to get done."

Like pleasure yourself?

"Oh, that makes sense."

She opens the door to the study, and we walk in. The room is equivalent in size to the bedrooms. Most of the walls are covered floor to ceiling with books, except for the furthest wall from the door, which is all windows. Two chairs sit facing the mahogany desk set in the center of the room.

"Wow, you have just about as many books here as the library," I say, looking around.

"Yes, Rick built it for me the same year he moved me up here," she says with unmistakable pain.

"Really, and why does that upset you?" I ask, wanting to understand.

She walks over to the desk and takes a seat as she looks sadly up at me. "I'm sorry, Chance, I don't want to talk about it." She wipes away the tear that slides down her face.

You hurt her again! You dumbass!

"What genre are you looking for?" she asks, glancing around the room.

"How about I try something in romance? Maybe something like what you are reading," I say, trying to get a smile on her face.

And I succeed as her shoulders shake with laughter.

"What? I might like it. Unless you have a better idea."

"Yes, I do, but if you are really wanting a romance novel, I will get you one."

"Bring it on. I want to see what you ladies all are into," I say, winking at her.

She looks down at her hands. "Okay, but if you don't like it, it's not my fault."

Emma walks to the ladder, pulls it to the far right side of the wall, and begins to climb. Halfway up, she stops and reaches for a book and I watch the ladder wobble.

"Do you need help reaching it?" I ask and walk over to hold onto both sides of the ladder.

She is wearing a pair of shorts with a loose plain blue T-shirt. The bare of her legs kicks up my body heat as they sit at eye level. The scent of lavender emanates from her skin and the image of her bath floods my mind again.

"Here it is," she says as she begins making her way down.

Hypnotized by the way her body moves down the ladder, I freeze in place. The mixture of citrus and honey wafts to my nostrils from her hair as she reaches the last step and turns to face me as her eyes lock onto the back of the book. A familiar burning, which I know I can only associate with Emma, erupts within me.

Completely absorbed into the back cover, Emma says, "Chance, I think you will like this one. It's a love story, but the setting is World War Two..." She looks up at me and jumps, hugging the book to her chest. "OHH, I didn't see—"

"Emma, how am I going to work with you? You make it impossible for me," I say as my voice vibrates low in my chest. Energy pulses between us, slamming hard against my body. My body begs for contact—*touch her.*

Knowing I am not going to be able to keep my hands off her much longer, I pluck the book from her grasp and pivot. I hastily make my way to the doorway without looking back. *Fuck, I don't have the strength to look back,* I think as I reach the doorway.

"Good night, Emma."

Chapter Fourteen

EMMA

These feelings are foreign,
Beyond my comprehension;
Too thick for absorption;
My mind distortion;
Stopping my respiration,
With all the flirtation,
Begging for clarification.
Feelings of fascination,
Keep breaking my concentration,
With thoughts of passion.
The depths of attraction,
almost making me madden.
Can you imagine,
If I called you handsome?
Would you proceed with caution?
Teaching me in moderation,
layers of compassion?
My first orgasm…

I drop my pen with the last line. *Emma!* I can't believe I am having thoughts about sex after I'd promised myself to never want a man in that way. My first and only experience with a man—Rick—was horrifying. Even years later, the pain still resonates through my bones when I think about him taking my virginity away.

My thoughts automatically drift to the romance novels that I love to read. They make it sound pleasurable, which makes me question if it could be like that for me. Or maybe it is all made up and the act of sex is supposed to be painful and only enjoyable for men.

My bedroom door flies open and my heart skips a beat as I quickly slam my journal shut and look up to see Rick in the doorway — shutting the door behind him.

"Good morning, my love," he says as he walks toward the bed.

I stand, hug my journal to my body, and look up at him. "Good morning."

"I will be home all day working. You will be staying here so we can have time together and start going over plans," he says as he puts his hands on my shoulders. His eyes fall to my journal. "Is something wrong?" he asks coldly as he eyes me questioningly.

I quickly change my demeanor and wrap my arms around him in a hug. "I was just missing you. So many things have been changing, it is just making me feel a bit off."

He pulls me to his chest and the woodsy musk that I recognize as Rick wafts around me. The recollection of something familiar oddly comforts me and soothes my nerves.

This is RICK…

But the familiarity of how our bodies fit perfectly together stirs my center. And my body heat kicks up a notch.

No, Emma … this is RICK… I remind myself. *RICK!*

"To what do I owe this pleasure?" he asks as he rubs his hands up my back in a gentle caress. A vibration ripples through me.

Oh God…

The craziness from the last few days feels as if it is melting away in his arms. I look up to his face and lock onto his lips. *I want to kiss him…* The realization hits me like a train as I find myself leaning into him. *What in the fuck am I doing?* I think as I

92

try to stop myself. I look away, trying to regain my composure. *Why do I feel this way? This is Rick!*

He kisses my cheek before releasing me. I hate myself for my involuntary desires. *Really, Emma, kissing RICK...? Get a grip on yourself!*

I flop down on the edge of the bed. *Rick...* I feel the bed shift as he sits down beside me.

"What's bothering you today?" he asks again, sounding concerned.

Could I really have feelings for Rick...? A chill breaks over my skin and I shiver.

I watch him quietly pick up my journal. Using his other hand, he brings my right hand to his lips and kisses the back tenderly before he rubs it against his cheek. The stubble of his five-o'clock shadow scratches against my skin, rough but gentle, warmth rocketing through me. *Yep ... I'm feeling something ... like I want him.*

"What is going on in that head of yours, love?"

Not with Rick. I can't want Rick! Remember what the first time with Rick was like ... remember ... but there it is ... a seed size of desire... Shit!!

"I'm just confused. I'm sorry."

"You can always talk to me. Please, what is it?"

The compassion that resonates through his voice causes me to look up. I'm not sure I am still talking to Rick. My eyes search his and I watch as his green eyes bore into mine with thick emotion.

"Umm..." I think for a moment. "I don't know how to explain it."

Was Rick always like this – this compassionate? Or am I just now seeing it?

"If you can't explain then I'm sure this can," he says before opening my journal.

I curl my arms around me as I watch him flip to the last page. I feel exposed—naked—as he reads the poem. Then fear courses through me. *What if he makes the connection to Chance?*

But is it about Chance? Or could it be about Rick? I think as I squeeze my eyes closed, shutting out reality. I just want to drift away. My heart and soul are scribbled on those pages—the pages in his hands! *Why do I have to write ALL my emotions? All the times I hated Rick — I wrote it down. All the times that I thought...*

I feel his large presence move in front of me and his long fingers skim my thighs, causing a wave of heat to my core.

I feel him on his knees before me as he pushes closer. Separating my knees, he moves his hands and grips my hips, gently digging his fingers in, pulling me to him. I hold my breath—wishing I could stop my body's reaction.

"Emma, please look at me," he says in a soft but demanding tone.

I open my eyes and slowly look up. I see his black trousers with a matching belt and his dark gray button-up shirt tucked in at the waist. I continue up to his wide chest, where he has the top few buttons undone, exposing a tuft of dark black curls and smooth tan skin.

He is so ... so handsome, I think as I focus on his face. Rick is a good-looking man in his own right, with a dark shadow covering his strong chin, narrow nose, and salt and pepper hair. His green eyes shine with softness—surprising me.

As his lips move to form words, I find myself staring at them again.

"Emma, it's normal to be confused. Desire can be overwhelming to the point it's uncontrollable. That is how my desire is with you. My desire for *YOU* is hard to control. Just like my love..."

Can I learn to LOVE this man...?

"I have been waiting for you to feel that same desire for me. In your poem, you said, 'to proceed with caution and in moderation.' I promise you that. I know that I haven't in the past and that is one of my biggest regrets. I want you to demonstrate your desires at the pace you feel comfortable with. And I know it will be better than satisfactory — we will be earth-shattering together, my love."

Holy shit, he thinks the poem is about him.

———

His desire burns bright in his eyes as he pulls me to the edge of the bed and pushes himself to the junction of my thighs. He seamlessly glides his hands up my back and kisses my neck, causing a bolt of unwanted shivers down my spine followed by another bolt of white-hot fire that hits my core, causing me to bite back a throaty sound.

As if reading my body's reaction, he draws his hips deeper into the junction of my thighs with urgency—parting them further. A low burning flame sparks deep within me as he glides his hips up my center. I feel the power of his arousal which demands acknowledgment as he glides it up my center again, this time stopping at my clit—as if pouring gasoline on the small flame. My whole body ignites.

Ohh... OH SHIT!

I plant my hands on his hard chest, wanting it to stop before having to recognize the authenticity of my body's reaction.

"I'm … I'm not ready… Shit…" I blurt out, stumbling over my words. I hide my face in his chest, taking in his woody scent.

"What can I do to help you be ready?" he says after clearing his throat.

His body's tension is unmistakable. With my head on his chest, I find the strong beating of his heart oddly comforting. Its strength gives me confidence.

"I'm scared," I whisper.

He wraps his arms around me and pulls me tighter. The heat of his chest warms me, easing my shaken reality. *I want him.*

"I will wait for you. I have learned that I cannot force you into wanting me. I will *NEVER* force you to be with me again…You have the power."

I have the power…

RICK IS SITTING at the head of the table with the paper in his hands when I walk in. He curls the corner of the page as he watches me enter the dining room. "You're five minutes late," he reprimands me.

———

95

"Sorry, I was checking in with Ms. May to see if she needed any help with breakfast," I say, taking my seat to the right of him.

"There is a reason they are called hired help."

Brutus walks in carrying our trays of food. He sets our plates down and I thank him before he quietly leaves.

"Enjoy, we have much to go over this morning."

"Mm-mm...." I moan in appreciation. Ms. May has outdone herself again. The French toast is beautifully arranged on the plate with a mix of colorful fruit on the side. Strawberries being one of my favorites, I pick one up using my fork and bite into it. The juice blasts into my mouth and I close my eyes, savoring the sweet taste.

"One of these days, I would love to feed you ... in bed," he says in a husky voice, almost making me choke on the succulent fruit. I cover my mouth and begin coughing from the shock of his directness.

Rick slams his fork down angrily, making me jump back. In a low growl, "Where is the ring I gave you?"

"Oh ... I ... I took it off yesterday... I ... I have it in my bedroom. I will go get it." I jump up but he grabs me by the arm and brings me back to my seat.

"Why are you not wearing it?"

"I was afraid to lose it," I say, thinking of the first thing that comes to mind.

He tosses all the plates in one swift motion—knocking them to the floor before he ejects from his seat and storms out.

Now that's the Rick I know ... this Rick I can handle. I know how to feel... Fear!

Shakily, I stand and begin to clean up the mess. *Fear him, Emma ... you can't love him!*

Brutus comes in to help. "Ms. Andrews, are you okay?"

"Yes, I'm sorry, Brutus." My voice cracks.

"Emma, your room now!" Rick's voice echoes from the doorway.

I look up to Brutus—frozen.

"Go," Brutus whispers.

Chapter Fifteen

EMMA

I HEAR THE thundering steps echo in the hallway as I stand in the middle of my bedroom with my body quivering and awaiting Rick's appearance. My eyes shift from the clock on my nightstand to the doorway and back again. *Ten minutes!* I have been waiting for ten minutes for him to appear. With every second my body tenses more.

Is he going to punish me? Which side of Rick is going to arrive?

A shadow fills my doorframe, causing me to focus once again in that direction. His face creases the moment our eyes lock. His flaming green eyes look duller as if in pain. *Pain – from me not wearing the ring?*

"Where is your ring?" This time his voice is more controlled with a tinge of — *regret?*

I had already retrieved it before he entered my room. With it in my hand, I open my palm to him.

"Do you not like the ring?" he croaks.

Fearing his reaction, I quickly answer, "No, it's not that."

"It's too bad I don't believe you," he says. His voice is low and slow. He shakes his head as he looks at the ring. If I didn't know better, I would think he feels defeated… "You are a terrible liar. I have to go. You will not be leaving the penthouse today. You are to work on plans for the library in your study. I will be in my office. I'll see you at supper." He grabs the ring from my hand and, fisting it, he walks toward the door. Barely audible, he says, "I'm sorry for my rage." He walks out.

AS I KNOCK on Rick's office door, my heart slams in my throat.

"Come in."

My palms sweat as I turn the door handle. I hate asking Rick for anything, but I have to with the library. I take a leveling breath, enter, and make my way to the chair positioned opposite Rick.

"I have a few ideas for the library I wanted to run past you," I say before he can say anything first.

He sets aside his work, giving me his full attention, causing my nerves to jump.

"Okay, let's hear it." Smiling, he waves for me to bring my notebook to the desk.

As I walk up to the desk, he motions for me to come around. Setting the notebook in front of him, he pulls his chair out. Surprising me, he pulls me onto his lap, then scoots the chair back into the desk. Tucking his head under my arm, he rests my arm over his shoulders. A giggle escapes my lips.

"What are you doing?" I giggle again.

"I love that sound," he says as he curls his arms around my waist.

Something blooms deep within me. I stomp it down and centralize myself. Why are you here...? *The library!* "I was thinking about the decor for the library. I was hoping to do something different from what we have." I open my notebook to the pages with all my sketches. Holding my breath, I wait for his answer.

"You want to use secondhand items and vintage decor?" he asks, looking over the pages.

"Yes." I point to some of the designs. "I'm looking for a comfortable, cozy cabin feel using secondhand items. Like a place you would snuggle up with a book and hot cocoa," I say as I envision it in my head — hoping my sketches portray my ideas accurately enough for him to see them clearly. "I want people to want to stay."

"It's not something I would pick, but I must say, Emma, these sketches are impressive." He pulls out a pencil from the drawer. "Can I add a few things on here? I have a few ideas, too."

"Yes! Of course."

To my surprise, it feels comfortable sitting with him. I watch as he elegantly moves the pencil on the paper. My heart swells in my chest seeing this side of Rick. *Is this the same man that stood in my room just hours ago?*

"I want to see some of your own touches and poems on display. You are incredibly skilled. You need to show it," he says.

"Thank you, Rick. So, does that mean you like my idea?"

"Yes, I want you to make it your own."

I giggle happily and throw my arms around him—instinctively hugging him. "I was so nervous."

"I don't want you to be nervous with me." He reaches up to tuck my hair behind my ear.

Yes … this Rick … this other Rick — I want to kiss — again…

I meet his green eyes, and my heart flutters in my chest. I search for his lips and feel an overwhelming urge to kiss him. His lips curl into a sexy smirk and a little dimple catches my attention. I follow a lazy path up to meet his eyes when I notice a small white scar just above his left cheek.

"You want to kiss me," he says in a throaty voice.

Heat coils in my center. I lift my finger to touch the scar. "What is this from?" I ask for a distraction and meet his intense stare. He reaches up for my hand and, gliding it to his lips, he kisses every one of my fingertips, sending sharp currents up my arm.

"Not a story I want to relive."

My thoughts go to what Ms. May told me about his father, and sympathy for the child Rick once was swells within me again. I lock onto his eyes, wishing to heal his pain, but in a split second his eyes change — the green of his eyes flames.

—

Rick pulls out his chair, stands up with me still in his arms. I let out a squeal of surprise. He turns me in his arms, setting me on top of his desk. He cups my face with his shaking hands and plants his forehead against mine. "Emma, please! Can I kiss you?" His dark voice shakes, matching the intensity of his eyes.

His need vibrates through me, causing my own to kick up a few notches. I nod, unable to fight my own desire. *Rick wants* ME!

His lips brush tenderly against mine, and sparks ignite in waves. He deepens the kiss, probing his tongue for mine. My lips move as if they have a mind of their own and match the tempo of his tongue with soft strokes. My body buzzes as I wrap my arms around his neck to stop my hands from shaking.

He breaks the kiss with a throaty growl, wraps his arms around my hips, and pulls me against the solidness of his thigh, applying just enough pressure as wetness pools at my center, causing me to let out an involuntary moan.

His tongue flickers gently over my collarbone, surprising me with the sensation. I whimper. With another growl, he rakes his teeth across my skin.

Oh shit...

I wrap my arms around his neck, holding on for dear life. His strong hands remain on my hips as he lifts me, grinding my clitoris up his thigh. I dig my nails in his back, feeling as if I were climbing higher and higher. If I let go—surely, I'd fall. Slowly this time, he grinds again with just enough pressure to make my mind spin. *Oh God, how is this possible?* All the new sensations send my nerves into overdrive, as if everything is hitting all at once. I let out another breathy moan, not even trying to hold it back this time.

A knock sounds on the door. Rick picks me up off the desk and holds me up against him as he slides me down his thigh, applying intense pressure to my clit. He covers my mouth with his hand as if he can read my body and knows how it will react. I let out a louder but muttered moan. Simultaneously, he hollers, "One minute," drowning out the sound of my pleasure.

He kisses me hungrily as my feet hit the floor. I stand on wobbly legs and straighten my clothes, my sex aching as it pulses for more... *More what?*

"Love, go into the bathroom. Cool down a bit. As sexy as you are in this very moment, this is for my eyes only. Understand?"

I nod and wobble toward the bathroom. My body flames as I feel Rick's green blaze lick over me with every wobbly step I take, making the cotton of my clothes feel like sandpaper against my skin, wanting to take them off.

I quicken my step in fear that I will react to my last thought, and nearly jump through the door. I press myself against the heavy door. *Think. What the hell, Emma? You want to – to get naked ... with RICK?* I feel as if I am a tight string about to snap. I push off the door and decide to walk a circle in the bathroom to loosen the needy tension.

I want him. But this is the same man that –

I hear Rick's voice with two other men bouncing off of the cold tiles of the bathroom. Walking back to the door, I push my ear to it to make out what they are saying.

"Boss, we have it done," a man's voice says.

"But did you *FIND* him?" Rick snaps.

"Umm ... no, Boss, but the first package has been shipped to its destination... As for finding *him* ... the last place he was located was out of the country... Lenny was checking..." another man says.

Lenny ... I haven't seen Lenny in months, I think as I can picture the man who shadowed Rick everywhere. *Where has Lenny been?*

"He has some of the best men to help him, that is why I hired you ... Do your job – you two pieces of shit are turning out to be worthless. So much for being highly recommended... He could be under your noses – " Rick snaps.

"But Boss, we – "

"Shut the fuck up. He is not getting the package no matter what threats he sends... And I don't want to hear another word out of your mouths until you are telling me that he is found!"

Rick snarls.

"What about the transfer —?"

"Lenny will take care of it. Now leave…" Rick says in a low tone.

A loud crashing sound vibrates through the door followed by the door slamming. My heart bangs wildly against my ribs.

I try opening the bathroom door, but it is locked. *Shit, what do I do…? Did they hurt Rick?* I pace the floor, all traces of passion gone. What transfer and package? I have always known that Rick was into something … but what? And what does Lenny have to do with this… threats … are we in danger? Is that why he upped the guards? Where has Lenny been in the last few months and why haven't I seen him around? My mind spins. All of a sudden — *click* — I hear the door open.

I run to Rick with a different twist of fear. "Hey, what is this?" he says, folding me into his arms. I land hard against his chest.

"I started to worry that something was wrong. I tried the door and it was locked and I heard —" I say, talking too fast.

"See, I'm fine. Somehow the door got locked by mistake and a pile of books fell off my desk. When you didn't come out, I thought I scared you with what just happened between us."

"Oh … right … about that…" I take a step back and level out my breathing.

"Look, love, it's okay; we can take it slow. I wanted you to see that there can be pleasure to it… I wasn't going any further." He holds up his hand. "I promised you."

"No further?"

"No further. Like I said, I wanted to show you the pleasure it can bring."

Holding out his hand, he leads me out of the bathroom.

Pleasure…

CHANCE

I WALK IN the direction of Rick's office to discuss his last email and to give him my list for temporary accommodations. I mentally prepare myself to run into Emma. *Keep her at arm's distance; think of her as a sister. Don't compromise the mission...*

I bring my hand up to knock on the office door, just as a woman's giggle seeps through, stopping me from knocking.

I look to see if anyone is around and drop my hand. *No one!* I push my ear closer to the door to hear. No mistaking Rick's muffled voice resonating through the thick wood.

Then a loud shuffle sounds and my hand flies to the doorknob as anxiety boils up. *I will fucking kill him if he is hurting her!* Just before I turn the knob, a moan echoes — Emma's moan — I instantly recognize it. I let go of the knob. *Fuck, what is she doing...?*

My temper burns white hot as my vision blurs. I want to throw my fist through the door as pain pierces my heart. *Are you fucking kidding me?*

She's not yours, Chance... My heart squeezes tighter, draining blood out with every beat — slowly killing me with the thought of Rick's hands on her body.

Footsteps bounce off the hallway walls and I quickly control myself. Turning, I see Brutus rounding the corner with two other men dressed in solid black. I walk in their direction.

"Mr. Fletcher, I'm surprised to see you. I didn't know Master was expecting you, too."

"I was hoping to find you. I have that list for you," I lie and hand it to him.

"Thank you. I will have it for you right away," he says as he takes the list and shoves it into his uniform jacket. "Is there anything else I can do for you?"

"No, I was just looking for you," I say, tipping my head to signal my departure. I add, "Thanks."

"Very well, good day." He turns in the direction of the office.

"Hey, Brutus, I haven't seen Rick and Emma anywhere. Do you know where they might be?" I ask quickly, unable to stop my roaring need to confirm my suspicions.

"Last I knew, they were in the office, going over the plans for the library. Did you need them? We are headed that way."

"No, it can wait until tomorrow. Thanks," I say as my nails bite into my palms, turning my knuckles white.

The fuck they were going over plans...

EMMA

RICK AND I enjoy light conversation with a delicious meal set before us. This side of Rick—this pleasantness—is something I find myself enjoying the more I spend time with him. *Just maybe, I could be with him – this Rick.* I eye him as he sits back in his chair, looking very relaxed. *Have I ever seen him relax ... ever?*

"Now, love, I have a few things I want to discuss with you. Or ask you..."

I stiffen momentarily thinking the old Rick is coming back. *The* OLD *Rick – when did I even start thinking about – the* NEW *Rick?*

He swirls the dark red liquid around in his globe before continuing. "It is important to me that you wear your ring. With that, I will be taking you ring shopping to pick any ring of your choosing and I want you to love it as much as I do you."

"Any ring?" I question teasingly hoping to keep the playfulness between us.

"Yes, my love, any ring."

"Ohh," I manage to let out as the intensity in his eyes sears through me. *No, Emma! Shut him out... This is a dream; this isn't Rick...*

"Secondly, I will be gone for five days and Chance will be ordered to stay with you—at all times."

Chance ... for five days...

"Five days is a long time. I will miss you," I say, knowing what Rick wants to hear.

His chest puffs out. "I leave tomorrow morning after I take you ring shopping. And after this afternoon, I am handing all control of the library to you. You impressed me today."

"Thank you, Rick," I say and feel my heart swell.

"I also want you to hire a part-time staff to help."

"Oh, staff, well, I don't know if—"

He interrupts me, "Trust me, you will need them. I couldn't manage without the help of Lenny."

"Where has Lenny been? I haven't seen him in months."

"He has been away helping on business. One more thing, and this is the most important and non-negotiable. With me being gone more, you will be staying in my room one night a week. I will let you pick the night, but I will get you alone one night a week."

"What?!" I choke out and my stomach drops to the floor.

"It's non-negotiable. I promise that you are in complete control of the situation. Meaning, if you just want to lay there and I can't touch you, then it's your rules and I must obey. But I get one night a week where you are in my bed."

I swallow the massive lump in my throat. "So ... what happens if *YOU* break the rules?"

"You punish me, in any way you see fit," he says in a low husky voice.

LYING IN BED later that night with my journal open and my mind numb, I can still feel Rick's powerful presence and his melting green eyes burning into mine. *Punish me in any way you see fit...*

I have always leaned on my writing to help me understand what the hell is going on in this thick head of mine. But tonight—I have nothing. Finally giving up, I curl up on my side and see the beautiful roses staring back at me.

Grr, NO feelings for Rick!! I silently yell at myself.

I squeeze my eyes shut, willing my imagination to whisk me away. I can always count on that—my imagination.

A tall frame of a man walks toward me. "Emma..." He is wearing a white button-up shirt that has been rolled at the sleeves, showing off strong arms—Mr. Ocean Eyes. "Emma, what can I do for you tonight?"

My eyes lock onto his sexy mouth and I know exactly what he could do for me. This is one man I know I can share all my worries with; he would never deny me because he is my dream man...

"Do you want to kiss me?" he asks, only his voice sounding eerily similar to Rick's. Rick would never deny you...

"But I don't know if I'm doing it right..." I say breathlessly.

"I can teach you." No, not Rick's voice! Mr. Ocean Eyes'—my dream man...

I look up to the perfect shade of blues and greens that mix like dancing waves. I could stare into them for a lifetime. Now he is perfect, I think as I start drifting away in the tranquility of the waves.

Yes, of course he would be perfect. I made him up – my perfectly sexy dream man, I think and settle deeper into the bed.

But just as I drift off riding the wave of the most perfect hues of blue-green, the color begins to swirl and smoke. When the smoke clears the color melts into a warm chocolate – Chance's eyes – then they flame with a brilliant green – Rick's...

Chapter Sixteen

CHANCE

I SHOVEL ANOTHER bite of Chinese food into my mouth and a soggy noodle covered in soy sauce lands on my outstretched leg.

Fuck, I need a bigger table, I think as I set down the half-eaten box and pick it off my pants. I toss the noodle and the rest of the box into the trash without even getting up. That's the nice part of a small apartment—everything is near, I think as I shuffle through another stack of papers that is scattered across the table.

Emma's moan rips through my mind for the hundredth if not thousandth time and I have to stop myself from picturing her body pressing up against Rick's. *I hate him … No, I* FUCKING *hate him*, I think as I try to roll my shoulders to loosen the tension that is building.

No man—no real man—has to play mind games to win a woman's love. *That's not real love … that's manipulation.*

And that is exactly what Rick is doing to Emma—fucking with her head. Just like how she talked about the scars on her skin; her perfectly smooth and flawless skin—skin I want to run my fingertips down. Hell, run my lips down … tasting her. I want to hear her moan my name … to show her a real man's love…

I scan the top few pages, stopping myself from letting my mind wander dangerously... *She's not yours...*

It reads: *Promissory note.* Then down a few lines: *Mr. Gage. I haven't seen that name before...*

After reading what looks like a legal contract between this Mr. Gage and Rick for the purchase of this building, I can't find anything that stands out.

Who is this Mr. Gage? I think and my gut squeezes as if telling me to keep digging into the connection between the two men.

My phone chimes and I toss the pages into a box that sits on the floor before picking it up.

Who is it this time? I wonder as I see there are two emails and a text from James saying something about going to the club tonight — *just like James.* My mind drifts back to Emma and Rick, and Emma's soft moan. My fists turn white... *I could use a distraction.*

I shake my head. No good will come from me drinking my problems away. *Problems... is she a problem? No — getting her away from Rick is the problem.* I open my emails to see one from The Lieutenant:

Fletcher,

This is the second time I am asking for that information from you. Don't forget your assignment — intel on Rick Stevens — that is all. With your placement, I want all reports about the girl as well. I need to hear from you immediately — or I will send in reinforcements to relieve you of your duties...

-Lieutenant

Something irks me about The Lieutenant wanting to know about Emma. My assignment has nothing to do with her. As The Lieutenant stated when I started this "duty," it is a simple intel assignment and the subject is Rick Stevens. So why does he want information on Emma? And he called her "*girl*" — she is far from being a *girl*...

Opening the last email, I force myself to focus on the words on the screen.

Mr. Fletcher,

Tomorrow morning you will have training with Mr. Marshall in the a.m. I'm sure he has already planned out a time with you. Afterward, you are expected to be at the penthouse at 1 p.m. to escort Emma for the day. I want to remind you of Emma's restrictions and the consequences for her breaking them. She will be punished. I also want to remind you of your obligations to her safety. Emma's regulations are for her own safety and you are required to inform me of any that are broken and ensure that she remains in the approved locations.

-Rick

I toss my phone back onto the table and my anger boils in my chest. *How can she want to be with this asshole?*

Chapter Seventeen

EMMA

I HEAR VOICES coming from the kitchen as I walk down the back stairway. Entering the kitchen, I see Rick, Ms. May, and a younger woman—approximately my age—standing around the island in deep conversation and completely unaware of my presence.

"I don't like someone handling my kitchen," Ms. May says to Rick.

"You know that with what we have going, you need her here to help when you're gone." Rick smiles down at the red-faced Ms. May.

"NO, I don't! I can prepare all the meals and Emma can heat them up when I'm gone," she snaps.

My stomach squeezes. *I have never heard someone talk back to Rick.*

Rick walks around the island and pulls Ms. May to his side in a gentle embrace. "You know you won't win with me. I have made up my mind. She is not to take over for you, just to help you and learn—that is all," he says in a soothing tone.

Taking advantage of the fact that they are completely oblivious to my presence, I observe them. I watch as Rick continues to comfort Ms. May with his arm over her shoulder; he crests and rubs her shoulder like a loving son. *How did I not see the bond between these two before now?* I gaze to the other woman; she, too, drinks in the scene between Rick and Ms. May, making me wonder who she is. I see her eyes lock onto Rick and then soften with affection. Something foreign builds in my chest and an overwhelming desire to knock her eyes off of him courses through me. *Who the hell is she?*

Ms. May huffs and shakes a finger at the other woman — snapping her to attention. "Fine, but I plan all the meals."

"Yes, Chef," she replies, sounding like a soldier at boot camp.

"Good, Ms. May. In time you will enjoy having the help. Now, promise me you will behave and not kick her out of the kitchen again," Rick says with a chuckle as he squeezes her shoulders.

In Ms. May's ornery style, she wiggles her hips. "No promises," she says as she looks over her shoulder and away from the island — catching me eavesdropping. Her whole face lights up. "Now, there's someone," she says as she strides in my direction, "I can promise not to kick out of *MY* kitchen."

Rick turns and our eyes lock, causing goosebumps across my skin and heat to my cheeks. Ms. May opens her arms and gives me a hug, breaking the intensity of his gaze.

She guides me back to the island to join them. "Darling, we have a lot to catch up on. I hear you and Rick are getting married," she says as she pats me on the back.
"Congratulations, you two! I didn't know that you two... Well, it doesn't matter..." Ms. May continues on as she glances to the new chef. "It's so exciting ... isn't it?"

"Yes, Chef," she says quietly, avoiding my eyes.

Oh, I wasn't misjudging her. *That bitch wants Rick.* I put a smile on my face and force out my hand to introduce myself. "I don't think we have met. I'm Emma, *RICK's* fiancée."

"I'm Molly Wright," she says, her eyes transfixed on Rick — again. *Breathe before you slap the shit out of her.* I look to Rick for a distraction from the anger that is building up in me. His bright smile greets me, and his eyes flame their brilliant green as if he can read my mind.

"Come on, my love. We need to get going," he says, picking up my hand and lacing our fingers together. He turns us to the door.

Just before we reach the main doorway, Molly hurriedly asks, "You don't want breakfast this morning ... Mr. ... *Rick*?" The way she says his name brings back thoughts of slapping her. Instead of reacting to her, I tighten my grip on Rick's hand.

Rick peers down to me before answering her. "It's *Master* and no. Ms. May will be training you all day. This morning I have to take my love to pick out the ring of her dreams," he says, kissing my temple before we exit the kitchen.

It isn't until we finally enter the elevator that I feel myself relax. The elevator door shuts and Rick leans back against the wall and stares at me. "Jealousy is flattering on you."

"*What!*" I snap. "I wasn't jealous," I say, rolling my eyes.

"My love, I will let the eye roll go—this time. But you were jealous of the attention that woman was giving me."

"I wasn't jealous." My voice rises an octave.

"Emma, Emma, Emma, what to do with you now?" He hits the stop button on the elevator and a cold chill runs down my spine. *Shit, I pissed him off—the* OLD *Rick.* Never before have I had an outburst and talked back to him. I quickly look down. "I'm sorry, Rick."

In one step, he picks me up by my waist and pins me against the icy wall, my feet dangling as his flaming eyes bore into mine.

"I don't want you to be sorry."

What! Why isn't he punishing me...?

"Love, it turns me on when you show possessiveness over what is yours. And *I AM YOURS.* It's even sexier that you don't recognize your jealousy. I have so much to teach you."

"Wait... I didn't..."

He crashes his lips on mine as he hungrily devours my lips. As he pierces his tongue into my mouth, our tongues collide with force. I moan into his mouth with pure passion as it rips open a piece of my heart. He jolts back just as quickly and drops me to my feet.

———

Taking a step back, he pushes his back against the opposite wall. He takes a deep breath, looking away from me. "I made you a promise. I will not break it. *I … promised…*" he repeats as if to remind himself more than to tell me.

My heart pounds wildly in my chest as my eyes run over him. His usually neatly combed hair looks disheveled as he runs his hand through it again. With the top few buttons of his wrinkled gray shirt open, I watch the flexing of his toned muscles with every intake of his labored breathing while he attempts to regain control. *Did I cause Rick to lose control?*

Oh holy hell … he is sexy like this. Vulnerable and sexy… Shouldn't I be scared? But I'm not… My heart slams from the raw passion of his kiss. No, I'm not scared of this Rick. The realization that I control this Rick makes my mind spin. I have always known that he wants me, but I never knew that Rick *WANTS ME…*

I step closer to him and reach out. *Just how much control do I have over him?*

He flips the button, bringing the elevator back to life before he holds out his arms, keeping me at a distance. "Not now, love. I need a minute."

Yes, I have control of Rick.

Chapter Eighteen

EMMA

"WHAT'S THE PROBLEM, sweetie?" the jeweler asks me as his wise eyes meet mine.

I don't respond and he nods in acknowledgment. He straightens the display on the top of the glass. "I'm willing to guess, if you are having a problem with picking the ring," he says, looking in the direction of Rick, who is waiting in the office, "it's not about the ring but the someone. Or maybe there is someone else on your mind..."

Warmth heats my cheeks and I look down to avoid his knowing eyes. "I guess all of the above," I say. *Why did I admit that to him...?* "But how did you guess?"

"I have been doing this for a long time, sweetie. I can tell if two people are in love or not."

Oh shit! Is he going to tell Rick? I don't even know how I feel myself. "Oh... You're not going to tell Rick?"

"No, sweetie," he says, reassuring me.

"Okay, so what do you think about Rick and I?" I ask, hoping for some of his wisdom.

"It's a given; the man is crazy in love with you. But I would bet my last dollar he has hurt you in some way—making you hold back." He crosses his arms over his thin chest.

"Somewhere deep down you love him, you're just scared of it," he says, smiling to himself. "How did I do? Did I get it right?"

My mouth falls open.

"I'm going to say I hit the nail on the head." He winks.

"How … How did you know?"

"Now, sweetie, I can't give away all my secrets. Sometimes for the best things in life — you have to take a chance on it…"

Chance… How can I marry Rick if I have feelings for Chance? Because Rick hasn't given me a choice. He demands it…

The jeweler interrupts my thoughts. "I want you to pick two rings that you love. Then let him pick from them — that way he feels he still picked it for you."

You can do this; you have no choice… "Let's do this," I say.

"Okay then, tell me what you like."

"Hm … well, I like small. I do like rose or white gold. I guess I would say something vintage." My excitement bubbles. "Oh, I love sapphires. If I were to pick a shape, I'd say oval."

"Now we are getting somewhere." He walks over to a display and starts pulling out rings. "I will be right back," he says as he walks to the back room.

A minute later, he comes back carrying another black velvet box and sets it down in front of me.

"Are you ready…?"

My chest tightens. "Yes."

"Close your eyes."

MY NERVES JUMP as we walk into the office where Rick is sitting with his phone in his hand. He looks up and slips his phone back into his pocket, smiling to greet us. "Any luck?"

"Yes, I had her pick two and she is to tell you what she thinks of each one and how they make her feel," the jeweler states, staring directly at me.

You can do this, Emma…

"Okay," Rick says without hesitation.

The jeweler opens the first box and I look down. An exquisite, large blue sapphire set with two larger diamonds on each side. The white gold twists into elaborate curves, making it look like it came from the mid-century era — *it's beautiful*.

"This is crazy…" I say as my cheeks heat.

Rick picks up my hand. "Ernie has been doing this for a long time. If he is telling us to do this, then there is a reason. I won't question his reasons."

"Okay," I say, looking back to the ring. "I like this one because it's beautiful," I say shyly.

"It is a beautiful ring, one of my favorites from my collection," Rick says, looking over to Ernie. "I see you were in my *PERSONAL* vault."

"Yes, sir," Ernie says quietly.

"Continue," Rick says to Ernie.

As Ernie opens the second black velvet box, my heart palpitates hard in my chest. My eyes lock on the single oval diamond that is set in the center of a rose-gold flower. The craftsmanship is breathtaking. I hold my breath, wanting to put it on.

That's when I notice for the first time that Ernie's hands are shaking slightly. A thick silence hangs in the room and I look to Rick. His eyes are fixed on the ring.

Ernie shifts in his chair. "Sweetie, what about this ring?" he asks as his voice cracks.

I look back to the ring. *How does it make me feel…?* I feel Rick's eyes on me.

"I love it," I say. "This is going to sound crazy but it's like it's calling me…"

Rick stands and quickly walks to the exit of the office. "Ernie."

I watch as they both exit. *Shit, what the hell…*

Alone in the room, I look back at the ring. *What is it about this ring?* I pull it out of the case and slide it onto my finger. It fits perfectly. My heart swells at the thought of wearing it. *Can I marry Rick? I could learn to love him, right?* I hold my finger out to admire it. *It's mesmerizing…* The more I look at it, the more I don't want to take it off. *I can fall for this* NEW *Rick.*

Out of the corner of my eye, I see Rick and he startles me. "Oh, you scared me," I say and put my hands to my chest.

His face twists as he looks down at the ring on my finger. He picks up my hand to take a better look. "Do you love it?" he asks with a thick tone but not meeting my eyes.

"Yes, I do. But I would be happy with whatever you choose."

"It fits you perfectly," he says, bringing my hand to his lips. "It belonged to my mother and now it belongs to you, my love." He kisses my hand tenderly as a single tear runs a trail down his cheek.

Chapter Nineteen

CHANCE

THE SMELL OF sweaty musk saturates the air as I wipe my dripping forehead. The last few days of sparring with Andy has surprised me. We are much more evenly matched than I thought. I begin to pack up my gear as my thoughts wander once again to Emma and what I heard in Rick's office.

Andy slaps my back as he walks past me. "Hey, what's with you today?"

I shove the last of the gear in the bag and zip it up. "What do you mean?" I ask, turning to him.

Andy tosses a water bottle at me. Catching it with one hand, I take a seat on one of the benches by the grappling mats.

"I'm just saying—you're unfocused today. I was about to pin you several times—you're usually more of a challenge for me... What's on your mind?" he asks, also taking a seat.

His question throws me off guard and I hesitate. *Can I tell him?* No, he'll report directly back to Rick.

"Oh, you know, man—a woman." I shrug, making little of it, hoping he won't press for more.

"Good luck with that. If you figure out the mystery to the creatures called women, hook a brother up with the intel." He laughs as he balls up his water bottle and tosses it to the trash can—making it.

"Nice shot."

"Thanks. So what's the deal with your woman?" he asks.

Your woman. She will never be yours... A stabbing pain jabs in my chest. I decide not to talk about Emma. *The last time I trusted someone with the knowledge of a woman I cared about...*

"So what's your story then? If you don't want to talk about your woman," he asks, noticing my reluctance.

"What story?" *My story of ... my past ... how I failed her ... failed Libby.*

He sits his elbows on his knees and leans forward. "You know, Rick gives me everyone's info. But I want to get to know my crew. And coming from Rick, you're trustworthy and that's hard to do with a man like Rick — who trusts no one."

"Yeah, I get it. Well, what do you want to know?" I feel my shoulders tense up.

"I'm not investigating you. I just want to get to know you. What do you guys do for fun around here?" he asks, leaning back in his chair.

I roll my shoulders. *Relax, he's not digging.* "About the only thing to do when you're off is go to the club. I have heard the parties can get pretty wild."

"I don't know about all that; it's really not my thing. I would rather shoot some hoops and kick back with a few beers," he says.

Maybe we will get along better than I thought.

SHE IS NOT mine. She is not mine. Fuck! I wish she were mine, I repeat to myself as I wait for Emma at 1 p.m. like Rick instructed. I pick up the book she lent me and open it for the first time. Judging by the cover, it looks to be more of a thriller than a romance.

Twenty minutes later, I am completely sucked in and don't hear as Emma enters the room.

"Are you ready?" she chuckles, snapping me back to reality.

I look up from the pages to see her standing before me smiling. My heart skips a beat.

"I'm ready," I say, forcing myself to build a wall around my heart as I repeat: *She is not mine. She is not mine.*

"Let's go."

As we make our way down to the library, I catch myself staring at her and repeat: *She is not mine...* and roll my balled-up shoulders as the library comes into view. *Thank God.*

Walking up to the reception desk, I see stacks of boxes taking over the space—stopping me in my tracks.

Emma bumps into me. "What the...?" she says as she looks around me. "Oh my gosh ... oh my gosh," she squeals as she nearly pushes me over to reach the boxes.

Her eyes brighten as she starts doing what I can only assume to be her happy dance, which causes my heart to slam in my chest. She stops and looks up at me, giving me her full attention. *God help me...*

Even God himself couldn't stop the emotions from hitting me. *She ...is ... so ... beautiful.* No matter how hard I fight it this time, it feels as if she has sucker-punched me in the gut as her blue eyes pierce into me. *I want to pull her into my arms!*

Instead, I smile back at her and pull out my pocketknife, handing it to her. "You better start opening all these boxes before they decide to run away," I tease.

One by one, she cuts the top of each box, looks inside, and does a little happy dance that I don't think she even realizes she is doing.

As she opens the final box, I walk up beside her. "So, what are you going to do with all of this?"

She smiles and shakes her head. "I don't know. I can't believe it came so fast." She steps backward and in her pure glee, she doesn't notice the box behind her, and she trips. Her arms fly forward and without thinking, I pivot and catch her, grabbing her hand that is holding the knife. I look down at her in my arms, but her eyes are squeezed shut. "Em, are you okay?"

She looks up at me and a rush of desire overwhelms me. I want to lean down and kiss her parted lips. A blush stains her pale skin, and I repeat, "Em, are you okay?"

She nods her head yes. I force myself to stand her up and pull her body away from mine. I take the knife out of her hand. Still, she remains silent. "Emma, are you sure you are okay?"

I scan her body for injuries when my eyes land on her left forearm, where she is bleeding. "Shit." I scoop her up and jog to the bathroom.

Setting her down on the edge of the sink, I reach for the paper towels to assess her cut. "Emma, are you going to pass out? You need to talk to me. Deep breaths. If you feel like passing out, I need to know so you don't get hurt from falling," I say, wiping the blood — *Emma's blood.*

Emma shudders. "I ... I'm ... light ... headed," she manages to say and sets her head on my chest for support. "But ... fine..."

I grab a few more towels and wet them down before applying pressure to stop the bleeding.

"It's deep but I think it will be fine once we get it to stop bleeding. A little bit of super glue should close it shut," I say, ignoring the desire to kiss her forehead. "Emma, are you feeling better?"

"Yeah ... I am," she says dreamily.

I pull slowly away, meeting her eyes. She blinks a few times and pulls her arm away from me as I apply pressure. "Ouch, that hurts," she snaps suddenly.

"Hey, don't move. I have to keep pressure until the bleeding stops," I say, firmly holding onto her arm.

"Fucking let go of me!" she yells, pulling harder this time. I let go and the paper towels go flying through the air.

Damn it! What is she doing...?

I put my arms up. "Emma, I'm not going to hurt you. I'm trying to help you. You're bleeding."

Her wild eyes look down to her arm as blood rushes to the surface and drips down her arm. She pales — and immediately faints.

"Damn it!" I say, leaping to catch her just before she falls hard to the floor.

EMMA

THE SMELL OF musky dust balls is the first thing my mind registers. I blink myself awake as a flash of light blinds me. As I sit up on the couch in the reading nook, my eyes land on Chance sitting on the floor with his back against the couch as he lazily flips through a book.

"About time," he says as he shifts to his knees and turns toward me.

"What happened?"

"Well, you fell back, tripping over some boxes with a knife in your hand — cutting your arm. Then you passed out from the blood."

I look down at my left forearm to see white gauze wrapped around it and it all comes back to me. "Oh, oh my gosh, Chance... I'm sorry," I say, hiding my face in humiliation.

He must think I'm crazy.

"There is nothing for you to be sorry about. How are you feeling now?"

"I'm sorry for freaking out on you. I feel fine ... I guess. How long was I out?"

"Not long — just long enough for me to stop the bleeding, glue you up, and walk around and eat a sandwich," he teases. "Only a few minutes."

"Thank you, Chance. I am sorry I freaked out."

Standing up, he says, "Really, it's okay. Everyone handles blood differently. But you're good now, right?"

I move my left arm to evaluate the pain. It stings but I know I am going to be fine. "Yeah, I'm fine, thanks to you." I stand up.

"Good, because we have a lot to do." He claps his hands together.

"Maybe, if I had eaten today, I wouldn't have passed out," I say, thinking out loud as I follow him to the desk. Again, I run smack into the back of Chance as he halts to a stop.

I look up as he turns around. "First things first—we feed you," he says, his tone sharp as he plants his large hands on my shoulders and turns me toward the exit.

THE AROMA OF pizza has my mouth watering the minute we walk into Mama's Pizza Shop. I stare indecisively at the menu. *I'm starving.*

"What can I get you?" a younger woman with her hair piled on top of her head asks. I watch her hair bob as she flips her focus between Chance and me. Her eyes light up with every glance she gives Chance, making it obvious that she is checking him out. *Really? I'm right here...*

"Chance, are you eating? I'll buy," I say.

"I can always eat pizza. I will take one meat lover's and two slices of your pepperoni. What do you want?" He looks down at me.

"I'm so hungry, I could eat the whole menu ... Umm ... I will do the same ... Oh, and can I get an order of the cheesy bread, too? Please."

The lady's eyes never leave Chance. "Medium or large?" she asks as if I'm not in the room.

"Large," I say, choosing to ignore the sliver of irritation that wants to surface and instead begin to bounce with excitement for the food.

Chance laughs and I feel the need to defend myself. "Hey, a girl needs to eat and I'm starving."

"It's $28.98," the lady says, fluttering her eyelashes at Chance.

Really? Could she be more obvious?

"It goes on account 1572, please," I say crisply.

The thought of Rick suddenly floods my mind—*Jealous ... I'm not jealous.*

"I bet you five dollars you can't eat it all." Chance winks at me.

I think about it for a minute. "I was going to split the cheesy bread with you. So is the bread included?" I say, knowing how much I can eat when I'm hungry.

"I'm not giving up my half of cheesy bread," he says with a mocking tone.

Arriving at a table, I stick out my hand. "Double or nothing." He smiles as we sit and shakes my hand.

"You're really going to eat all of that?"

"Oh yes! If I haven't eaten all day, you would be surprised how much I can eat. I'm winning that bet. Besides, I had lots of practice when I was little, sometimes going days…" I stop myself abruptly and look to the food counter.

I hear Chance shift in his chair. *Shit, I said too much … What is he going to think – ?*

"Here," he says, and I watch as he pulls out his wallet and pays me for the bet.

"But I haven't even started yet…"

His chestnut eyes soften. "I know you will win."

Just then they announce our food. He stands, retrieving the tray, and brings it back to the table. I look up at him. "Thank you."

"So why haven't you eaten yet?" he says, sounding bothered by it.

Taking a bite of my pizza, I cover my mouth. "Just busy this morning," I say as heat crawls up to my face.

He pauses before speaking again and takes a leveling breath. "I thought Rick took care of you," he murmurs.

I set my pizza down and pick up my napkin. An overwhelming sense of protection builds up in my chest and I feel the urge to defend Rick. "He does. We didn't expect this morning to take as long as it did."

Why do I need to explain this to Chance? It's not his business!

His warm eyes shadow to black. "What is more important than to meet your basic needs?" he asks tersely.

"It wasn't like that. We went ring shopping and time got away from us."

Chance's nostrils flare for a brief second, as he looks to my left hand. Silence stretches between us and he forces his gaze out the window.

"Do you love him?" he asks, his voice just barely above a whisper.

I square my shoulders and challenge his question. "And what does it matter to you if I love him or not?"

The golden hues of his chocolate eyes illuminate as he meets my eyes. "It matters."

I divert my gaze, unable to stand the intensity of his. "It shouldn't."

Chapter Twenty

CHANCE

FRUSTRATION PINCHES EMMA'S face, bringing her eyebrows together as she is submerged in boxes. She's spent the last three hours sorting and unpacking, but it still looks as if she's gotten nowhere.

"Emma, why don't we put all the boxes in the back room for now and get rid of the things you don't want? That way you will have room to think."

She looks over the top of the stack. "You know, that's a great idea. Grab yourself a box," she says, picking up one for herself.

We head to the back room and open up the door. I follow her inside as she flips on the light. She almost drops her box at the sight of the room.

"Really?" she says, sounding deflated.

The back room is stacked floor to ceiling. Everywhere you look, there are stacks of boxes.

"I guess that plan is out. Have you not been back here?" I ask in shock.

"No, I just helped her in the front. What do we do now? I will never be able to meet deadlines with all this crap."

"Honestly, you need to hire a few more hands. Do you have any idea what all this crap is?" I set my box down, looking over the piles that are stacked as high as my head.

"Rick told me to hire help, too. I don't have any idea what all this is. How can one small lady have so much shit?"

"I would rather you not touch it. I don't want it to fall on you. It's an accident waiting to happen in here. One pile falls and it is going to be like dominos." I look down at her. "I don't want you to get hurt again."

She avoids my eyes. "About that... Can you please not tell Rick how it happened? You know, the part about me holding a knife." A blush flushes her cheeks.

"Why should I have to do that?" I ask, feeling ill at the level of lies she has to weave in order to protect herself from a man that she is marrying.

How can she love him...?

"If Rick knew I was using a knife, he would be extremely upset with me."

"And you don't want him to punish you," I say, finishing her sentence.

Her beautiful eyes turn cold. I tread lightly, unable to stop myself. "I know, Emma. Rick emailed me *ALL* the details of your arrangement." *She can't really believe that this is love.*

Every atom in my body wants to scoop her up and show her what *a REAL MAN'S* love should feel like. I would cherish her, nourish every inch of her body, and teach her what she is worth. How could she possibly think that Rick loves her? *What if I use this to my advantage ... to understand what Rick has over her? Maybe if I understand, I can get her out of here.* "Okay, I will lie for you, but you must answer three questions for me."

"Anything," she says with little hesitation.

"First, let's get out of here," I say. *How am I going to ask just three questions when my head is swimming with them?* "Let's go to the reading nook."

"You're that serious with your questions?"

"You don't know what I'm going to ask." I take a seat on the couch. "How are you *NOT* worried?"

"It will be worth it." She smiles as she sits down on the opposite end of the couch and curls her legs underneath her.

"It makes you this happy over me not telling Rick?"

"Yes, was that your first question? If so, then this will be easier than I thought." She smiles mischievously.

"No it's not," I answer dryly. *How do I ask my first question without upsetting her again…? But I must know!*

Deciding to make myself more comfortable, I turn to face her. "First question. Do you love him?" I ask, nearly stumbling over my words. My chest squeezes as if I am suffocating.

Her smile fades. "Umm… I guess I should have seen that coming…" She closes her eyes for a moment. Opening them again, she says, "I guess I truly don't know how to answer. I mean, I see the good he can be and maybe I could grow to love that side."

She traces the floral design of the couch with her long elegant finger, avoiding looking at me. I can hear the truth in what she says, suddenly understanding the stupidity of my question. *How could someone in her position understand what real love feels like? Someone who seems so innocent and naïve…*

"Emma, have you ever been with anyone before Rick?" I ask without thinking.

I watch her cheeks turn a soft pink. "Rick moved me to his penthouse on my eighteenth birthday and I never dated anyone before that." She shifts uncomfortably in her seat. *That explains it.* He moved her the day she became legal age. *That fucking bastard…*

I ask the last question cautiously. "Emma, how has Rick hurt you?"

She sits up straighter. *Good, she does have fight in her.* "That's none of your business."

"Emma, it is my business. I'm guarding you and protecting you. I must know everything I can about you." I hit her with a low blow. "If we are attacked, I need to know how you will handle it—like how you freaked out when you cut your arm." Most of what I was saying was the truth, but part of it was me selfishly needing to know.

She slouches her shoulders and focuses on the floral design again. "I understand. Well, you know about the punishments.

129

If I get in trouble, I get hit. Once, I was whipped... " Her voice sounds empty.

I navigate my way around the information. "And besides the other day, when was the last time he hurt you?" I fist my hands at the thought of him using a whip on her.

I'm going to kill him.

"It's been a while, actually. Maybe even months, but when I first moved in—it was all the time." I can feel her walls come down—brick by brick—the more she opens up. "A few years ago was the worst. I don't remember it but I was in the hospital..."

Ice fills my heart with the image of Emma lying there unable to defend herself against Rick's beatings. I tense. "Emma, is that your scars? Is that when he whipped you?" I ask cautiously.

How do I make her understand that I didn't see any scars...?

"Umm, yeah, I don't remember it, but—"

"Emma, I never saw a scar on you..." I hold up my head to interrupt her and continue, "I'm not questioning if it happened, I'm saying that the scars you talked about, I didn't see them."

"I know," she breathes out. "After the thing in the pool ... I made myself look ... but I remember the pain ... I know it happened..." she says shakily.

Unable to stop myself from comforting her, I reach for her hand and pull it to mine. "I believe you. But I must know all of it, Emma. What else has Rick done?"

She pulls her hand sharply from mine. "That's all."

"No it's not, Emma!" I stand. "Is it?"

Fuck, she can't marry him!! How can she think about loving him?

I pace in front of the couch. "Tell me. I want you to say it."

Maybe if she were to say it out loud, then she would truly understand the severity of Rick's actions. Just maybe she will realize that she can't love him.

"No," she breathes out.

"You will say it, or I will tell Rick," I snap, feeling an inch tall.

Her eyes widen. "No ... no, you wouldn't."

"Yes. I need you to say it."

She stands, anger boiling in her eyes. "Why, why do I have to say what that monster has done to me?" She shoves at my chest. "No one wants to hear it. *NO ONE*. Do YOU want to hear how he has held me down? Is that what you want to hear?" She shoves me again and her eyes cloud as she continues. "*YOU* want to hear how he has stolen all my first times from me? I will never know what a real first kiss feels like. Or how my first time should have felt..." She buckles at the knees and falls to the couch, covering her face with her hands. She sobs.

I kneel down, careful not to touch her, knowing she needs space. "No, Emma. I was hoping I was wrong." I pause to give her a moment. "I want you to be *REAL* with yourself — to *FIGHT*."

Chapter Twenty-One

EMMA

MY PEN SCRIBBLES lazy circles all over the pages of my journal as I lie on my bed. The memory of Chance's voice echoes. *I want you to be real with yourself.*

Do I love Rick? Is there any love for him in the depths of my heart...? I turn the page, letting my subconscious paint me a picture...

Why do I not understand?
Is this all part of your plan?
I wish I was told,
The secrets of the heart;
Wishing I could guard,
The thoughts in my head.
Praying I will forget,
The feelings that you took.
When you read my book,
Stealing like a crook;
Can I love this master of deception?
Does he deserve redemption...?

Maybe if Rick wouldn't have read my poem about desire, I wouldn't have been vulnerable and let myself get close to him. *You broke your promise to yourself – to forever hate him... all the pain he has caused you…*

But how did he slip into my heart? How!?!

Chance is right about one thing—I need to be *real* with myself. And to be real I have to acknowledge that deep down—as stupid as it sounds—I have a sliver of love for Rick—*this new Rick*—and that scares the hell out of me. But I can't help but see the man he could be…

And then I have my feelings for Chance to try and understand as well. My heart slams in my chest as he appears in my mind's eye. Fighting this energy between us is like pulling two strong magnets apart only to be forced back together. *Does he feel that same pull?* The way he looks at me, sometimes, it feels as if he can read my soul.

But the last few days, after our conversation in the library, he has been avoiding me and keeping his distance. *I told him too much and scared him.*

A knock sounds. "Come in." I look up to see Brutus walking in as I climb off the bed.

"Ms. Andrews, supper will be ready in ten minutes. Ms. May had to leave again this afternoon to accompany Master. The new chef, Molly Wright, has requested supper be served in the dining room," he says in his proper British accent and smiles.

"You know what, Brutus? I'm not feeling it tonight. Please have my meal brought to my study. I have to finalize some of my projects for the library."

"Very well, Ms. Andrews. But I'm sure Ms. Wright won't be happy with your request."

"I have to get this done before Rick is back tomorrow."

"Yes, Ms. Andrews, I will let her know." He bows and leaves the door open as he walks out.

Grabbing my things to head to the study, I turn toward the door. Just as I reach my doorway, I look up to see Chance in his room with his bare back to me. With every blow to the punching bag, his muscles flex, causing his tan skin to glisten in the low light of his room. *Boom, boom, boom.*

With every boom, my heart races. *He is so…*

I'm completely powerless to look away. His graceful movements are hypnotic, and his sheer agility causes my mouth to water. I follow the lines of his back to his narrow waist — *to his ass ... Oh holy sh —*

"Ms. Andrews, can I help you with something?" Brutus asks, peeking around the corner and causing me to jump.

"Oh … ahh … no, I was just heading to the study."

"By the way you were staring into Mr. Fletcher's room, I thought you needed something," Brutus says, smiling a little too broadly.

I feel my cheeks flame. "No, just lost my train of thought … I…"

Damn it, Brutus, why did he call me out? My skin burns as if Chance's eyes are running wildly across my skin. *How can I feel him looking at me? He is looking at me … Right?*

"Well, Ms. Andrews, if you are on your way, I will bring your supper to you as you requested," he says with a bow.

"Thanks, Brutus," I mutter. *Don't look, Emma. Don't look to see if he is staring.*

But I never seem to listen to my own advice, and I glance back into his room. *Please don't be looking — please…* My eyes lock on his. *Shit.*

His lips curve up as if he can read my thoughts. I would love to know what he is thinking right now. And by the look on his face, I'd bet it is something along the lines of: *You like what you see?*

CHANCE

The image of Emma's rosy cheeks heats my drive, and I land a loud smack with my fist to the worn leather bag, arousing me even more. *God, what I would love to do to her…*

She's not yours… I remind myself, like I do every time I see her. Keeping my distance from her over the past few days has proven to be harder than I anticipated.

The flush of her skin clouds my subconscious and I envision all the shades of pink I could make her skin. My dick stiffens instantly. *Fuck, how does she get to me this quickly?*

I land my last jab and decide another cold shower is due to extinguish the fire building within me.

I FOLLOW THE smell coming from the kitchen. *Damn, I'm hungry,* I think as I walk through the kitchen doors. Ms. May's new chef, Molly, a petite woman with black hair that she wears pulled back tightly in a bun, stands behind the island with plates steaming in front of her. Her eyes are glued to the dishes as she prepares them, not seeing me enter the room.

"Hey ... Molly ... so what are we having tonight?"

Her amber eyes sparkle, and she looks up at me, setting aside her dish towel. "We are having my family ravioli tonight," she says, beaming.

"It definitely smells amazing and I'm starving." I pull up a seat.

"It took me forever, it seems, to talk Ms. May into letting me cook this meal. I can't wait for you to try it."

"Then I can't wait to start. Are we all eating in the dining room?"

Her eyes fall back to one of the plates. "Not now. Ms. Andrews wants to eat in her study." She sighs.

"I can eat with you in here. Then you're not eating alone," I blurt out without thinking.

"Really! I mean... Yes, that would be great."

Brutus enters suddenly. "Ms. Wright, you called for me? What can I do for you?"

"Can you please take Ms. Andrews her food?"

"As you wish," he says, taking the dish and leaving the room.

Molly picks up her plate and takes a seat next to me. "Enjoy," she says, picking up her fork.

I pick up mine and take a bite.

It's good—but more than that—it's one of the best meals I've had here. "Holy shit, this is amazing."

"I'm glad you like it. It's one of my favorites to cook." She giggles.

"Yeah, you definitely got the cooking part of it down."

"Thanks."

I finish my plate and push it aside. "Where did you learn to cook like that?"

"From my grandmother. She practically raised me."

She stands and pulls out a bottle of wine from the refrigerator.

"Was your grandmother a chef, too, then?" I ask.

She smiles as she fills up two wine glasses. "No, but it was her dream and she taught me everything I know." She walks back around the island and hands me a glass of red wine.

"Thank you," I say, tipping the glass in appreciation.

She sits down and turns her chair in my direction as she overexaggerates crossing her legs at the knees and slides against my thigh. "You're welcome," she says as she takes a sip and looks up at me from under her eyelashes, leaning closer.

Is she making a pass at me?

I ignore my gut. *No ... it's just been longer than I want to admit since I've been with a woman...* "It must have been hard without your parents around."

"Yes, it was. No siblings either." She pulls out her full bottom lip in a pout. "I didn't have anyone to play with me," she says in a low, seductive tone.

Her lips land hard, slamming against mine—catching me off guard. *What the...?*

A loud crashing sound comes from the doorway and pulls me to action. I push away from her and see Emma's back as she retreats through the doors, leaving a pile of broken dishes in her wake.

"*Shit!*" I murmur.

"I have never had that reaction after kissing a man before," she says in a salty tone.

"No, I mean—I just wasn't expecting it," I blurt out and my mouth instantly dries. Standing, I grab the wine glass and tilt it back—downing the remaining liquid. My eyes water from the sting and I divert my focus back to the empty doorframe.

Emma...

I hear the sharp metallic sound of Molly's chair move and I force myself to look her way. *Emma's not coming back... You fucked up... You don't deserve her...*

"Look, Chance—" Molly says softly.

"I'm sorry. It's just that I—"

She holds her hands up, stopping me. "Just go."

Chapter Twenty-Two

EMMA

I HATE HER, I think as I storm to my room. *She's a —* My throat tightens at the image of Molly's lips on Chance's. *I hate … I hate…* "Grrr," I yell as I wipe the wetness from my face. *He is not my — not my anything … so why am I crying?*

Turning the handle to my room, I head toward the bathroom. *Bed.* I'm tired and need to go to bed. My heart swells with pain. *Of course he would want her … she is beautiful.*

I start the shower and hop into the hot spray. A hundred thoughts run through my mind at once. *What is going on with my emotions…? I hate her… I don't ever have a chance against her, she's so beautiful … but the way she looked at Rick … but she clearly wants Chance — and Chance wants her…*

I sink to the floor and pull my knees to my chest, hugging them. My chest quakes as I let everything out — everything I haven't wanted to admit.

He doesn't want … me…

CHANCE

I QUICKLY SCAN Emma's study and find it empty, so I make my way to her room. The sound of the shower echoes through the bathroom door. I reach for the handle and swing it open. *We need to talk; I must know if she has feelings for me.*

"Emma." I feel my palms sweat when my eyes land on a shadowy form in the shower. She is on the floor, curled underneath the water, and an overwhelming desire to storm in and cradle her into my arms slams me.

"Emma, please talk to me..."

"Go away, Chance," she whispers.

"I'm not going anywhere until we talk."

Marching to the opposite wall, I sit on the floor and lean my back against the cold marble tiles. The icy surface penetrates to my core, smoldering my flame.

"I'm not going anywhere until you talk to me, Em."

Her silhouette stands and I watch as she moves around reaching for things. A light floral scent fills the room, adding fuel to my flame. My body ignites all over again as I watch her lather her hair—the smell fills my lungs. I think about how it would feel if my fingers were doing the work for her, running my hands through her beautiful blond waves, washing away all the tiny bubbles as they flow over her curves. *Fuck,* I think as the seam of my crotch begins to feel restraining.

I force myself to focus. "Emma, please tell me why you won't talk to me? What did I do?"

I need her to work through her web of emotions. I could tell her that she is jealous of Molly kissing me, but I need to be sure and she needs to determine that for herself.

"Chance, I don't want to do this. Go away," she says, her voice cracking.

"Please, why are you upset? Let me help you, Em, I just—"

"I don't know. Okay. I just don't. What do you want from me?"

I stand up. "What are you feeling now?"

"You're not going to leave, are you?"

"I told you I wasn't"

"I'm angry. Angry because you won't just leave me alone; that's what I am feeling now."

"I can tell," I chuckle. "But I want to know why you are angry with me."

"What does it matter? Why don't you just go back to Molly? She seems more than willing to capture your attention."

My eyes shoot to her silhouette again. *I knew it — I knew she was jealous.* How do I get her to understand it is her that I want?

"I don't want her."

Suddenly, the water turns off and Emma reaches through the cracked door for the towel, hugging the frosted door — her body becoming visible. I swallow the lump in my throat, and I lose all rationality as I snatch the towel and bring it out of her reach. "You're not going without us talking this out."

"Chance, it's none of my business who you want. Now, please give me my towel."

"You have two options. Listen to me or step out to get your towel." I watch as she retreats back into the shower, making her decision. *That's what I thought...* My voice thickens with passion and I continue, "Like I said, I don't want her. We were eating and I was asking her about her family and upbringing."

I begin to pace. "She's not even my type. I mean she is pretty but the next thing I knew, she was kissing me."

"Didn't look like you were fighting her off."

"Emma, you're not understanding. I don't want her. I want—"

"I can't do this," she says as the door to the shower flies open. I jump in surprise. I look up to see Emma — beautifully naked — stepping out with her eyes focused on her target — her towel.

The sight of her causes my head to spin. Her skin is flushed from the heat of the water. I follow the path down as beads of water lick her skin. The image of licking them off her skin causes my dick to jump — to be able to pull her into my arms and follow the descending of the droplets with my tongue. *God, she is breathtaking!*

Her nipples are taut little nubs as she approaches, and with every step she takes, the weight of her full bare breasts causes them to jounce. I suck in a rigid breath. *Oh, the things I want to do to her.*

She stops before me, pulling her towel right out of my frozen hand. She wraps it around, concealing their perfection. My eyes look to hers — searching. I'm met with a storm, longing — raw and thick — as her powerful need overtakes me.

I inhale sharply. *She wants me...* I pick up on the scent of her arousal, her sweet nectar permeating my nostrils. I step closer, our bodies inches away. Lifting my right hand, I slowly skim the top of her shoulder, wrecking the tiny droplets with my fingertip. She takes a hissing breath.

I reach behind her neck. Closing the space between us, I wrap her wet hair around my wrist and gently tug it, tipping her head back. I search her face; her pink lips part and I lock my eyes on hers. My need for her burns like an inferno and I watch her own battle within her icy blue eyes. She lets out a moan that ignites my flame. I enfold her deeper into my arms and her magnificent breasts press against my chest, heavy and full. *Damn...*

I lower my lips to hers, closing the distance, painfully slow. "Emma, you are who I want my lips on," I say in a raspy voice I don't recognize as my own.

I lower my lips to meet my salvation — *Emma.* The connection silences her whisper of a moan.

I take my time, savoring the softness of her full lips. My need for her heightens as she wraps her arms around my neck, pulling me into her. Deepening the kiss, I gently tug on her hair, tilting her head farther, giving me full access to her mouth. A deep growl vibrates in my chest as her passion matches my own — feverish and hungry. I feel a pulsing energy building between us. Using all my power, I control my momentum, slowly probing her lips with mine.

She moans again as my tongue traces the inside curves of her lips, begging to taste her. She gives in to my tongue's demands. She tastes like the sweetest fruit, driving me nearly over the edge, wanting to taste every inch of her body. My dick hardens some more, straining and testing the durability of the zipper of my jeans.

I squeeze the curves of her ass and lift her up to me. She parts her legs and straddles my hips as she lets out a high-pitched moan and grasps tighter around my neck, breaking the kiss.

My chest heaves as I flick my tongue down to her collarbone, lapping the pool of droplets — teasing her. The heat of her sex burns through the only layer separating us — my jeans. My cock aches to be released to feel her silky wetness.

I glide her sex up the length of mine. "Christ you're driving me mad ... I want you — "

She moans into my mouth as I claim it with my own. *God, help me...* This time, I feel her body shake as she glides up my length, whimpering in need. Shifting her, I palm her ass in one hand, holding her against my hips tighter. I reach up and tug on her towel, freeing her beautiful body as the towel falls to my feet.

Breaking the kiss, I take in the sight of her straddled against me. *She is perfect...* I cup the weight of her full breast and rub my thumb over her nipple. Her intake of breath tests my restraint. My voice traps in my chest as I feel her wetness soak through my jeans.

Her body starts trembling in my arms as she glides harder up my dick. *Yes, baby, I know what you need —* "Emma," I whisper, kissing down her neck. "Please let me show you what you ... need." I kiss the top of her breast, causing her to hiss. "Emma, please let — "

"Chance ... I need you..." she whimpers.

My mind clouds as my body's desire takes control. Without hesitation, I grip both of my hands on the succulent curves of her ass and build up a rhythm by dragging her sex against my cock. Her soft moans echo off the wall, driving the pace — building hard, faster. My own yearning for release heightens to a near breaking point. *Fuck...* Her whole body quakes and she screams as she rides her wave of ecstasy, ripping through me, tearing at my soul — bringing me to my own undoing — my heart.

She goes limp in my arms. "Em?" I carry her to her bed and lay her down. She curls sleepily with a glow on her skin and my chest fills... *God help me ... I love her...*

Chapter Twenty-Three

EMMA

SITTING IN THE middle of the library, I look up to see endless rows of shelving. There are books upon books as the shelves seem to fade out in the distance up to the heavens.

Lying down, I rest my head back. The smell of honeysuckle and lilac fills my nose and the soft grass tickles from underneath me. I cross my ankles together and place my hands at the back of my head, making myself comfortable. Enjoying the serenity, I close my eyes. "This is my safe haven," I say out loud.

Opening my eyes, I turn to lie on my side, watching as books fly through the air, hundreds of them, spines facing upward like birds – their pages open and gracefully fluttering with different-colored wings in all sizes. They fly to and from the shelves – mesmerizing.

A man's voice echoes – "Helloooo…" – distracting me from the beautiful magic. I sit up, trying to find the voice's origin.

The shelves seem to suddenly disappear. A large apple tree replaces the shelves, startling me. I run to hide behind the trunk that is so thick it would take two or three people hand in hand to reach all the way around it.

"Hello." He sounds as if he is just around the large tree.

I slide my hands on the tree. The bark feels rough but warm and I lean over to peek around. The apple tree smells of earth and wood. There is no one there.

Bewildered, I step around the tree, this time looking in all directions for the man. All I see are wide open green fields. Grass that goes on for miles. Just me and this tree, I think.

My feet bump something on the ground which catches my attention. I look down to see a blue blanket spread out with red roses embroidered around the outside edges and a wooden tray sitting on the corner. I walk around the blanket investigating. It looks to be my favorite wine in two goblets set alongside a fruit dish and, sure enough, my favorite book.

I sit down on the blanket, picking up the book to examine it closer, and fan through the pages — not a single word written in it. I feel my chest squeeze as I set the book back down and reach for the glass of wine. A hearty chuckle sounds from above me.

I look up to the tree — again, I see no one. I decide to lie back as my eyelids feel heavy. Closing them, I take a deep breath.

A whisper of a breath stirs against my neck, sending goosebumps across my skin.

I open my eyes and a pair of blue-green eyes stare down at me. A pulse of energy courses through me as if his energy has built to lightning, shocking every nerve in my body.

He leans closer, nearly inches away from my lips — igniting me.

In a low sultry voice, he whispers,

"…Wake up, Ms. Andrews."

"Ms. Andrews, it's way past time for you to get out of your bed. It's almost noon." Brutus's muffled voice snaps me out of my dream.

"Noon?" I repeat, bolting upright in bed and hustling out as fast as I can. "Brutus, please tell me you're joking."

"It's eleven thirty-eight a.m., Ms. Andrews. You missed breakfast. If you don't hurry you will be late for lunch with Master."

I head toward the closet and stop mid-stride — *Rick is back.* And all my memories with Chance from last night rush in. *Holy shit!* My body shakes. "Where is Chance?"

"Master sent him home for the day. You best hurry to not be late."

CHANCE

FOCUS...

Papers and folders are strewn across the table. I try concentrating on the puzzle before me — everything I have on Rick Stevens. *What am I missing...?* I lean back in the chair and bring my hands up to rest behind my head. The image of Emma overtakes my consciousness for the thousandth time today — again, breaking my concentration.

Just the thought of her, I can feel her lips on mine, how her body teases, the sounds she makes — *Fuck, I'm in deep...*

I stand up — *focus, damn it.* Pulling the chair away, I look down for a new angle. "What am I missing? Why is The Lieutenant having Rick investigated?" I say to my empty apartment.

I pick up my phone and reread the last email from The Lieutenant. It is only one line:

"What is the connection between Mr. Rick Stevens and the girl?"

The girl ... Emma's no girl. Is he talking about another girl ... maybe? My gut tells me he is talking about Emma. But I find it odd, The Lieutenant calling her — *girl.* And if he is asking about Emma, how is she tied into all of this? Is she in deeper than I think? That's the part I'm so puzzled about. Everything that I found on Rick — is legitimate.

What am I missing...?

EMMA

RICK IS SITTING at the table as I enter. He stands with a

smile.

"Love, how I have missed you these last few days," he says. Walking over to greet me, he wraps his arms around me.

"Thank you, I have missed you as well," I say but not meeting his eyes.

He holds onto my shoulders and takes a step back— examining me. "There is something different about you."

My stomach drops. *Could Rick know what happened between Chance and I?* He would kill Chance if he did. He probably would kill me, too, for the betrayal. I swallow the bile that threatens to rise and do the one thing I know will distract him.

I kiss him.

He pulls me into his arms as he deepens the kiss and a pull tugs at my heart as if a string is attached. I close my eyes, wrestling my body's reaction to the familiarity of Rick when the image of Chance's face comes into my mind's eye. I part my lips, inviting, thinking of Chance's not Rick's tongue. My center heats like a wildfire and all thoughts of Rick disappear.

Rick breaks the kiss. "As much as I would love to continue, this is not the place," he says, stepping back. "That is, unless you want to continue ... somewhere else..."

"Umm—" I mutter.

Rick locks his eyes on me and grabs my hand, bringing it to his lips. He kisses it tenderly, causing the string connected to my heart to vibrate. *What have I done?*

"Love, it's okay. I have a few things we need to go over. Let's just have a seat," he says as he ushers me to the table, and we take our seats.

The table has three piles of paperwork on it, one in front of Rick, one in front of me, and the last between the two of us. Where the silverware usually sits are pens and I look inquisitively at Rick.

"What is this?"

"We have important matters to go over before we eat," he says, gesturing toward the papers.

I look down and the word *Will* is written large across the top. "What is this for? I don't have any belongings."

"We are getting married; I want to bring you into the paperwork process of that agreement. I need you to understand what I am expecting from you with our marriage and what it is you can expect of me." He looks to me and continues. "This is a contract, Emma. A contract for life. And I need you to sign before we go any further."

A contract for life... My breath catches. *Life with Rick...*

"And if I don't want to sign?" I ask as if I have a choice.

"You will sign. Now," he says, looking at the page, "I will go over the major parts with you. I am to advise you to take your time. Read it thoroughly. The first page states what I expect of you."

I skim the first few paragraphs as he reads it aloud.

"You are to be loyal to me and only me. You are to show physical affection daily. You are to bear an offspring within the first two years of marriage..."

I continue scanning the first page. There are at least fifty things he expects from me... *It is a contract for LIFE...*

"Most of this will not be abnormal for you—with the exception of sleeping in my bed every night." He turns the page. "Let's move on for now. On the second page, you will see everything I will provide for you."

I turn the page and the size of his list surprises me. It's larger than mine. I skim down that list as he continues reading aloud. "I will provide a shelter. I will provide a living. I will provide an heir. I will provide love. I will provide—"

"This is more of a prenup," I state in confusion.

"It is both. I wanted to go over what we are both expecting from one another moving forward. The will starts on page four," he says, turning the page. "On page three, you will find some of the conditions." He pauses, waiting for me to catch up.

Only two paragraphs are displayed across the crisp white page. I skim across—*approved time frame*. And as I read deeper, he is willing to wait for us to be married, or so he says. I see the expiration date on this contract, giving me three months. My knees shake under the table. *That's soon...*

"Three months to marry you ... but what if—"

"Yes. That is all I am willing to wait. I said I will let you pick the day and if you read on, I have promised to wait till the wedding night — *to have you*."

My stomach squeezes and his words bounce off the walls of my brain — *to have you...*

"But you are required to stay in my room one night a week until the wedding day. That part is non-negotiable with or without the contract," he says in a low, gravelly voice.

I flip to the next page to distract my mind from thinking about being in Rick's bed. *I don't want to be in Rick's bed ... I want to be in Chance's bed —*

"From page four to page eighteen is the will. It is a full list of my assets. I do not have any family, Emma, so the minute you sign, everything will go to you. If something were to happen to me, married or not, it's yours. You just have to sign."

Shit! I feel like I am about to sign over my soul to the devil himself. *A lifelong contract...*

I flip over the remaining pages; Rick has more assets than I could fathom.

"All you have to do is agree and sign," he says.

I look up at his handsome face. *A lifetime with this man ... with Rick ... will I get the old Rick or the new?*

"Like I said, you can take it with you and read it thoroughly, before signing."

I push the papers aside and my heart lodges in my throat. "It's a lot to go over."

"Take your time," he says.

"Okay, I will. What if I wanted to make some changes?" I ask. *Am I really considering this...?*

He pauses for a brief moment. "Then I guess, if they are important enough for you to bring up, we will discuss them."

I smile. *This Rick, the new Rick, I could sign, right...?*

"Okay. What is this folder for?" I point to the other folder between us.

He quickly retrieves it and slides it over to him. "This is for another day."

Rick snaps his fingers and Brutus appears out of the corner of the room.

"Yes, Master." Brutus bows at the waist.

"Remove the paperwork from the table and put it all in my office. Then you may start bringing out our lunch," Rick says with a wave of his hand.

"Yes, Master."

I lift my hand and set it on top of mine. "Brutus, can you put mine in my study, please, so I can read it later?"

"Yes, Ms. Andrews."

I look over at Rick, expecting to see distaste for giving an order over the top of him, only to be met with—*approval.* And the string of my heart tugs again.

Brutus leaves with the paperwork and Rick picks up my hand. "You are incredibly sexy when you make demands."

Chapter Twenty-Four

EMMA

MY FINGERS STRUM the solid wood of my desk. *Thump, thump, thump… Okay, I can do this,* I think as Rick's contract stares back at me.

With the last few days being so busy with planning, I have been avoiding this tiny stack of papers.

Come on, all you have to do is read it…

It's a contract for life … with Rick … What about Chance? What would a life with Chance look like? Would it all be on a handful of papers? He said he wants me, but would he want a life with me? I haven't seen him since that night… Does he still want me?

And who do I want … Rick … Chance? With Rick, I at least know where I stand … He wants me in his life … for life…

My chest heaves and my palms sweat as I reach out and flip the top of the folder open. *This is a contract for life … FOR LIFE, Emma.* My breath quickens and I force myself to read the first line.

"Ms. Andrews, Mr. Davis has arrived and—" Brutus's voice announces, and I quickly slap the folder shut.

I look up to see Brutus eyeing me and I ignore his gaze. I look to Mr. Davis, a.k.a., Lenny. He is following closely at Brutus's heels. Lenny is Rick's personal secretary—no, assistant. Whom I haven't seen much of in the last few months. *Where has he been?*

153

After Rick's continued persistence to have Lenny help with the renovation of the library, I reluctantly agreed because of my looming deadlines. *I will take any help I can get ... even Lenny's...*

I push the folder happily aside. "Thank you, Brutus, you may leave."

Lenny walks over to the chair in front of the desk. "Rick has assigned me to help you with the library and party planning." He sits down in the chair, femininely crossing his legs at the knees. He claps his dark hands together in excitement. "I just love planning a fabulous party."

I look up from my desk and feel a weight lift at seeing this middle-aged man sitting across from me. I can't expect the two ladies Brutus hired the other day to handle everything for me.

I hold out my to-do list to Lenny. "I need you to go check on the progress of the library. This list has everything that needs to be done today in order to stay on track with the grand opening. Please ask Jordan and Leah if there is anything I am missing."

He plucks the list from my hands. "Darling, is this all?" he says flatly.

"Yes, for now. Thank you."

I look to the clock—2:30, time for my meeting with Rick. *And time to talk about some changes... I need to have time in the library...*

I stand. "Where are you going?" Lenny asks, following me toward the doorway.

"Rick asked me to meet with him in his office."

"Oh, I want to join. You know, just to make sure Rick doesn't need anything from me as well," he says as we walk in the direction of Rick's office.

My stomach squeezes. Lenny's upbeat demeanor makes it hard to miss his feelings for Rick. *Am I jealous of Lenny's feels...what is wrong with me...*

Rick looks up at both Lenny and me as we walk into the office together. "Good, I need to talk to you both," Rick says. "Love, where are you with the plans on the library? Are you on track with the grand opening?"

"Yes, Lenny is checking to make sure Jordan and Leah have everything. But last I knew, we should be at the final details," I say, trying to sound confident. "It would be faster if I could check it out myself—"

"Lenny, report back to me tonight. Also, did you get the email on the details for the engagement party?" Rick says, ignoring my comment.

"Yes, it will be lavish."

"Good, I will be leaving tomorrow morning—"

"Wait, what engagement party?" I ask.

"I am planning a masquerade party to celebrate our engagement," Rick says then turns his attention back to Lenny. "I want you to stay here to assist Emma."

"But I'm not needed at—"

"No. Stay with Emma," Rick snaps.

"Of course," Lenny says with a flip of his wrist.

Rick's eyes blaze into mine. "Have you had time to go over the contract?"

A blush creeps up my cheeks and I feel Lenny staring. "I was going to look over it this afternoon."

"I will be leaving for seven days this time. I would like it signed before I go. So if you wanted any changes, I need them by four."

"Okay," I say, looking away.

"Good, that should be all," Rick says dismissively.

Lenny and I stand and turn toward the door.

Just as I reach the door frame, I hear Rick. "Love, tonight you will be in my room."

BACK IN THE safety of my study, I tell myself to breathe and try to slow my racing heart. *You can do it. Just read the damn contract.*

No longer able to avoid it, I pull the folder open and scan the first page. Rick is right when he says there won't be many changes for me—except for me moving into his bedroom... My breath catches.

———

My focus falls to the next page — what I am to expect from him in our *CONTRACT marriage*. It is a contract marriage, I think, refusing to think of it as — *our marriage*.

I look over property after property that he owns, all over the U.S., with a few located outside the country.

I never imagined that Rick held this amount of wealth. He also lists several bank accounts with no amount. It just states that all money is to go to me.

I flip to the last page — searching. There it is. The fine print that I'm looking for. *I know him all too well.*

It reads: J. Gage no longer has possession of any property and is considered void of any future payments in regard to E. Andrews. Total debts paid.

What the hell? Possession ... future payments ... debts? What is Rick talking about and who is J. Gage?

I read on to the last paragraph:

"For you
will be my love for always,
and it is you that I will protect.
I just ask one thing of you.
With all my heart, I love you.
I ask you to find a drop of love in yours.
I can live a lifetime with the hope to make your heart completely
mine one day."

My heart pulls like a game of tug-of-war. On one end, I have my feelings for Chance. They feel warm like a summer's day, promising more, promising light — to light my way in the dark. And Rick is the dark — the unknown, scary but intense. His love is always over the top and I never know exactly what to expect from him. His love is demanding — and hard to ignore.

Do I love Rick? I feel the string tug on my heart. *Shit ... yes, I do ... somehow.* How did I let that happen? I don't want to... I want to love Chance...

My body warms... *Love Chance... Do I love him...?* My heart blooms like a flower on the brightest day basking in the rays of the sun. *Oh, yes, I do —*

Brutus opens my door and announces supper is ready.

Thank God...

RICK AND LENNY are already at the table when I walk into the dining room. As I reach them, Rick stands and pulls out my chair.

"Thank you."

He leans in, kissing my cheek. "Anything for you."

Heat burns my cheeks when my eyes meet Lenny's. I push at Rick's chest to stop him from going any further.

I take a seat across the table from Lenny, who is beaming. He looks as if he is about to bust at the seams.

"Did you go over the contract, love? You didn't come in at four," Rick says.

I look to him, then to Lenny, then back to Rick.

Sensing my discomfort, Rick turns to Lenny. "I will have you go to the kitchen to eat tonight."

Lenny's face drops and he opens his mouth to protest, but instead he picks up his drink and marches out of the room.

"Better?" Rick asks, sounding amused.

I tuck a strand of hair behind my ear. "Umm ... yes, thank you."

Brutus walks in with trays of food, deposits them, and leaves.

After a long moment, Rick finally encourages me to open up. "You have me to yourself now; please, ask away."

I clear my throat before blurting out, "You talk about physical affection and how it is required daily. What do you mean exactly?" I ask, paling. *And that's my first question? Really, Emma...?*

A hearty laugh roars through his chest. "Love, I'm sorry, I forget just how naive you are. I'm promising you that I won't make you have sex with me — that is, unwillingly. However, I do need you to show me attention and some form of affection.

———

Even if it's as simple as wanting to hold hands, I will take it." He reaches for my hand, pulling it to his lips and kissing the back ever so softly.

The small gesture sends goosebumps up my arm and his eyes dance with longing, chipping at the wall I have built around my heart.

"The smallest acts of love are the key in opening a broken heart," he says as his eyes flame. "You are teaching me this— how to love."

I gasp for air and pull my hand slowly away from him. My heart tugs as his words echo through my head.

"Let's eat. If you have any more questions, just ask. I don't want you to sign it until you're ready. Even with wanting it signed tonight ... it can wait."

"Thank you," I say breathlessly.

I pick up my fork and eat, letting all the creamy sauce from Ms. May's fettuccine overtake my senses.

"I have to make an appearance at the club tonight to announce the upcoming engagement party. Lenny has arranged the announcement around eleven. Do you want to go early for a few drinks? It may help you relax for tonight."

"Can I stay home tonight? I have a lot I need to get done."

"Yes, you can this time with all that is coming up. I will have to get ahold of Chance to come to the penthouse while I am gone."

"No! Umm I mean. I have had people non-stop around me." I'm hesitant to add the last bit. "Just time to myself. I miss the time when I didn't have someone watching me all the time. And, and I miss my swimming."

He pauses and I hold my breath. I don't want him to think something is wrong with Chance. I just need time. *Time away from everyone. Time to think...*

"I will let you have tonight to yourself. I shouldn't be gone long. I expect you to be in my room when I get back. As for swimming or wanting time out of the penthouse, you are permitted to go with Chance, only to approved locations."

"You are letting me go anytime?" I ask as excitement builds with this newfound freedom. Chance or no Chance—Rick has never let me leave as I pleased.

"Yes, but only to approved areas of the building. I will send Chance the locations and the changes." Rick stands up and his face pinches as he looks down at me.

I jump to my feet and throw my arms around his neck and kiss his cheek.

"Thank you, Rick!"

After Rick leaves, I head immediately to my study to sign the contract—forgetting all about the one line I had the most questions about...

J. Gage no longer has possession of any property and is considered void of any future payments in regard to E. Andrews. Total debts paid.

Chapter Twenty-Five

CHANCE

THE LOW LIGHT of the club mixes with the strong scent of alcohol, heightening my buzz from the six-pack Andy and I consumed in his apartment. The young blond waitress with tits up to her ears waves us to the edge of the bar. With her flirtatious grin, she looks back and forth between Andy and me as we pull up a seat.

"Hey, handsomes, what'll it be?"

I look over to Andy. "I will take a Bud Light. I got the first round," I say, paying no attention to the waitress.

Andy nods. "Same. Thanks," he says, scanning the room.

I evaluate Andy for a minute, thinking how he reminds me of someone, but who? I can't put my finger on it... But it's like we have hung out before...

Looking around, I'm surprised not to see James out on the prowl for some honey for the night. "Hey, have you seen James around? Most nights he is down here."

"Nah, he told me he plans to go out with that girl again tonight."

"Really? Good luck to her. I have never seen James keep them around longer than three dates. Then he is off to the next."

Scanning the VIP area, I spot Rick. I look all around for Emma, but she is nowhere. *Where is she?* I think as a ball rolls in my gut.

I haven't seen her since — that night. The last thing I want her to think is that she was just a hook-up. *She is so much more...*

"Rick's here." I elbow Andy.

He follows my gaze. "Yeah, and it looks like he is waving us over."

Shit. Rick isn't someone I want to see. My whole *job* is to be guarding Emma when Rick is not around. And if he is here, then where's Emma? If Rick really thinks she is in need of 24/7 protection, why is he doing a piss poor job at protecting her now?

"Chance, he just waved us over again. Let's go."

"Yeah," I bite out.

Rick's muzzle-headed bodyguard lets us into the VIP. We step around the large oblong table and take a seat on each side of Rick; that's when Rick's pain in the ass sidekick, Lenny, slides in beside Andy. *Come to think of it, I haven't seen Lenny around much...*

"What are you guys drinking?" Rick asks with a slur.

"Just beers tonight, sir," Andy answers.

"Eeee. They are manly men, Boss," Lenny says in his annoying high-pitched voice.

I look back to Rick, watching as he picks up a shot and throws it down his throat. "No, real men drink hard alcohol," Rick says.

What the fuck...? Rick's drunk... And where the hell is Emma...?

My chest tightens.

I control my reaction and glance at Andy to gauge his. His cool demeanor is as easy to read as a mask. He hides his own awareness of the situation — soaking up every detail.

I look back to Rick. "I didn't see Emma here," I say, trying to act indifferent.

Lenny hands Rick another shot. Rick shrugs. "She wanted to stay home."

My fist tightens around my beer can. *What the fuck.* "I thought she isn't to be home by herself and she isn't safe—*alone.*"

Andy snaps a look in my direction, and I register his warning—*Fucking chill out.*

"No, she thinks she is home by herself, but Mr. Nash is keeping guard."

The beer can crinkles in my fist—*Fucking Nash!* My anger rises thinking about an incompetent jackass like Nash watching the woman I love.

Andy, not missing a beat, stands up. "Sorry, sir, we will have to take a rain check on the beer. We have an early day in the morning with training." Andy snaps in my direction. "Chance, let's go."

Without a word, I get up and leave.

Standing outside the club in the crisp night air. Andy slaps my back. "I don't know what that was back there with you, but let it go, man."

Only one word escapes me. "Gym."

Andy grunts in agreement.

EMMA

I WAKE TO the sound of a fist pounding on my bedroom door. I jolt up in bed and my journal falls to the floor, my heart deafening my ears as it slams against my ribs.

Oh my God...

I see Rick standing there against the door frame, looking like a wild beast with his clothes hanging and wrinkled. His cloudy green eyes track over my body and he stumbles in.

"Why are you *NOT* in my bed!" he growls.

Shit, I fell asleep writing in my journal. I quickly climb off the bed. "Sorry, I fell asleep."

"Shut up. I don't want to hear your excuses."

He stops just before me and the smell of booze flogs around him.

"Yes, Rick, I'm sorry," I say, shaking.

Rick's face twists as his eyes glass over and he looks down his nose. He reaches out and grips my arm tightly. "Let's GO!"

I start to pull away, my stomach rising and my breathing quickening.

He growls again. "If you're a good *little boy* — it wouldn't have to be like this…" His tone is eerie.

Run…

I start pulling harder. *What is he talking about … little boy…?*

With him being unstable on his feet, I slip out of his grip.

I take a step back. Rick's fist lands on my upper thigh, hard, knocking me to the floor. I instantly curl in a ball and try to protect myself from another blow.

Rick's fingers encircle my waist as he pulls me to my feet. He sweeps me up into his arms and I feel his body shake as I grab onto him in fear. *Where is he going…? Shit … his room…*

Fear courses through my limbs as we near his door. He opens to blackness and I fight the urge to free myself from his grip, knowing it will be futile — *I can't get free…* He shuts the door behind him, and I hide my face into his neck — wishing to disappear.

Rick walks about the room, like a cat being able to see everything in the dark, weaving around any obstacles in our way. He stops abruptly and lowers me to my feet.

"This is not how I wanted to start the night with you," he says, straining. "Please…" He lets go of me and the heat of his body vanishes.

I feel bare standing in the blackout sea. The room hums with waves of energy that vibrate around me. Hugging myself, I arm against the darkness that tries to consume me.

A flicker of golden light cascades a soft glow around Rick's masculine frame, causing more shadows to dance as he turns toward me. I watch as he makes his way back to me, keeping his eyes on the floor.

He sits on the bed that is inches away and pulls me into his arms. "My love, I'm sorry. Will you forgive me?" he asks, his voice cracking.

My insides tremble and I place my hands on each side of his rugged face. "Yes," I say, not trusting myself with more.

I don't know what to think ... or say ... I don't want to make things worse.

Our eyes meet. And the image of a scared little boy flickers as I watch a hundred different emotions darken his gaze. He opens his mouth to say something, then stops and shakes his head. He looks into the blackness that surrounds us. *He wants to tell me something ... I can feel it.*

"I have something for you. That is, if you will still stay with me tonight..." His voice sounds pained. The sincerity of his need for me to stay with him seeps through each word.

I nod.

He walks into the darkness and I lose sight of him, causing my throat to tighten.

When he returns, he holds a golden box with a crimson bow. "For you ... open," he says, handing it to me, and his green eyes flame to life.

I take the box from him and turn to the bed. Setting it down, I pull the bow and open it. Matching crimson tissue paper lines the inside of the box. Underneath the tissue paper a silk crimson negligee presents itself. *Oh ... my ... God!*

I rub the silk with my thumb; it feels luxurious. I lace my fingers into the straps and lift it out of the box.

"Wow. Rick, it's beautiful," I say as my body flushes. *He wants me to wear this.*

Rick's hands rest on my shoulders as he stands behind me. He slides his hands down my arms and his touch heats me from the inside out. He steps closer to me, pressing my back against his hard chest.

"Will you do me the honor and wear it for me?" he asks in a husky tone.

The heat in my cheeks deepens with the realization that I do want to wear the beautiful garment. I nod.

Rick gently pulls the negligee out of my hands and lays it on the bed in front of me. His hands make their way to the hem of my oversized cotton gray nightshirt.

"Lift your arms," his voice gently demands.

I lift them as he pulls my shirt over my head. My palms tingle as he bares every inch of my upper body and tosses the shirt. I suck in a breath as he reaches the waistband of my matching cotton shorts. A mixture of fear and exhilaration courses through my veins like I'm playing with fire.

He hooks his thumbs on each side and bends as he follows my shorts down my legs. I feel them pile at my feet and I move to step out.

He is eye level with my ass, and I feel his breath tick over my skin, hot—taunting me. My skin blazes, begging for his touch. It feels like an eternity, waiting and anticipating.

His hot lips sear as he kisses my thigh, just below my ass cheek, first one than the other. I let out a gasp, surprised by the gentleness, and my sex sizzles. *Oh...*

I feel him stand. He reaches around me and picks up the garment. His breath brushes beneath my ear, causing goosebumps to explode.

"Lift your arms, again, love," he whispers.

I do as I'm told, feeling every nerve in my body vibrating. Rick slides the cold silk of the negligee down my arms and over my body. The coolness of the silk in contrast to the burning need flames me hotter. I suck in a breath.

My nipples harden from the sensation and my mind loses the battle against my body. *I want him, I want Rick...*

I feel Rick's gaze lick over every inch of my body as he walks around me—admiring.

"You're fucking beautiful."

His eyes never leave mine as he leans down and pulls off his shoes, then his socks. I break the intensity of his stare when his hands finish untucking the last bit of his white shirt. His long fingers make their way to the remaining buttons and he pulls off his shirt. *Oh...* I look over his well-sculpted torso covered with black hair and follow the path up his equally defined pecks and wide, tanned shoulders. *He is gorgeous...*

His belt chimes as his hands bring me to attention when his pants hit the floor. His arousal standing large and unashamed. I feel my own sex swell and wetness pool. *I want ... him...*

I take a step back, my mind and body at war with one another. *Yes, I want him...* Hitting the bed with the back of my legs, I stop. *Oh, I want him... I ... I can't, I'm not ready –*

"Love, I'm not embarrassed to desire you. I know you're not ready for me. Not just yet... I can see the battle in your eyes," he says softly. "Tonight, I just want to hold you. But it's up to you."

He pulls down the covers and climbs in, waiting for me to decide.

My mind spins. The events of the evening crash in and sleep creeps in the corners of my eyes. *Yeah, I need sleep...*

Going against all better judgment, I climb into bed next to him. I feel his weight shift the bed as he pulls himself closer to me. My eyelids are heavy as the familiarity of his body heat comforts my nerves. I sink deeper into the mattress.

He drapes his arm heavily around my waist and pulls me closer. I take a deep breath, matching the rhythm of his chest as it rises and falls. I surrender to the feeling of sleep. Just before I give in completely, he kisses my shoulder and whispers, "I love you entirely."

Chapter Twenty-Six

EMMA

I BOLT UPRIGHT in the blackness. *Shit.* I feel my heart thundering through my chest. *Where am I?* I search for a light — a light to rescue me from this feeling of doom.

I slide my legs off the pillowy bed and blindly reach out my arms. I make contact with something cold and hard on the nightstand. *The lamp!* I reach up and hear the tong sound as my hand lands on the metal lampshade. Light explodes through the room.

Blinking a few times, I take in my surroundings. *I'm in Rick's room.* Slowly, the events of last night rush back to me.

Last night, I think, and a tug pulls at my heart. I never knew Rick was capable of being … *gentle … passionate … so much more…*

I take in the room. It is painted in a rich burgundy with gold sparkles glittering the walls that resemble stars in the warm light. Unlike most of the rooms in the penthouse, this one has several pieces of large furniture. The four-poster bed is set as the focal point of the room and is covered in black silk sheets and burgundy pillows.

On Rick's pillow lies a single red rose and a note. I bring the rose to my nose and open the note.

To My Love,
   Words cannot begin to express my love for you.
      Your patience gives me serenity;
         Being my remedy,
      You are my only destiny.

Love, Rick

My mind fogs and my chest squeezes. I feel the room closing in on me. *I have to get out, NOW...* I immediately climb off the bed as if it is burning me.

I turn the handle to the door and enter the dark hallway. Turning in the direction of my bedroom, I slam into a solid chest.

"AHH," I say, stumbling back.

A pair of large arms whip around me. "Are you okay, Em?" Chance whispers through the darkness.

His heat penetrates as he tightens his arms around me.

"Uhh ... yes," I say, stepping backward, trying to control my frayed nerves.

"What are you doing here?" he asks.

My mind goes blank as I search for something to say.

The sound of shuffling echoes off the hallway walls and a beam of light flips on in his hands, lighting up the hallway and momentarily startling me. I close my eyes.

Opening them again, I watch a display of emotions play across Chance's face as he examines me still dressed in my negligee. His expression transforms from lascivious, to a sense of awareness, then to anger.

A throaty growl vibrates through him. "Did you *stay* in Rick's room last night?"

I look away. "Yes."

With a click of the flash, the light is gone, leaving everything eerily black and cold.

"Chance." My heart slams in my chest.

"It's four in the morning; go back to bed, Emma," he says. A faint light illuminates the hallway, bringing Chance's tall frame to a shadow in the doorway to his room.

"But Chance—"

I watch him duck into his room, shutting the door behind him and leaving the blackness to engulf me.

Chapter Twenty-Seven

EMMA

AFTER GETTING SOME much needed sleep to clear the mess of emotions in my mind, I walk to the study, welcoming the distraction. Lenny is sitting at my desk waiting for me. *Great, not the distraction I was hoping for…*

"Good morning, Ms. Emma. Did you sleep well?" he asks with a wicked grin. *What is it about this guy? It's like he knows everything that goes on here.*

Walking up to my desk, I choose not to answer him. "I have a lot to go over today. Is there something you need, Lenny?"

He pushes out of my chair, walking around me like a shark circling its meal. "I was just waiting on you. Remember Rick left me here … with you, but as I see, you are an hour late coming in. I was thinking that Rick must have worn you out last night."

What the hell! How did he know I was in Rick's room? "It wasn't like that, for your information, and it's none of your business. How did you—?"

"Oh, darling, I know all when it comes to Rick. And I mean ALL. It's a crying shame you haven't shagged that sexy man." He takes a seat in the chair opposite of me. "Anyway, the grand opening is a little over a week away … let's get this all done … I have more important things—"

"We should be done in about four days, if everything goes

as planned. That reminds me … where have you been…?" I ask, remembering the conversation I overheard in the office. I haven't seen Lenny for a few months…

"Just been busy, you know, Rick and his demands. What's on today's list?"

I hand him today's agenda. "Here's your list. I will be working in the study most of the morning. This afternoon, I need to go over to the library in person."

"Okay, this is all you need from me today?"

"Yes, for now. I will know more once I look over the library."

"I have another party to be planning, so I will work on your list first," he says, standing up.

"Okay, see you later then."

He stands and turns to the door. "Oh, Emma, before I forget … the next time you're in a room alone with a sexy man – use him right. You would be surprised how an orgasm can clear your mind."

I watch him leave without another word. Immediately after he is out of sight, Brutus enters the room.

"Ms. Andrews, I was told to let you know breakfast is ready."

"Thanks, Brutus. I'm a bit busy this morning. I don't know if I will make it down there."

"Very well, I will let the chef know to start without you," he says, leaving me alone.

I wasn't completely truthful to Brutus. Yes, I do have work to do, but I also want the distance from Chance right now. The more time we spend together the stronger the pull I have to him.

It took me a while, but lying there in my bed this morning, I began to understand that my newfound longing need was awakened because of Chance. He sparked something in me – something buried underneath all my pain. Now the problem is that I recognize it and it is consuming me. But does Chance want me…?

As I lay there restlessly, I also tried to sort out my emotions for Rick. He loves me; he wants me without question. But my feelings for him range from resentful, to heated lust with bits of love. The longer I think about it, the more I understand that I love Chance just as much, if not more, and that scares the hell out of me.

After this morning in the hallway, I wonder if I can even tell him. Will he listen? How do I tell him that I'm falling for him? Does he even care?

The smell of eggs and bacon fills the study just as a plate of food is placed in front of me. I blink a few times, bringing it into focus, and look up to see Chance. The longing I was just thinking about heats my face.

"You have to eat, Emma." His voice sounds flat. His eyes look cold, missing their rich warmth.

"Umm, yes. I was going to. Just wanted to finish a few things."

"Yeah … sure you were. Just eat. I have a meeting in Rick's office this morning. Let me know when you need me," he says, not hiding his disdain.

"Chance … I—"

He holds up his hand, stopping me. "You don't owe me anything."

"But I want you to understand I didn't—"

"Emma, stop. Lenny already told me. Just let it go."

What the hell? What does Lenny know?

"No, Chance—"

"Emma, I said I don't want to hear it," he says bluntly while avoiding my eyes.

My stomach squeezes. He is withdrawing from me, not only physically as my eyes follow his broad frame out the door, but emotionally.

What the hell did Lenny say to him?

Chapter Twenty-Eight

CHANCE

I WALK OUT of Emma's study in a haze, pissed off at myself for even thinking she could be mine. *She will never be yours…*

And after seeing her this morning, it became clear—she's not mine. And the thought that she stayed with him—*in his fucking room*—is like a punch to the gut. But when Lenny showed me her contract with Rick, accompanied with her signature and date—dated *after* I confessed my feelings to her—it fucking killed me…

As I walk into Rick's office, Lenny is sitting at Rick's desk and Andy, James, Dean, and Brett are standing around the room looking impatient as they pace or fidget with random items. I look to my watch—*late again, damn it.*

"Sorry, guys," I say.

"You need better time management," Andy says.

"Yes, sir. Just doing my job," I say sarcastically.

Andy glances at me with his brows pinched together.

"Yeah, babysitting duties…" James chuckles and slaps Dean's back. Dean averts his eyes and bites his tongue.

"That's enough. Let's get started with Rick's objectives. Brett, where are we with the new security surveillance that Rick wants throughout the building?" Andy asks as he looks around the room and takes a stance, dominating the space.

"Just waiting on the last shipment. Then all equipment will be installed. Should be ready in two weeks."

"Great, let me know as soon as it is up. Dean, James, how about intel on all the building staff? Do you have information on the leak yet?"

"Nothing yet, sir. The club's staff and the business floor's staff all checked out. We plan to work through departments going up the building. And my guess is it's someone closer to Rick," Dean says as he uncrosses his feet.

"Has Rick said who the information has been leaked out to? I mean, we are in the dark here. And we would be able to work faster if it wasn't so … vague," James says and Dean nods in agreement.

"No, Rick hasn't. Just make sure you're doing thorough background checks and dig as deep as you can. Something will come up."

They nod and Andy continues.

"Chance, Rick dropped this off for you this morning, said it's a list of new approved locations."

I grab the list from Andy's outstretched hand. I absorb everything, trying to figure the key components I am missing. Looking over to Dean, I have the sense he is trying to connect the dots as well.

I can't help but probe further for answers. "Andy, do you know why Rick is being paranoid with adding all this security? I mean, have any of us found any real threats? It just feels extreme. It just doesn't add up."

"I agree with Chance," Dean joins in. "I feel like Rick is either extremely paranoid or he is into something big. I put my money on the latter."

"Do any of us know what the hell is going on with all the extra goons Rick has hired?" James adds. "Some of those men are sketchy as fuck."

Andy looks at us, then back at Lenny, who is sitting quietly behind the desk. His gaze silently signaling that this is a discussion — without an audience. But he says something else entirely.

"It is not our job to know Rick's business," Andy says. "Our job is to find where the leaks are and to ensure the safety of anyone in the penthouse. We are required to do our job and our job only. The job that Rick has asked of us."

In unison, we answer, "Yes, sir."

Andy nods his head. "Good. Now you all have your schedules for this week's training. As for now, you know what is expected of you. Dismissed."

WITH ALL MY willpower, I strain to keep my focus on anything but the sweet round ass I follow to the library. *She's not yours...*

My phone buzzes in my pocket with an incoming email. Welcoming the distraction, I pull it out to read Andy Marshall's name with the subject line reading — *Meeting.* Opening it, I see only one line. *Plan a meeting in my apartment in the back of the gym tonight, 2200 hours.*

I knew it. Either Andy knows something, or he is beginning to question what the hell is going on here. But I have a feeling Dean is right. Rick has gotten himself in a fucking mess ... and what will that mean for Emma? It would explain the contract. *What does she know? Could she know what Rick is doing?*

The smell of fresh paint and old books wafts through the air in waves as Emma opens the door to the library. I look up to see that the place is almost unrecognizable.

I watch people bustling around, working on what look to be the final touches. I survey the once dusty cream-colored walls — now painted in warm grays. The lines of the room are accented with vintage-looking wood that creates a welcoming feeling.

The dim lighting accentuates the cozy atmosphere, which somehow suits Emma's personality. Two large men are moving in what look to be the last of the shelves, made of the same older wood, while others are stacking and organizing the last of the boxes of books.

The desk is no longer in the middle of the room; instead, it is at a small corner by the door. A lanky man, looking no older than his early twenties, is working hard at setting up the computer system without glancing up at us.

I continue to follow Emma. In the middle of the room is now an open space surrounded by half shelves. I look to where the desk once sat, and a large shaggy purple rug lies on the floor and extra-large pillows are strategically placed about the space.

"It's exactly as I pictured it," Emma says, her eyes sparkling.

"It looks bigger without the desk in here."

"Yes, I was hoping it would."

"What are you planning to do with this space?"

"I want to read for kids—hopefully start a youth book club. And," she says as she ducks behind more shelves, "I wanted a homey feeling." She continues turning, revealing private nooks in every corner with seating ranging from oversized chairs to hanging board swings.

Her excitement bubbles as she smiles broadly, causing her laugh lines to deepen. *I would die to keep that smile on her face... I love that smile.*

She finds a little nook in the far end of the library. This one is large enough for a twin mattress to lie on the floor with a lamp that sits next to it causing a glow to cast across her skin. *She is beautiful ... but she will never be yours.*

"It's perfect," she says, peering up at me. She throws her arms around my neck with excitement. "I can't believe it's all coming together."

I wrap my arms around her and savor the feel of her body against mine. *She feels perfect ... like she was made to be here...*

Her body heats with our closeness, and my groin hardens. My senses heighten with the weight of her soft breasts against my chest and my heart squeezes.

She gasps for air as the realization wakens within her eyes, causing her to slightly part her lips. In an animal-like reaction, I pull her possessively to me. *Mine ... she is mine... My everything...*

Fighting through my need for her, I quickly let go of her as if she burned me, and I guess in a way—she did.

"Sorry, I shouldn't have," I mutter.

"No, I'm sorry," she says quietly, turning away to hide her blush. "I was just excited about the library."

"Well, you should be excited. It's all coming together."

"Thanks. I wanted a space where people can go to get away from it all. You know what I mean?"

"Yes, I get it. That is the gym for me."

"Explains why you are beating on that damn punching bag all the time. I guess following me all day must be dangerously frustrating work," she teases.

I laugh. "It's more dangerously frustrating then you could imagine…"

Chapter Twenty-Nine

EMMA

CHLORINE FILLS MY lungs as I pace the locker room. *What were you thinking? Okay, so Chance wouldn't take no for an answer... Now he is swimming... And you're wearing this...*

"Grrr," I say, echoing off the cold tiles.

I look back down at the visible marks on my upper arms — fingerprints. And then to the black plum-colored bruise on my upper thigh the size of Rick's fist. *How can I hide all this from Chance?* I think as I study my revealing swimsuit. *Stupid bikini...*

Taking a deep breath, I crack the door. "Chance... Close your eyes."

A ripple of water answers me back. I peek around the door and see Chance already swimming laps. *Great, maybe I can do this... Just run for it...*

I look back at Chance and my body heats when my eyes lock on to his long, toned arms as he reaches over his head, performing graceful strokes that cause the muscles in his back to flex.

I press my desires down. *Run for the water — now!* I bolt to the pool and pull my knees to my chest in a cannonball. The cool water calms my rigid nerves and I sink for a brief moment.

I come up only to see Chance still busy with his laps. *Thank God!!*

Having the distraction of Chance swimming so close to me

does nothing to help me focus on my laps. I have to redirect my line countless times but end up in the deep end, half treading the water and half floating. *Just relax ... you want to swim ... remember* – Water splashes across my face, startling me.

I look around to find Chance. But he is nowhere in sight. *Now, where did he go?* I think just as something grabs hold of my ankle and pulls me down. I quickly take a breath just before my head completely submerges underwater. My body shakes and I feel my heart slam in my chest. *Where is he?* My eyes land on Chance grinning back at me.

Two can play that game. I swim back to the top to catch my breath.

I tread the water's surface waiting for my revenge. *What is taking him so long?* I spin, looking all around for him – *Where is he?* Panic boils in my veins. I dive back under the water.

Where is he? Where is he?

I find him sitting on the bottom of the pool with his legs crossed.

I swim down and sign to him. "Are you okay?"

His smile widens, letting bubbles escape as he nods. In a split second, he pushes off his feet and grabs me around the waist, jetting us to the surface of the water. I wrap my arms around his neck trying to hold on. *Holy shit...*

When we break the surface, I quickly push away. His deep chuckle vibrates off the walls.

"It's not funny, Chance. For a second, I thought something happened. You were down there a long time."

"Were you worried about me?"

"Chance! You were down there for like ... ever... How can you hold your breath that long?"

He moves closer – inches from me. I watch his warm eyes deepen and the swirls of water that lick my skin feel exotic. I secretly wish it was his hands touching me.

"I was a MARSOC in the Marine Corps. It's an elite specialized group of men."

The minute the words leave his lips, I can feel him withdraw, even though he doesn't move.

———

Why would he be ashamed of that?

I move closer to him and reach up to touch his face.

"Don't be ashamed—"

He places his hand over mine. "No, Emma, it's not that." He pauses. "No one here knows I was in the military with specialized training. You understand...?"

"No. Why? There are many people here who have."

"Yes, but I have *specialized training* that most of the men don't have a clue about. It was all top-secret assignments," he says, closing his eyes. "I don't even know why I'm telling you. I have never told anyone before."

That's when it dawns on me—the seriousness of his position. Rick would use him—probably in the ugliest ways.

I move closer, peering into his eyes. "Chance, I get it. Your secret is safe with me. I won't let Rick use you..."

He encircles my waist with his arms closing the gap between us. We sink into the depths of the water in silent understanding. I open my eyes to see him smiling at me. His eyes shine as he cups my nape and pulls me closer.

My body reacts instantaneously as our lips meet. I feel his feverish need as he devours my mouth, claiming it as his. He takes hold of my hips and pulls me closer. I part my thighs and welcome the feeling of him against my sex with a burning longing.

I need him.

His arms glide up my back, deepening our contact as his own arousal presses against mine, causing sparks to ignite. I part my lips and the last bit of air escapes as I moan.

Chance claims my mouth once more. My heart swells, fueling me with a deeper need. Burning to show him the intensity of my yearning, I thrust myself on him. His passion is equivalent to my own as his hard shaft jumps in response. The flimsy layer of our swimsuits exposes his sheer size as he poises it against me, stimulating my clit with his head.

Unable to stop the moan from escaping, I close my eyes. I feel him push off the floor with his strong legs, jetting us back to the top. I tighten my grip around his thighs with my legs, pressing deeper against his cock, building me higher to bliss.

The second we break through for air, he frees his arms around me. I squeeze tighter around him and my body begins to quake as I grind against him. I take a needed breath and begin kissing his neck, making my way down to the hard lines of his chest.

He lets out a growl as he swims us to the shallow end. The movement of his hips heightens me, causing an overwhelming frustration at the thin layer that separates us. *I want him.*

His hands find my ass and he squeezes with his long fingers as he glides my pussy up the length of his cock, making the most sensitive places swell with need.

The coldness of the wall presses against my back and I shudder. "Chance... I want you... I need you—"

An animal-like sound escapes from his mouth as he confesses, "My need for you is inescapable."

Cupping my hands around his face, I kiss him passionately, expressing all the words I am unable to say. His hands glide up my back as he grinds against me. Palming my breast in his hand, he rubs his thumb over my already hardened nipple. I whimper in need.

He shifts against me, parting my legs further as he skims his hands back down my body, stopping just as he reaches the junction of my thighs.

"Emma, I want—"

"Please ... Now!"

Without hesitation, he hooks his finger into the crotch of my bottoms and moves them to the side. The coolness of the water hits my sizzling hot center and sends a shock to my system. His lips land hard on mine, stifling my moan as my body begins to shake. His thumb skims up and makes contact with my clit. I deepen the kiss.

He circles my clit, building me higher, and his other finger enters me. I feel myself stretch against the thickness of his finger. My muscles contract around him sending me over the edge as I climax. I let out muffled screams as he silences them with his lips, kissing me passionately.

He continues kissing me until my moaning stops. My body quivers as he lifts me and sets me on the edge of the pool. He begins kissing down my neck while his hands glide up the tops of my thighs.

My hands run down his chest and the fine hairs tickle my palms as they descend. I inhale sharply, surprised at my own readiness once again. *I want to please him, to feel him against my palm and watch him climax...*

I slide my fingers into the narrow waistline of his shorts and my other hand pulls at the front strings of his trunks.

His body shakes and I momentarily hesitate, having never before touched a man in this way.

"I ... umm ... I never ... but I want to—"

"There is nothing you can do wrong. I already feel like I'm going to combust, Em."

He gives me the confidence I need, and I pull open his trunks, freeing his cock. He closes his eyes and leans his forehead against my shoulder as he shudders. My eyes widen at the pure size of him. I pull his trunks down even further and run my thumbs along the dimples of his hips. I feel my own arousal heighten once again. I circle my fingers around his cock and slowly begin stroking, making my way up to his head. He remains frozen and I begin to set a pace stroking him.

Just when I start to question if I am doing everything right, while he's kissing my neck in between breathy groans, he whispers, "Oh ... God ... Em..." He releases his own climax and I watch goosebumps spread over his skin as he moans out my name one last time.

He claims my mouth once again and squeezes the tops of my thighs.

Pain shoots up my thigh. "Ouch." I wince and pull away.

He looks down to where his hands are, and I jump into the water as my bruises from last night come to consciousness. *Shit!* I push Chance backward in the opposite direction and start swimming away.

He quickly catches up to me and grabs my shoulders. He effortlessly lifts me up over his shoulder and hops out of the pool with me.

"Chance," I say, hitting his back with my fists. "Put me down now."

He sets me down and examines my back side. He firmly holds onto my shoulder to keep me in place.

"Let me go, Chance."

He turns me to face him and lets out a growl as his eyes land on the bruises along my arm. The tone deepens when his eyes come in contact with the bruise on my upper thigh.

"Did Rick do this last night?" he asks in a low tone.

Unable to look at him, I lock my eyes on the door of the locker room. "I am fine. Just let me go."

He releases me. "Emma, did he do this to you last night?"

"It doesn't matter. I'm fine now."

He takes a step back and flips a chair, sending it flying.

"Damn it, Emma! It does matter! You matter!" His voice cracks as emotion I am sure he wants to hide comes forth.

Our eyes lock and the intensity of his storm touches me. It feels as if his soul is speaking to mine, whispering truths of the depths of his emotions. *Does he love me…?*

I'm frozen, not in fear — I am not afraid of him — I'm frozen by the raw yearning in his eyes.

He loves me…

My soul burns to sing aloud my love for him. But I feel as if someone has stolen my instrument and I stand there merely staring at him.

Chance —

He turns away. "Go."

Chance, I love you…

I watch him disappear into the men's locker room.

Chapter Thirty

CHANCE

PACING THE SMALL cramped space of Andy's kitchen, I dig my nails into my fists as I replay the image of Emma's bruised body. *I must get her out…*

I feel like a caged animal as I pace. *I'm going to make that bastard regret ever looking at her wrong.*

I turn again. How am I going to help her if she won't tell me anything? *Fuck!!*

Andy, Dean and Brett all sit at the table.

I ignore them, even though I can feel them staring at me.

I turn again. If Emma won't ask for help then maybe I can find a way for her to help herself.

"Chance, what's gotten you so pissed off?" Dean asks, breaking the silence.

I huff and clench my fists. I turn.

"Just let him be," Andy interjects.

"If you ask me, he looks like he just needs to get laid," James teases as he walks into the room.

Ignoring James, I take a deep breath.

"Dude, do you need to go a few rounds on the mat before we start this little meeting?" Brett asks.

"If I want to beat someone, it might as well be your ugly ass," I spit out, trying to ease my tension.

"First, let's get started with this meeting. Then we can talk about beating someone's ass. Chance, is Nash watching Emma right now?" Andy asks.

I feel my fists tighten again. *I fucking hate that asshole just about as much as Rick ...* "Yes, but I don't understand why. It's not like he is skilled with protecting a life. What the fuck is this meeting about?"

"I need you to bring it down a notch, this is important. I called the meeting here because I know this place is not bugged. Not to mention, Rick's weasel is not looming around us," Andy says, standing as he dominates the space and I take a seat.

Andy continues. "I was the one to ask Rick to place you on this team. He thinks it's for his better interest but that is where he is wrong. I have been waiting for some signs that you guys were seeing through Rick's scam," Andy says, looking in each of our eyes before continuing. "I have been investigating Rick for a long time. Trying to create enough evidence to lock him away for good. However, we didn't expect how deep Rick's pockets go and how many people he has paid off, even some in my division. That is why I have selected you men after reading all your qualifications. I know as a team we can take him down." He pauses briefly.

"I have honorable men here before me and I understand this is not what you were expecting, so before I go into further details, I am giving you an opportunity to walk away. Or stay and we join together to take this whole operation down. To take Rick down, but it's your choice." He looks at each of us.

"I've hated Rick from day one. Fuck yeah, I'm in!" James hoots.

"Me too. Rick is in something and I bet that something is bad," says Dean.

"Count me in," says Brett. "It's about time we do something more than this petty shit Rick has us doing."

"In!" I growl.

"Good. Each one of you were positioned where your strengths lie. I've been keeping Rick in the dark about your past training. I purposely led him to *think* you all needed advance training, but I know otherwise. From now on, our training sessions will be strategy meetings to understand Rick's operation. If we are going to take him down, we are taking down this whole fucking thing."

"Will our training continue as one-on-one sessions?" James asks.

"Yes, for now. Rick is already on edge. I don't want to flag his paranoia and jeopardize what we have here. Our position can give us the upper hand because of our access to the building."

"Access to everything but the guarded floors where he hides his goons," Brett scoffs.

"That is another obstacle we must tackle," Andy adds.

We all nod.

"But, as of recently, I learned the power behind Rick's operation. With that kind of power, you're bound to create a few enemies who are just as powerful. Unfortunately, I haven't figured out who Rick is so scared of. I need all of you to gather everything you have on Rick and we will be going over it in our meetings this week. But that is all we have time for tonight. There will be a lot to get you guys up to speed."

We rise and Brett turns back to me. "Hey, man, I was serious about going a few rounds if you need to." He slaps me on the shoulders as we enter the back side to the main gym area.

"No," Andy says. "I got it. Chance, meet you out on the mat in a minute."

"Okay." Brett waves as he exits the main entrance with the others.

I turn to Andy as he enters the gym.

"I don't want Nash anywhere around Emma, so I will take a raincheck at kicking your ass..." I say to Andy as I wave him off.

"You're no good at keeping her safe like this."

"Yeah, well that may be, but I'm better than that worthless scum watching her now, especially if Rick's not just being paranoid."

"Okay, but Nash is safer than having Rick around her," Andy says to my back as I make my way to the door.

I stop in my tracks and turn back. "What do you know?"

"I know Nash won't lay a finger on her without Rick's say-so. I know something is eating at you and I'm going to place my bet that it has to do with Emma. I can see she is affecting your judgment, like when we were at the bar... And I know *your past —* "

"What do you know about my past?" I ask, my chest tightening.

"I know about *her.* And I know how it affects you to see a woman with someone like Rick, that's why I put you in the position to watch over Emma. I know you won't let it happen again — will you?"

Libby...

My fists shake as pain shoots through me and tears me in half. *Ten years. Ten years, I have pushed it away ... locked it away...* And just the mention of her brings back the pain as if it were yesterday.

But Emma's not Libby... Emma's alive —

"Still want to throw down, Chance...?"

"You have no idea, but I don't think you can handle me tonight. I won't hold back, not tonight!"

"Bring it on."

EMMA

BOOM, BOOM, BOOM...

I drift awake from the thundering sound, irritation boiling within me. *Damn, I was having a sexy dream with Mr. Ocean Eyes ...*

Boom, boom, boom...

Rolling over, I cover my head with the pillow. *Come back to me ... damn it!* I try to envision him again. His thick black hair is cut short in a military style that my fingers burn to run through. *My perfect dream man —*

Boom, boom, boom...

I bolt upright and throw my pillow at the door. "Argggh," I say, looking at the clock, "four thirty a.m. Are you flipping kidding me!"

I flop back onto the bed. *For Pete's sake, who in their right mind is up at this hour?*

Boom, boom, boom...

I jump off my bed, stomp to my door, and throw it open.

Boom, boom, boom...

The sound vibrates through Chance's door, nearly rattling it off its hinges. *What the hell is he doing in there...?*

Boom, boom, boom...

Boom, boom, boom...

"Chance, people are trying to sleep," I yell as I beat on the door with my fist.

The pounding stops. I smile to myself.

Boom, boom, boom...

It sounds as if an elephant is storming around his room. This time I turn the knob and swing the door open. Stepping in, I shut the door behind me. After yesterday, he has been avoiding me—again. But this time, I'm going to give him a piece of my mind.

I look up to see Chance bouncing and gracefully switching positions, wearing nothing but a pair of shorts. Sweat rolls down his sculpted muscles. A pair of white headphones blasts in his ears, loud enough that I can almost make out the song. He power hits the worn bag with such force that it vibrates in my chest. *Wow...*The poor bag doesn't have a chance in hell.

Boom, boom, boom...

The velocity of his strike causes me to jump back. He pivots on his feet and moves around the bag, landing a kick to the middle of it. That's when he spots me, just before he lands his next assault.

My face heats instantly, feeling like a creeper in his room. *Shit...* I force myself to look down at my feet.

A pair of beaten gloves come into my view.

He places his gloved hand up under my chin and tilts it up,

making me meet his eyes. With his other hand, he pulls the earbuds out with one tug.

"What are you doing in here?"

I watch as a sweat bead slowly descends down his handsome features. *Focus, Emma, he asked you a question … remember you're mad at him. He woke you up … but God he is handsome –*

"Emma?" His husky voice echoes through my head and my body reacts instantaneously, sending a ripple to my core.

His eyes deepen.

"You woke me up," I blurt out.

His lips curve into a mischievous smirk – a smile I'm starting to become all too familiar with. The one that heats my spark.

I hold my hand up between us and take a step back. "No, I want sleep. And having you over here murdering that poor bag is keeping me up. Do you even know what time it is? It's four thirty in the morning!"

His eyes cloud as I watch all traces of humor vanish and he starts pulling at the Velcro of his gloves. Pulling them off, he tosses them to the floor.

"I guess I didn't realize I was hitting it so hard. I was trying to get to sleep."

"Get yourself to sleep … by punching a bag?"

"Yeah." He shrugs.

"And how does that get you to sleep?"

"It wears me out, I guess. You know, kills some demons ..."

"Kill sounds about right; your poor bag is going to rip in half," I joke in hopes of lightening his visibly tense body.

I look up to his face, which is vacant of his signature smile, and a stabbing pain hits my heart. My eyes search his.

He smiles faintly as he looks to the bag covered in duct tape. "I have done worse. It's still in one piece."

"You have broken one of those in two before?"

"Yeah, I have. It's been a few years … but I have."

"Holy shit."

This time he laughs deeply, and the sound warms me.

"I can teach you," he says.

I step back. "Oh ... I could never hit like that."

"Actually, I have seen many powerful women, no bigger than you, kick a man's ass with the proper training. It's not about your size." He steps forward and grabs my hand. I feel heat sizzle up my arm. "You are strong, Emma. I can train you. It would make me feel better if I knew you could protect yourself. Maybe even help me sleep at night," he says, staring down at me. "Will you think about it?"

I nod.

"Thank you." He raises my hand to his lips, kissing the back of it—just like Rick does. *This is Chance, not Rick.* But the unwanted familiarity slithers to my core.

"I have to hop in the shower, Em ... but please, *please* think about it..." He releases my hand and turns toward the bathroom.

"Yes! I will do it," I hurriedly answer before I can change my mind.

He spins back on his heel. "We start later tonight." A fire flicks in his eyes.

I clear my throat. "Okay. And Chance..."

"Yes," he says with a genuine smile.

"Never ... kiss my hand again."

Chapter Thirty-One

EMMA

WELL, FUCKING DAMN, I think as my dream of Mr. Ocean Eyes leaves me with an ache in my chest. Instead of lying on a beach like most of my steamy dreams I have with him, I was picking up shards of glass off the floor in the foyer when he finally appeared. My chest squeezes as the familiarity of the dream strikes a chord. *Why does it feel like a memory?*

A knock at the door announces Brutus. "Good morning, Ms. Andrews. It's getting late and your breakfast is getting cold."

"Thanks, Brutus," I say, climbing out of bed. "But it's best I get to work. Can you bring it to my study, please?"

"Very well, but, Ms. Andrews, Ms. May will be awfully disappointed, seeing how excited she was to have some alone time with you."

Excitement bubbles in my chest. "I thought Ms. May was with Rick. And where is Molly?"

"I'm not entirely sure where Ms. Wright is. I just know Ms. May kept pestering me as to when you were going to join her."

"Tell her I will be down in ten minutes," I say, ducking into the bathroom without waiting for a response.

I enter the kitchen to see Ms. May sitting at the island with her nose deep in a cookbook. I sit down in the empty chair beside her and look at the covered plate before me.

"Is this for me?" I ask.

"Oh, yes, sugar." She pivots in her seat and pulls me in for a quick embrace. "Oh, I have missed you, dear."

My heart fills with her motherly affection.

I pull the cover off to reveal French toast. "It's been so crazy. I've missed you, too," I say, shoving toast into my mouth.

I must have been hungrier than I realized, because I ate my entire plate in mere minutes. After finishing, I stand and place the dish into the dishwasher.

"What are you doing with all your cookbooks?" I ask, taking my seat again.

"Planning food for the party and making plans for Molly for the rest of the week when I'm gone."

"Where are you going and why can't you just stay?" I pout playfully.

"The where doesn't matter, hon. I wish I could, but while I have you now, I want to hear what's going on with you. I feel like I have been missing out on so much with being gone."

"Well … yeah, a lot has happened … lately," I say, tucking my hair behind my ear.

"Oh, girl, start from the beginning." She waves her finger and adds, "And don't leave out anything."

"I, umm…" I tell her everything—the good, the bad, and everything in between. At first, I am shy about telling her all the things that happened between Chance and me, but the more I talk, the faster everything spills out. And it feels good; I guess I didn't realize how much I needed to talk to someone. *And I'm so glad it's Ms. May,* I think as my heart warms.

Taking a deep breath, I look back up to her face. She sat quietly the whole time. *Did I say too much?* I think, half expecting to see a repulsive glare. Instead, she is beaming at me.

"You're not repulsed by me? I mean, here I am confused about feelings for not one man but two. And one of them being Rick… I thought you wanted me to marry Rick—"

"Hell, you're starting to remind me of when I was your age. Although I was never as shy as you. So tell me what is bothering you the most with all this."

My heart swells. "I guess I don't know what to do with all the confusion and all the pent-up energy I feel. What do I do with Chance? And what if Rick finds out—?"

"Slow down. It's easy," she says, standing up and swaying her hips.

"How can this be easy? What about the twisted ways I'm feeling for Rick? Then I have Chance, who I think I'm starting to fall—"

"Sweetie, stop thinking so much and just have some *FUN*."

"Fun?" I question her. "But I thought you wanted me with Rick—?"

"I want you happy! And *YES*, fun! This is the most smiles I have seen on your face in seven years... So just enjoy the attention." She sways her hips at me.

She has to be kidding me...

"I want you to get out of that beautiful head of yours. We can talk more about it next week when I'm back, but for now, just listen to your body and do whatever your heart desires. Stop thinking so hard about the what-ifs."

She walks around the island and holds her hands up. "What if ... you fall for Rick? What if ... Rick finds out about Chance? What if...? How will you know what your heart needs if you put all these walls up with the what-ifs?"

"So you're saying..."

"I'm saying go have fun and enjoy your time. And if something should happen and it feels right ... explore it." She searches my face to see if I understand.

Chance walks in as if on cue. "Emma, I was looking for you."

Chapter Thirty-Two

CHANCE

PACING EMMA'S STUDY, I wipe my sweaty palms on my jeans as I think about the one-on-one meeting I had with Andy this morning. *How the fuck am I going to ask Emma...* I think as all the information Andy has on Rick bounces off the walls of my brain. *Emma can't possibly know...*

"Chance, what's going on?" Emma asks as I watch her take a seat on the couch.

Her icy blue eyes stare up at me and cause a stabbing feeling to my gut. *No, she can't possibly know... How do I tell her about the potential danger that she is in? Does she know what Rick is into? Do I tell her about my past? Do I tell her that I'm a failure? Can I protect – ?*

"Chance..."

I kneel down and take her hands in mine. *I will protect her with my life!*

"Emma, I need you to understand. There are things about Rick ... Rick has legitimate concern for your safety. He is not playing around here," I say as I feel my blood pressure rising. *Emma will not end up like her, not like Libby... No, I can't lose her... It won't happen again, not on my watch. Emma will live...*

Her icy blue eyes freeze in fear. *Fuck...*

"So ... so ...you don't think this is him being overly controlling?" she asks as her voice cracks.

"I wasn't sure at first but no, he's not. He has been receiving real threats."

She stands. I watch her eyes cloud over.

"This whole time, you were thinking there was a real concern and you just let me walk around thinking I was safe," she says and begins to pace the study.

I drop my head. "It's not like that. I didn't think Rick's operation reached out as far as it does, Emma. He has some shady people working for him. And if he has caused a ripple... Think about it. Look at all the extra guards Rick has brought on, and what kind of people do you take them for?"

She stops mid-step. "Killers..."

"Yes!" I stand and grab her by the shoulders. "Rick is scared of someone and apparently that someone is bigger than he is."

"How do you know all this—?"

"That's not important right now. What's important is that you trust me. Rick is receiving death threats..."

A shadow haunts in the depths of her eyes. "Yes, I believe you ... I have never seen him act the way he has been lately—"

"Emma, do you know something, anything?"

"No," she snaps. "He has always left me in the dark when it comes to his business..."

Thank God. Maybe her not knowing anything means there is no immediate danger to her. But, damn, I was hoping she could answer some of my questions. "Do you know what Rick has been doing on all his trips?" I try again.

"No, but it is odd, he never before had to travel like this. What do you think he is doing? I mean I have always questioned how he makes the kind of money—"

"I am trying to piece it together myself." I pause. "Look, Emma, I need you to make me a promise." She looks up at me with her wide eyes and my heart squeezes.

"Okay, what?"

"You have to promise me ... if I say it's time to run because it's not safe for you that you will go with me. I will keep you safe. Please promise me you will leave with me..."

Her eyes glaze over.

"Emma," I say as my breath catches and my mouth dries. *She has to promise.*

"Yes, Chance. I trust you."

She leans up and brushes a feather-like kiss across my lips, easing the tension building in my gut.

Emma will not be her...Emma will live...

EMMA

THE REST OF the day, I have this nervousness I can't shake. I was hoping the library and a good swim would distance me from the fear stirring though my mind, but I have no such luck.

I take a deep breath and roll my shoulders. *Run away with Chance...* I shovel through the last bit of paperwork for the library in my study. *What has Rick gotten into?*

"Are you about ready?"

I jump and my heart pounds in my ears. I look up to see Chance sitting down in the chair across from the desk.

"SHIT!" I say and quickly cover my mouth. My cheeks heat. "Umm, sorry. You scared me. I didn't see you come in."

He laughs. "You have no idea how cute you are, do you?"

I look down to the papers piled on my desk and try to change the subject as I feel the heat already coil to my center. "What am I supposed to be ready for?"

He stands and walks to the desk, his hand coming into view as he plays with the folders. "Have you already forgotten what we are starting tonight?"

"Oh, you're going to teach me to defend myself. Make me an ass kicker... Is that what it is called?" I laugh.

He picks up a folder, laughs, and flips it open. "Yeah, something like that," he says as his eyes scan the page.

I look at the folder and realize it is Rick's contract—our marriage contract. Bolting upright, I hurriedly make my way around the desk and reach to pluck it from him. "I believe that is mine," I say and pull at the folder, but he doesn't release it.

"Umm, this is interesting," he says flatly.

"Chance, it's none of your business."

He moves it up out of my reach and continues scanning the front page of the contract, ignoring my protests.

"Chance, give it back." I jump, aiming to retrieve it, but he pulls it away. "Chance … please."

He drops the folder onto the desk. Turning, he walks toward the door. Just as he reaches for the doorknob, he says, "When you're ready … I will be in my room."

CHANCE IS ALREADY giving the punching bag a workout as I walk into his room. He is wearing his usual shorts with his earbuds blaring. I approach him slowly, feeling heat rising to my cheeks as I enjoy the view of his flexing muscles.

I continue approaching, unaware of the distance I am closing between us. Chance spins unexpectedly and swipes a leg behind me. I begin falling backward and squeal in surprise. *Shit…* I close my eyes, preparing myself for impact.

His arms wrap around me and he pulls me to his body. Heat radiates off him in waves of earthy woods that swirl around me, causing my sex to swell in anticipation.

He places me back up on my feet, his demeanor presenting a much different reaction than mine. His face is absent from any emotion and his lips are in a thin line. "You must be prepared at all times," he says as he pulls out his earbuds.

What the hell…?

He walks over to the small mat on the floor. "We will start the basics of self-defense. Once you are completely confident with that, then we will move on."

TWO HOURS LATER, I sit on the loveseat drenched in sweat. Our whole session proved to be surprisingly more difficult than I was expecting. And Chance didn't hold back. In fact, he was focused and driven the entire session.

He tosses a water to me. "Let's do twice a day, until you have the self-defense down. Then when you're ready to learn attack, we may go to once a day," he says, sitting down beside me.

I take a large drink of water and manage to slow my breathing. I look at him and my chest swells with determination. "I can go some more tonight ... if you just give me a sec," I say, taking the hem of my shirt and wiping the sweat from my face.

"No, we are done for today."

"Is everything okay, Chance?"

He stands up and walks to the door, opening it slowly. "Tomorrow morning, I want you here by seven."

He is cold as he addresses me. *What did I do wrong?* He stands there holding the door and avoids making eye contact.

I stand up, bottle in hand, and make my way to the door. My body shakes with need as I step through the door. He catches my arm, stopping me. My heart lodges in my throat.

Say something, damn it, Emma...

"Wear tighter clothes tomorrow, you will need to move more freely," he says in a warm voice.

I look up and see compassion shining bright in his eyes. *Chance... I...* I open my mouth and he stops me.

"Good night, Emma." He shuts the door in my face.

Chapter Thirty-Three

EMMA

MY TRAINING WITH Chance progresses tremendously and I start to feel more confident with each session—more confident in my training, at least; I have no confidence with Chance. Ever since he saw my contract with Rick, he's been avoiding talking to me.

I am sore, though. So much so that the weight of the folders strains against my sore arms as I pick up the last of my things to head to the library. I turn toward the door just as Lenny walks in.

"There you are." He marches in my direction.

"I was just about to find Chance and head down to the library for the rest of the afternoon. Have you seen him?" I say and adjust my grip.

"Uh, yes, he is down in the kitchen talking with Molly."

The image of her lips on Chance's explodes in my mind and I immediately drop the stacks of folders on the desk and storm past Lenny to the kitchen.

How dare he give her attention and yet avoid me like … like some contagious disease…

Laughter booms through the kitchen doors. *You've got to be kidding me…* I grip the handle and send it flying open. They both turn to me, wide-eyed in surprise. Molly stands at the stovetop frozen in mid-stir. I lock eyes with Chance, who is sitting at the island.

Our energies buzz around us, making everything in the room disappear. His face looks calm but his eyes flicker with unspoken emotion, instantly causing a flame to ignite in the deepest layers of my heart.

He rises out of his chair and I hold my breath. He stops a foot away from me, causing my heart to skip as his chestnut eyes peer down at me with longing that hovers just below the surface.

I blink—it's gone. *Everything ... gone.* I take a step back, feeling him withdraw. My stomach tightens.

"I, umm..." I say, trying to gather my thoughts.

I look over his shoulder, remembering Molly is in the room. She is paying no attention. *See, it's nothing, Emma. He wasn't doing anything with her...*

"I was just going to tell you that I'm ready to head down to the library..." I say, looking back at him.

He averts his eyes—as he has done many times these past few days.

"Let's go," he says in a low tone and turns us back toward the door.

Just before we exit, Molly shouts, "See you tonight, Chance..." I think I hear a scandalous snicker as we leave.

Rage blinds me and I turn just as Chance's grip tightens on my arm and he guides us out into the hallway.

I focus my rage on him. "What the hell?" I say, poking at his solid chest; he doesn't move an inch.

He continues to bulldoze us down the hallway in the direction of the elevator. I slam my fist down on his chest. "*See you tonight...*" I bite out as the elevator doors open.

Without a word, he swoops me up like a sack of potatoes and enters the elevator.

"Damn it! Chance, put me down ... now." I pound on his back.

"No."

I try to wiggle my way free and feel his grip tighten around my waist. "Put me DOWN!"

He bumps his shoulder and hikes me up to get an even tighter grasp. "Stop moving," he snaps as the doors open.

I look out to see we are on the second floor of the penthouse. He walks out and heads in the direction of our rooms.

"No, put me down!!" I say, hitting his back even harder. He lessens his grip momentarily as he adjusts his hold. I take advantage of the opportunity and quickly wiggle my hips down, searching for the floor for leverage.

Chance walks into his room and wraps both of his arms around me, locking me in place. My breath seizes, and I buck harder, trying to pull free.

"For fuck's sake, Emma." He quickly lowers me to my feet and turns his back to me.

I slow my breathing and throw my arms in the air.

"Do you have any idea just how difficult you make things?" he asks with his back still turned to me.

"*ME…?* I make things difficult?"

Like a switch went off in his head, he pivots and charges at me. The dark shadow of his face causes a cold chill to run down my spine. *Oh, God…*

He comes flying at me, his hands aiming for my neck. I shift my stance and dodge his attack. Before I can turn to face him, one of his arms wraps around my neck and the other crosses my chest. He locks me against him.

My adrenaline kicks in and without thinking, I use full force and pound my heel into the top of his foot. Simultaneously, I jerk my head back and throw him off balance. With the momentum of his weight being off-kilter, I bend at the waist and throw him off my back, causing him to somersault and land on his back.

I wildly look around for my escape, then realize I already scanned for my exit, as if on autopilot, and I immediately run for the door.

Just as I reach the doorknob, I hear a gasp from behind me. "You passed."

I turn to him. Chance is lying flat on the floor with his

hands on his chest. He takes a deep breath. *He's fucking SMILING!!*

I stand over him and look down. "What does that mean?" I ask in a bitter tone.

His eyes warm as he peers up at me. "You passed. Now we can move on to attack," he says and leans up on the back of his arms, revealing his signature smile.

"You mean this whole thing was a test?"

"Yep."

"Even the part about … Molly?"

"Yep. I knew you would come…"

I kick him in the thigh.

"…Oouch."

"You deserve it."

He laughs as he stands and dusts off his jeans. "How else am I supposed to see if your training is working?" he asks dryly.

I cross my arms over my chest.

"Hey … you passed. Now we can start working on attack and that's going to be a bit tricky."

"What about it is tricky?"

"Well … I don't have the equipment we need here, and I don't want Rick to question why you are going to the gym."

"Let me guess, it's not an approved location."

"Nope, and don't forget the security system he is installing. I have a few ideas, but it will take me a few days to get it all together."

"Okay, is there anything I can do?"

"No, just focus on this weekend with your grand opening."

"Okay." I look to the clock. "Shit, I'm supposed to meet the girls for tomorrow's agenda. I'm late."

"Let's get a move on it, then."

We step into the hallway and turn quickly only to smack into each other. He wraps his arms around me and studies me. I set my forehead on his solid chest. "Umm, sorry … my study … first …"

THOUGH I'M DETERMINED to call it an early night, my mind wanders deceivingly. I was tired before I had even laid my head down on my pillow. *Sleep, I need sleep...*

The day seemed to disappear with the chaos of all the last-minute preparations. The library's grand opening is planned for the mid-morning and Rick's damn engagement party follows that same evening. *How am I going to make it through the whole day...?*

I recap Lenny's email with the final details for tomorrow. Rick isn't going to make it to my grand opening and a stir of unexpected disappointment pulses through me.

My phone chimes again and I look to see another email from Lenny, this one reminding me, once again, that my appointment for hair and makeup are planned at two and I mustn't be late. *Yes, sleep ... I'm ready for tomorrow to be over already.*

"Have FUN," Ms. May's voice rings in my ears. *Fun* is something I need right about now...

I stretch out in an attempt to release the tightness in my shoulders. *Yes, I should take Ms. May up on that...* FUN will be tomorrow's motto...

CHANCE

"OKAY, SO LET me get this right. You have been training her and you want to start bringing her here for advanced training?" Andy asks in shock.

The smell of Lia's Chinese food fills Andy's small kitchen and empty food boxes and files are strewn across the table. Brett, Dean, James, and Andy stare at me, waiting for my answer.

"Fuck, do I look like I'm joking?" I say and run my hands through my hair.

All at once, they sit back in their chairs. James and Andy

toss empty boxes down onto the table, as Dean bitches out loud, "Come on, man. We don't have time after I just found this folder in Rick's office —" Dean waves the four-inch folder in my direction. The folder is labeled *Shipment.*

"Chance, we need to be going over this folder. There has to be thousands of names of what look like young girls and women. This folder alone will take us hours —"

I stand up to protest. *We have to make time...*

"You guys don't understand," I say, pacing. "You haven't seen what the fucker has done to her. He has her believing she is covered in scars, from only God knows what. So, fuck yes, I'm going to do this with or without you. I will make time." I slam my fist on the table, causing the clutter to dance and an empty box to fall on its side. *With or without them ... I will help her...*

I look back and take a deep breath. "Look, this is the way I see it. Rick sees us as untrained and if we are working together, he won't find out. I can use some of my training time to work with her. But with your help, it will be easier to sneak her around the building."

"Your stubborn ass will do it no matter what, so the hell with Rick. If we are going to take him down, why not help her," James says. "Plus, I'm more than happy to work with her on some ground and pound," he adds with a crooked smile.

"I can work the surveillance; Rick will never know that she was here," Brett pitches in.

"What about Nash? He has been watching her when you're not there. What's your plan there?" Dean asks. "I don't know. I want to help but we have a bigger mission here."

"That's where I come in," says Andy. "If I were to change the schedule around, I can tell Rick that Brett will be watching her, that I need Nash for another assignment, but instead, she will be here with Chance and I as we train her together. This will free time for James and Dean to run intel."

"Come on, man, I wanted to roll around with her on the mat," James protests.

Over my dead body, I think before Andy turns to James. "No, this will be the time to get Nash away, giving us more time for you and Dean to bug the penthouse." Andy meets my eyes. "I will help you. We will make time. Plus, I can't stand a man who beats on women any more than you, Chance."

My nerves settle a bit. "Thanks," I say and take my seat.

Andy stands and walks up behind me and pats me on my back. "Don't let this get personal like your past... Now, Dean, let's start going over this folder you found..."

I FIND MYSELF flipping to the first page of the file again. "Dean, this was in that folder?" I ask to clarify.

"Yes, it was categorized *the system,*" he says.

"It looks like Emma's foster care history..." I state as I flip the pages again. *Why would Rick have Emma's — ?*

"Yes, it was with hundreds of others. They all look like foster care papers," Andy adds.

"There has to be a connection..." I say as I scan.

Why does Rick have hundreds, near thousands, of histories on young girls? I scan further down the page and read "J. Gage." *Who is J. Gage and where have I seen that name before?*

"Chance, do you know why Rick would have this file on Emma, along with this stack?" Andy questions.

"No, the only thing that stands out is the name Gage. I've seen it somewhere," I rasp out as my gut twists.

"Gage, I think I've seen that name —" Dean whispers.

"Oh shit," James yelps from the other side of the room.

We all look up to James, watching as he flips through the file.

"What is it?" Andy demands.

"Did you know Emma's mother was murdered and Emma was the one to find her?"

Chapter Thirty-Four

EMMA

"HAVE FUN, EMMA. Have fun, Emma... Have fun..." I repeat to myself as I set the last folder for the library in my briefcase.

"Good morning!!" Lenny says, waving his arms flamboyantly, announcing his arrival into the study.

"Good morning."

"Darling, that didn't sound very enthusiastic. We have a big day ahead of us."

"Umm. Yes. I'm as ready as I will ever be. I'm just running through my list of things to remember," I say, bringing my attention back to him.

Lenny is sporting a dark navy suit with a fashionable dusty-rose vest and bow tie. "You look amazing, Lenny..."

"Oh, I know," he says and waves his finger at me.

I make a show of looking at the clock. "We really need to get going. I have things to go over with Jordan and Leah before it all starts," I say and pick up my things and walk toward the door.

With every step, I silently chant, *Have fun, Emma. Have fun....*

CHANCE

THE LIBRARY IS full of people when we arrive. In every turn, in every nook, there are people. *Damn, I wish this day would be over already.*

I watch Emma. She is breathtaking as she interacts with guests. *This is her element.* Her shyness is replaced with a glowing smile and lively eyes. *She is beautiful.* The only hint of timidness is the soft pink that flushes her cheeks, making it hard to take my eyes off of her.

I watch as she shakes the hand of an older woman. My chest tightens. *She is perfect – just how deep pink could I turn those cheeks…?*

"So this is what your job entitles you to…" I turn to find James leaning against a bookshelf. "So while the rest of us work our asses off, you get to go to parties and—"

"What are you doing here? I thought Andy wanted you working intel today?"

James rolls his eyes. "Relax, man, I know. I can snatch that chick you're drooling over in a minute, if I wanted her. But lucky for you, I am officially off the market."

"So you and Jenny?" I ask, trying to take the heat off of what he is implying.

"Yes, but let's hear about this little filly, you know, the one you can't take your eyes off. How are you guarding Emma if you are distracted by another woman…? I told you, you need to get laid. Where is Emma anyway?"

"That is Emma," I whisper.

"No way, man. I didn't recognize her. She looks … different. But more importantly, don't tell me you have a thing for the one girl in this building you can't have?"

"What do you want and why are you here?" I ask, not needing another reminder as to the importance of keeping my distance from her.

A waitress stops by carrying a tray of nuts and James grabs

a handful. "Andy sent me to let you know that we are on for training starting Monday morning," he says and tosses a few cashews in his mouth. "And, as a side note, I can't wait to wrestle with Emma," he taunts me.

"You're not," I say and take a controlled breath. "In two days, it's on for training... Is that all?"

"That's all," he snickers and tosses a few more into his mouth.

"Why didn't he just send an email?" I whisper.

"He wants everything done in person from now on. So why is it that you get to go to all the parties?"

"You're all invited for the party tonight, remember?"

"The one where your girl is celebrating her engagement to another man—to Rick, of all men. You know, the one we are taking down..."

I ball my fists and walk away from him toward the back exit.

She's not mine...

EMMA

LENNY PULLS AT my arm for the second time in a five-minute stretch. Without a word, he signals it's time to leave by pointing to his watch.

"Excuse me... Thank you for coming," I say to the older man I am speaking to and sign to Jordan that I must be leaving. I make my way over to my small office and pick up my things. Lenny is already at the door, crossing his arms and impatiently tapping his foot.

"Let's go," he says.

Joy swells my heart as I take another look around to see the library full of people. *See, you did it!*

From across the room, Leah smiles brightly at me and gives me a thumbs-up. I wave back to her before turning to a very impatient Lenny.

I wish I could stay longer and my heart sinks as I realize I don't see Chance anymore. *No Chance and no Rick... But at least Chance showed up for a bit ... that's more than I can say for Rick.*

The last I saw Chance, there was another man speaking with him, before he stormed off. *I wonder what that was all about?*

"We are already three minutes late," Lenny huffs.

"Have you seen Chance?" I ask before we walk out as an uneasy feeling sits in my gut.

"No. And no! We don't have time to go looking for him. You are late!" He pulls at my arm.

LENNY SPINS ME to face the full-length mirror in my bedroom, causing my jaw to drop. I don't even recognize myself in the mirror. My eye makeup is done in charcoals, creating a smoky-eye that frames my icy blue eyes, making them stand out. My hair is pinned back in a waterfall of blond curls that cascade down my back. "Wow..."

Lenny bounces with excitement. "Now let's get you in your dress."

I follow Lenny to the middle of the closet where my dress is hanging. My hands fly over my mouth. *That's my dress?!*

The dress has layers of delicate black lace over a shimmery red fabric that peeks through the eyeholes of the lace.

"Oh my *GOSH*!!" I say.

"I designed it myself," Lenny says.

"What? Really? I didn't know you knew how to—"

"Yes, Emma darling, there are a lot of things you don't know about me." He winks.

"Well, it's beautiful... Thank you."

"Then let's get you in it..."

I spin, checking my reflection. The deep heart-shaped cut in the front cups my breasts with high boning. The sides of my shoulders drape with a matching lace to the corset back. The length of the dress is perfect, letting my red heels peek out.

Lenny's cell rings, distracting me momentarily, and I look over to him, hearing the last of his conversation. "Yes, sir," he says before hanging up.

He gestures for me to sit and he picks up a black-laced mask. "Rick is going to be late," he says in a low tone and ties on my mask.

What...? Now he is going to be late to our engagement party? My chest drops.

Lenny crests my shoulders.

I look down to my hands folded in my lap. "Thank you for … everything. I wouldn't have been able to do it without you," I say.

Taking my hand, Lenny stands me up. "Girl, it's been my pleasure," he purrs, causing me to giggle.

"Now," he says, his eyes sparkling, "Rick has directed me to take you there, but you have to close your eyes," he says, pulling me into a spin.

"What, aren't we just going to the masquerade—?"

"Yes, we will, but... Oh, just you wait." He picks up his metallic dusty-rose mask and leads me out the door.

"OKAY, YOU CAN open your eyes," Lenny says.

I open them and see brilliant colors of reds and pinks. *Oh my...* We are standing in the middle of an elaborate garden. I look up to see nothing but dark crisp sky. *We are outside!* The sound of a water fountain makes music behind me and I spin. "Wow!"

In the middle of the fountain sits a concrete angel, her face gazing up to the heavens. I look beyond her to a labyrinth of stone and hedge walls.

Where did he take me? We didn't walk far...

"Where are we?"

"We are on the adjacent lot from the building; the one that was once an old parking garage. Rick had it redesigned into this garden … for you. The garden sits on the top level of the old garage and is attached to the ground-level entrance of the club. For tonight, he has made it available to the public."

Walking around the fountain in disbelief, I find a bench to sit down on. The cold of the stone chills my legs through the fabric of my dress.

I sit there taking it all in. The front entrance has a large display of roses that vine around the archways. I look down to see a raw stone path, covered in moss. Opposite the entrance is the labyrinth.

I meet Lenny's face. "I don't know ... what to say... Why — ?"

"He said that you weren't much for the club so he wanted to give you a place you could go ... that is all I know. He was supposed to be the one to bring you here."

If Rick made all the effort for tonight ... why isn't he here? What is he doing?

"Lenny, do you know what Rick is doing? Why has he been so — ?"

"Different? No, I don't ... but there is more."

"I don't know if I can take more tonight, Lenny."

He sits down next to me. "Rick has requested that I host the party."

"What? None of this is making sense. It's not like Rick." Rick likes to be in charge and show off. My nerves jump.

"Look, Emma." Lenny lowers his voice. "I'm going to be honest. I don't know what is going on with Rick. But if I were you, I would take advantage of tonight."

My stomach tightens. *Is Rick testing me again? I thought we were past that side of the old Rick. What if I fail?*

"Look at it this way, I am the only one here tonight who will know who you are — not even Rick. That reminds me, he wants me to take your ring to ensure he won't recognize you."

"But I thought this was to be our engagement party. Now he doesn't want me to be wearing my — "

"I'm just following orders. It doesn't make sense to me. But the way I see it, tonight is your last night of freedom. Why not have a bit of fun?"

"Now you're sounding like Ms. May. It's all about the *FUN*." I laugh.

"Well, the old broad is wise."

I take a deep breath. If no one will know who I am...

"What about someone guarding me? I thought—"

"Emma, no one will know that it's you. No one!"

"No one...?" I say and meet his dark eyes. "I will be safe?"

"Yes. Now, go have fun tonight. Be free."

"Fun ... Free."

Chapter Thirty-Five

CHANCE

"SO WHAT DID Rick's email say?" James asks as we walk down the hallway to enter the club.

I white-knuckle my fists in frustration. "He wanted me to leave Emma at the library. No one is to know who she is tonight. And it is total bullshit, if you ask me."

"What's his angle? He can't be that careless with her safety, especially after learning that he is receiving death threats, right?"

"I don't know, but I don't like it."

I step into the club, immediately scanning the space for any potential threats. *What the fuck is Rick doing...? Fuck, it's packed.*

"So are you going to listen to him?" James asks.

"Fuck no. As soon as I find her again, I plan on laying back to watch over her. Problem being—I have to find her." I scan the club again.

"It just doesn't make sense. You don't think that this could be to disguise what is really going on tonight ... you know, to throw things off... Like something is going down—"

I nudge James and point in the direction of the VIP. "I'm going to start looking around up there. They took down the VIP area for tonight, she may be up there..."

"Yeah, okay. I will walk around the bar. I have to find Jenny anyways. I will keep an eye out for your girl."

"She's not my girl…" I growl. *If she were mine, I would never be so careless with her safety.*

"Yeah, whatever, man." James nods as he walks past me.

EMMA

LENNY AND I make our way to the bar for drinks. He waves the waitress over and turns his attention to me.

"I'm going to loosen you up a bit. Then I must go and do my thing. What are you going to do tonight?" he says, eyeing me.

"I got it … *fun*," I say, still trying to understand how this is an engagement party if no one knows who I am. I'm not complaining about the freedom, though. *Is that what Rick is trying to accomplish here – letting me feel one night of freedom before being sucked into a forced marriage?*

"Rick wants you to have fun. Trust me," Lenny says and wiggles his black manicured brow at me.

"What can I getchya?" the waitress asks, leaning up against the bar, causing her breasts to nearly pop out of her top. Lenny leans in and whispers our order.

The waitress returns a few minutes later carrying a small tray with six shot glasses—two with some type of blue liquor concoction, two blood red, and the last two are taller shot glasses with half blue and half pink liquor.

My eyes widen and I look over to Lenny. "I can't do all these."

"And you won't. Half of them are mine." He slides the tray in between us and points to the blue shots. "Start with the Masturbating Smurf." He points to the dark red shots. "Then to Cherry Popper. And lastly, chase it with the Battle of the Sexes. On the count of three… two…."

"Wait! Lenny, I can't drink all *that*. I will be on the floor drunk."

"Fun, remember ... plus, they contain more sugar than alcohol. Trust me, Emma, you will be fine. One..." he says, downing the first one.

Okay, maybe he is right, I can do this. I watch him slam down the empty shot glass. *Well, here goes.*

I down all of the shots. The last one is sweet, but the burn of the alcohol causes me to choke.

"That one was strong..." I manage to choke out.

"Yes, foreplay is always sweeter than the rough sex," he says and hands me another drink; this one is clear and bubbly.

Inhaling sharply, I push the drink back at him. "No, I'm good, thank you."

"It's a vodka soda-water."

"No..." I say, already feeling a buzz rush to my head.

"Emma, it's light on vodka. The purpose is to look like you're drinking. The shots were just to relax you and take the edge off."

I take the drink from him and sip. It is refreshing and I don't really taste the alcohol.

"Thank you."

"Now, go have *fun*," he says with a snap of his fingers as he turns and leaves me at the bar.

Alone.

An odd feeling of awkwardness starts within me but suddenly a sense of freedom overcomes me. *I have no one to answer to.* I close my eyes and let the beat of the music reverberate through me. *Yeah, I can do this tonight ... alone and free.*

I look up to the balcony level, searching for anyone who looks familiar. Lenny is right, there is an indescribable sensation knowing that no one knows who I am.

If I could be anyone else, who would I be? I eye all the masked faces whizzing around the room, colors of black, red, and gray all blending together and causing my heart to race in my chest.

I decide to make my way to the second level. *If I am going to be anyone, who will I be?*

"I would be *fun*," I say out loud as I turn up the stairway.

I walk past a couple pushed into the corner and tiptoe around them as they grind one another in a frantic lust. I feel their heat blazing my own nerve endings.

I enter the second floor and take one of the seats at the small island bar. A gentleman wearing a charcoal gray and white suit slides up next to me. His brown eyes openly drift to my cleavage from behind his mask.

"Can I buy you a drink?" he asks in a thin voice, his eyes never lifting to mine.

"No, I'm good," I say and tip my full glass in his direction.

"Then I will buy you the next one," he says as he leans in closer and slicks back his blond hair.

"Thank you but really I'm good."

His eyes flash darker and he snatches my hand. I watch in slow motion as he raises it to his dry thin lips.

"You are the most beautiful woman here. And I just want to buy you one drink," he says and attempts to kiss my hand before I sharply pull it away.

I land a hard smack across his sleazy face and watch his eyes widen in shock.

Stunning myself at my own quick reaction, I dig deep and square my shoulders. "I said no," I snap and turn my attention away from him.

Adrenaline courses through my veins and I take a deep breath before taking a few large gulps of my drink, emptying my glass.

I watch the waitress walk in my direction, just as someone sits down next to me. *This fucking guy again,* I think as I ask her for another soda vodka. *Can he not take a hint…? Hell, that wasn't even a hint. I couldn't have been more direct…*

The waitress brings over my drink and a man's voice says, "I got it," to the waitress.

I set my pocketbook back down. "I said n—"

"Can I get a beer, too? Thanks," he says, cutting me off.

His voice is deeper than the other man's and my stomach tightens.

"Now ... don't hit me. I was going to buy myself one anyway," he says.

The sound of his voice echoes in my subconscious, sending sparks of lightning to my brain. *Yes, I know that voice... But it couldn't be him ... he's a phantom of my imagination.* No, no, no! Surely the booze has officially hit me.

The waitress sets his beer down and I watch his long lean fingers circle around his bottle. *No wedding ring – good. Good for what, Emma?* I think, mentally shaking myself. This is just another one of my sexy dreams. *Mr. Ocean Eyes is NOT REAL.*

"You know, most girls just say thanks when a man buys them a drink," he taunts.

"Well, most men ask first... Thanks for the drink."

I watch from the corner of my eye as he takes a sip. My body heats with the memory of my dreams and how his lips feel against my bare skin. *I have to be dreaming...*

"You are welcome..." he says, and his arm rubs against mine, causing a spark to shoot through my body.

"God, is it hot in here ... or is it — ?"

I feel a feather-like touch glide up the inside of my wrist, causing me to catch my breath. I look down to see his finger draw a lazy path across my skin. *Oh, shit...* A wildfire ignites up my arm. My head spins from the heat and lack of air.

Air...I need air...

I turn and run to the stairwell. Weaving around people on the dance floor, I head toward the garden.

As I open the door to the garden, the cool air rejuvenates me. *Yes, I needed air.* I feel my senses clear immediately. *That wasn't him...* It is my buzz making me imagine his voice. *Yes, that's it, see, your imagination is getting the best of you again...*

Walking past the rose vines, I follow the broken stone path. I pass the water fountain, wanting distance between me and the party, and head to the maze. As I round the first wall, I find a stone bench and take a seat.

"Hello."

I shudder and move back on the bench. Looking up, I meet a pair of perfectly colored ocean eyes. *It is HIM!*

"You are jumpy," he laughs.

"I ... I didn't hear you," I say, feeling heat rise to my cheeks.

"You ran off. I wanted to make sure you were okay," he says, sitting down beside me. I can't help but notice an overwhelming confidence which resonates from him.

I must look like an idiot sitting here just staring at him. I try to look away, but I'm powerless. I watch as his sexy lips form words that my ears are not hearing. *Oh, the things that mouth has done to me...* I think as my steamy dreams rush into consciousness, causing my body to heat with anticipation.

He lightly glides a finger across my knee to get my attention. "Are you okay?"

"Yes ... um ... I just needed some air... I'm not much for parties..."

"I'm not one for parties either," he says as he flattens his hand on my knee and begins drawing small circles with his thumb, sending sparks up my leg.

I try to distract myself from his touch. "If you're not a party person ... why did you come tonight?"

"I could ask you the same, but to be honest, it sounded ... fun."

"*Fun,*" I repeat.

"Yes... Plus, if I didn't come tonight. I wouldn't have met you," he says and turns to kneel down in front of me. My entire body ignites, and I hold my breath as he leans forward. *Is he going to kiss me?* He glides his hands up my thighs.

My stomach tightens as he cups my face. *Yes ... he is going to kiss me...*

"You are so stunningly beautiful," he says as he leans closer.

I can be anyone tonight, I remind myself. I lean in. "You're not too bad yourself."

He smiles. "I'm glad you think so." His breath tickles my cheek. "But what is it about you? I feel like ... I will die if I don't kiss you —"

"Then do it."

He presses a feather-light kiss against my lips, teasing me.

I part my lips with an intake of breath. *More, I want more.*

The blues of his eyes flame with shards of apple green. Need, pure and hot, flashes in his eyes as he looks down at my parted lips. He suddenly crashes his lips against mine.

My head spins with desire. *God, I've wanted him … forever…* He moves his hands down to my waist and pulls me to the edge of the bench. *Oh…*

I gasp, tipping my head back. He kisses a path downward as sparks of pure desire coil to my center, creating a dying hunger. *I have to have him.* I suck in a ragged breath as a moan escapes my lips. With every kiss, his mouth teases as he licks across the top of my breasts, causing wetness to pool and my body to quiver with need.

Reading my body's reaction, he reaches for the hem of my dress and lifts it to my thighs as he explores with his needy hands, making his way back up my legs.

"I feel like you're my drug … and I'm going to die if I don't have you…"

He pulls me closer to him and I feel his cock press against my thigh, my sex swelling in response. *Yes, I will die if I don't have him…*

His long fingers dig into my bare ass and he lets out a muffled growl as he kisses the tops of my full breasts.

"You're going commando, beautiful."

"Yeaahhh," I manage to get out. *Thank heavens for my last-minute wardrobe change.*

In one measured step, he lifts me up and turns me, pressing me against the opposite stone wall. *Oh my…* The bare skin of my shoulders makes contact with the cold stone, creating a shudder to explode within me. *Yes … I have to have him…*

His body covers mine as he claims my mouth with his. He hunches his large frame to match mine as he fervently unleashes his tongue to meet mine in a duel of lust, both with equal need. The need overtakes him, and he quickly pulls away. His eyes flame as they stare into mine.

I watch as the blues and greens of his eyes dance as if they complete one another. As if our souls are dancing.

***

He drops to his knees. Placing his hands around my ankles, he glides up, painfully slow, as he pulls my skirt up. I feel his eyes burn my skin. He stops at my thigh and leans in to kiss a path upward as he reveals my nakedness.

A moan escapes as my sex feels the coolness of the air. His hot mouth moves slowly across my hip as he licks and teases with his tongue, causing a burning sword to pierce through me. I lay my head back, feeling weak with need.

His breath flicks across my skin. "That's the sexiest birthmark I have ever seen," he says as he tongues across it.

My hands search for something to hold on to, to steady myself on my shaking legs. "Ahhh..." I moan and find my fingers entwined in his thick black hair.

He bends my knees with his hands, lifts me as he sets my legs up on his shoulders, cupping my bare ass and holding me in place. He buries his face into my wetness. My toes curl with the sensation as he flicks his tongue over my clit.

A pulse of pleasure waves through me, causing me to involuntarily rock my hips upward to deepen his contact. *Holy ... shit...* He sucks on my bead and I feel my body build higher.

I moan louder and close my eyes as I buck my hips upward, creating a rhythm. He shifts and balances me against the wall and his wide shoulders. With his free hand he reaches for my mouth and covers it, silencing me.

He circles my entrance with his other finger, teasing as he builds me higher. *I'm ... I'm ... going to die...*I think with overwhelming need just as he flicks my clit with his tongue, sending me over the edge, and I let out a muffled squeal of pleasure.

Chapter Thirty-Six

CHANCE

I SCAN OVER the dance floor again. *Fuck, Emma is nowhere in sight*, I think as my body tenses. Having advanced training makes it easy to read and memorize people's body language, which I hoped would help me navigate around this party, though I thought I would have found Emma by now. I walk around and take a sip of my beer. I bring my focus back to the VIP area and take a seat at the bar. *Where is she?*

My phone chimes and I pull it out; The Lieutenant, with a subject line that reads: *Urgent*. I shove my phone in my pocket. *Not fucking now… I have to find Emma first…*

I shake my head. It boggles my mind – *why is Rick being so careless with Emma and out of all nights, tonight?* Something unsettling rattles my nerves, but I just can't put my finger on it. Maybe, if I find her, I can be sure she is safe and that would put my mind at ease.

During my last meeting with the men, we were able to learn why Rick was on edge. Dean uncovered some intel about what Rick has been hiding on the guarded floors and it looks to be a black market of some kind, like a sex trafficking operation. That explains Rick's reputation for hiring all the young women and that fucking folder. *Bastard… Men like that have a special place in hell.* And according to Dean's source, Rick screwed up on a shipment, causing his client to be rather unhappy with him, and from the sound of it, that client is even wealthier and more ruthless than Rick.

I spot James in his light gray suit. He is sitting on a barstool with Jenny in a matching colored skintight dress. She pushes herself between James's knees and pulls him in for a kiss. I watch them, as the two of them make no hesitation of their display of affection. I'm happy for James but I can't stop the squeeze in my chest. *I wish one day I could openly demonstrate my desires with Emma.*

I turn and make my way around the crowd and enter the back hallway. Rounding the corner, I spot Rick as he makes his way to the back doors that lead to the club's main office. *What is he doing?* I follow him a few steps to see Lenny, Nash, and two other men I'm unable to identify.

I stop in my tracks. *Do I follow them, or do I continue my search for Emma? Fuck...* I groan, knowing that I need to follow Rick, because the sooner I expose him, the sooner I can free Emma from this nightmare.

EMMA

I STRAIGHTEN THE skirt of my dress as heat burns my cheeks. *Thank you, mask, for disguising my naivety.*

His broad frame closes in as he encircles his arms around me and pins me against the wall, causing lightning-sharp heat to course through my veins. His eyes find my lips and I feel his need vibrate within him. He crushes his lips onto mine, vigorously and hard. The sweet and tangy taste of my sex heats my center and I feel my body ready again. *Holy ... hell...* I think as I deepen the kiss.

"Helllooo, is anyone out here?" a man's voice sounds and is followed by footsteps and a girlish giggle. "Hellloooo," the man's voice repeats, sounding closer this time as if just around the corner.

I pull away and a frustrated sound unhinges from his lips.

"Oh… They are going to catch us…" I breathe out as he leans his forehead against my shoulder.

Taking a leveling breath, I reply to the calling man. "Hello."

He frees me from our position and I push off the wall and turn to run my shaking hands down my dress to smooth out the wrinkles, just as the couple rounds the corner to where we were.

"Aw … hello," the man says, dressed in a light gray suit with a lanky woman connected at his hip, wearing the same color gray with a matching feathery mask.

"Sorry, we were just going for a walk," I lie.

"We?" the man questions.

I turn around to find myself standing alone. *What the hell…? Where did he go?* I shudder and pull off my mask and make a complete circle. *He was real,* I think as my body trembles.

"Miss… are you okay?" the man questions.

I straighten my shoulders. "Yes, ummm, I meant me. Or I." I turn back to face the couple. "Sorry, I had a few drinks. I just needed some air." I nod my head shakily. "I was just on my way back now … going home." I giggle nervously.

The man looks over to the woman before walking past me to the maze. "Well, we're going to get lost in this maze, maybe even get a little … lucky," he says with a chuckle, and they disappear around the corner.

My body begins shaking. *Where did he go? Shit, it felt real. He was real…*

Not knowing what else to do, I start walking back to the club. *I'm sure the hell not going to look like an idiot and call out to a man, even if I know he felt real.* I feel like a bigger idiot now as I realize I don't even know what to call out. I don't even know his name.

Damn, Emma, what would Ms. May think now? That is, if I even tell her. I won't, she wouldn't believe me anyway. Hell, I am having a hard time believing what just happened myself. I can still feel his lingering touch on my skin, arousing my senses, making me hyperaware of everything around me. That alone tells me it was real.

Chapter Thirty-Seven

CHANCE

I TAKE A drink of my black coffee as all the guys stare at me after I unloaded all the events from last night. I had been able to breathe easier the minute I read James's text last night saying he saw Emma heading back to the penthouse.

"So you're saying Rick just let you walk in on the meeting?" asks Dean.

"Yeah, well actually I didn't walk, I more stumbled in when he saw me sneaking around so I acted inebriated. I just can't believe he didn't dismiss me to leave."

"I told you that the masquerade was a distraction. I knew something was going down," James snaps. "But you didn't listen to me. You were more concerned about—"

"Fuck off, James. I followed them to the meeting, didn't I?" I snap back.

"Good call there, Chance, but you are sure you didn't catch the names of the other two men?" Andy asks for the fourth time.

"No, Rick never addressed them by name. And I didn't recognize them with their masks on. I'm sure, mask or no mask, I didn't know these men. They made demands that Rick deliver the *PACKAGE*, or they were ordered to take a life for a life…"

"*A life for a life?* Could the package be a person—or persons?" Dean asks.

"I would say person ... one for one," Andy interjects.

"Yes, I agree. Chance, is there anything else you remember about them—you know, something that stands out?" Brett asks.

"Seriously, guys, I would have told you. There was nothing noticeable about the men other than the conversation."

Andy stands up. "Okay, so let me get this straight: We now know that Rick is working an underground sex trafficking ring. And he pissed off the wrong client by not delivering a package that we are going to assume is a person. And somehow Rick allowed you to listen in on the whole meeting?"

"Yep," I say.

"So ... the pissed off client who has been threatening Rick is giving him forty-eight hours to deliver the package? But they never said exactly what or who the package is?" He raises his left eyebrow.

"No, they didn't say exactly, but a *who* is the only logical answer. And yes, I'm guessing, but it has to do with the sex ring, so it only makes sense."

"So at this point, all we know is something is about to go down, but we don't know what. They didn't say what would happen if he didn't deliver?" Andy says as he begins to pace. "They were just ordered a life for a life..."

"Whose life ... Rick's?" Dean asks.

"Again, I think that only makes sense that they are threatening Rick's life."

"We all must remain on high alert. Let's meet at midnight after we do some more digging. Hopefully we can come up with more. Chance, keep an eye on Lenny, I have a feeling he knows more than he is letting on," says Andy.

"Yes, I agree. Also, Rick just sent me an email to meet with him this morning. It was vague, just said, 'We need to talk.'"

EMMA

"MS. ANDREWS," Brutus says from across my bedroom.

I squeeze deeper into my pillow-top mattress and cover my head with my pillow. *No, no, no. I don't want to get up and face reality.*

"Ms. Andrews, you must get up. Master is in one of those moods today," Brutus snaps with urgency.

Oh, shit... I quickly sit straight up in bed.

"Give it to me real, Brutus. How mad is he?" I ask, preparing myself for the worst.

Brutus's eyes fog over without a word. *It's bad, I know it. If Brutus is worried...*

"Brutus," I say. *He is holding back!* "What is it?"

"My dear, I hate to worry you, but ... well ... he has torn apart your study. He kept repeating, 'I won't do it. I won't hand it over.' Do you know what he is talking about?"

"No, I don't. I was thinking he would be mad that I didn't find him last night."

Shaking his head, he squares his shoulders and regains his composure. "Okay, very well, I wish to request you to join him to defuse the situation."

"Okay, I will be down in fifteen."

BOOKS, FOLDERS, AND loose papers are thrown all around my study as if a tornado made a path through it. *You have to be kidding me.* I scan the room in search of Rick, but he is not there. *Damn, where did he go now?* I begin picking up books and scattered pages that litter the floor as I make my way to my desk. *What has gotten into Rick?*

With a heavy sigh, I set the pile down onto my bare desk. I look at my belongings which are now scattered on the floor, as if Rick made a swipe of his arm to clear it. I bend to gather more of the mess.

"What happened in here?" I hear Chance's voice call from

the doorway.

Popping my head up, I meet Chance's chocolate gaze. A warmth flames as I watch his sexy frame lean over to pick up a few books and make his way over to me.

My stomach suddenly drops with memories of last night. *Chance... What about Chance? What would he say if I told him what happened last night? Hell, was last night real?* It felt real...

"Earth to Emma."

I force myself to focus. "Oh, sorry. What did you say?"

Amusement shines in his eyes. "I asked you what happened in here."

My heart skips a beat. *God, he is handsome...*

"Em..."

"Oh," I say as heat waves up to my cheeks. "Brutus told me it was Rick. But I don't know where he is now."

His eyes darken before he looks down.

I stand to reassure him. "I wasn't here... Brutus asked if I would help him," I say quickly.

"Help him? Why would you want to help him?" he snaps and his eyes drill into mine.

His question takes me aback. I haven't seen this side of Chance. I don't cower like I did with Rick, though; instead, I feel like he is bringing out a strength in me. I plant my hands on my hips and square my shoulders.

"Yes, help him."

Chance drops the stack of books on my desk with a loud thud and throws his hands up.

"A man that is so disgusting to you. A man that doesn't even value your safety." He gestures about the room. "An asshole that—"

I pull at his arm. "You will not call Brutus names... He is the sweetest and most loving man. And he is like family to me—" I say, tearing up.

"Brutus? I thought you were talking about Rick."

I shake my head. "No, the only reason I would help Rick is if Brutus were to ask me."

He wraps his arms around me and pulls me into his warmth, causing my head to spin. *God, this feels … so …right…* I think as I inhale the smell of earthy male. "I'm sorry," he says.

I wrap my arms around his waist and bury my face into his chest. *I needed this – the feeling of comfort he gives me.* I inhale his scent again, letting it soothe my nerves. There is something about being in this space which causes my guilt to slowly crawl up my throat.

Shit, I'm going to tear him apart when I tell him about last night … but do I tell him if I don't even know if last night was real?

He pulls away and I feel an invisible wall go up between us.

"Did Brutus say why Rick was pissed off?"

I hug myself to ease the ache of his absence. "No."

He brings his focus to the destruction of the room. "Rick did a number in here. Let's get your books picked up first, then go and find Brutus to see what he has to say about Rick."

"Okay…"

Chance's phone rings. He pulls it out then makes an irritated sound before he silences it and slides it back in his pocket. No more than a minute later, it starts buzzing again and he ignores it.

"Do you need to answer that?" I ask.

"Nope," he says and changes the subject. "By the way, I put the book I borrowed on your desk. So it should be here somewhere."

"Did you like it?" I say as excitement soars through me.

He turns and picks up some more loose papers. "It was good but you're right, it wouldn't be my first choice…" he trails off.

I look over at him and follow his line of vision to the torn piece of paper in his hand. I stop in my tracks… *Please, please … don't be my journal.* But I know it is, and I can only imagine what Chance is reading.

"The confusion of the yearning is equivalent to the burning," he says and glances up. His eyes burn hot with need.

My cheeks heat, knowing the poem is about the need I feel

for him.

"Emma, is this about me?"

I walk over, wanting to hide my vulnerability, and reach for it. He pulls it out of my reach and steps closer to me. I feel his breath tickle my cheeks as he leans in.

"Emma, is this about me?" he asks in a husky whisper.

I'm not ready to face what I'm feeling for him… Not right now…

"Please, Chance, can I have it back?" I say shyly.

He smirks. "I guess if you won't tell me, then I will have to keep it … for evidence." He folds the tiny piece of paper and slips it into his pocket.

Embarrassed and a bit shocked that he is keeping it, I turn on my heel and leave him and all the mess behind as I walk out the door.

"Where are you going?" Chance calls out.

"To find Brutus."

I WATCH CHANCE stride into the living room. His face changes from sexy mischievous to disappointment as his eyes land on Brutus.

"As I said, Ms. Andrews, I don't know what got into Master this morning."

I bring my focus back to Brutus. "Thanks anyway. Do you know where I could find Rick?"

"I believe Master is in his suite now. But I don't know if I advise you to join him in there…"

"Brutus, just earlier you wanted my help with Rick."

"I agree with Brutus on this one," Chance chimes in.

I straighten my spine. "I decide if I am going to…" I say, challenging Chance.

He raises his eyebrows in response.

Before second-guessing myself, I step around the two men and march in the direction of Rick's suite.

Halfway down the hallway, I start to rethink my decision. *What am I doing?*

I reach for the door handle and hear heavy footsteps behind me.

"Emma, wait—"

Chapter Thirty-Eight

EMMA

I DIVE INTO Rick's bedroom and press my back against the hard door. Blinking, I'm surrounded by pure blackness. My heart pounds viciously against my rib cage. I hold my breath in hopes of slowing it down. I am enveloped in a humming wave.

Quickly, I search my memory for the location of the bathroom. Fear courses through my veins and every ounce of my body starts to pull me in that direction. *What am I doing? Turn ... run ...* But my body continues forward, slowly and deliberately.

Suddenly, a blinding light pierces my eyes, causing me to shield my face. Someone pulls me into the bathroom. I squeal in fear.

"My love, it's just me," Rick says as his breath whispers across the back of my neck, causing a chill to dance across my skin. He chuckles as he places his hands firmly on my hips, steadying me. As I slowly peel my hands away from my face, the warm glow of the bathroom seeps into my vision, welcoming in comparison to the cold blackness of the bedroom.

The bathroom is decorated in elegant colors of creams, surprisingly more feminine with all the rose gold color orchids that are strategically placed about the space. *Oh, my ... it is breathtaking.*

I walk over and touch the velvety petal of an orchid. "They

are so beautiful."

"My mother … had a love for them," he says in a whisper. I turn to him. *His mother…*

Rick stands in the middle of the bathroom in a pale-yellow towel that is wrapped low on his hips. My eyes run down the V cut of his abdomen. I follow the path of black hair that covers his chiseled abs. I drink him in as I follow a lazy path up to his well-sculpted chest. *Yes, Rick is sexy … in his own right.*

I force myself to look away. *Shit, Emma, what was he talking about…his mother…?* "Rick, I'm sorry —"

"Don't," he says.

I watch him move closer to me from the corner of my eye and I feel my body heat.

"I don't want to be talking about her. I want to know what you are doing in my room," he says, his voice throaty.

I bring my attention back to him, feeling his nearness. He is most definitely an attractive man. I admire his caramel-colored skin in contrast to the pale yellow. *Oh, holy hell…*

"My love," he says in a lower husk. "Is there something I can help you with?"

"I, umm…" I feel heat spill into my face. "I was just checking on you," I say, nearing the doorway that enters the bedroom but stop abruptly.

He takes a step away from me. "Love, I made you a promise."

I take a deep breath to control my thundering heart. I focus on his feet just as the towel drops. A wildfire explodes to my core. I close my eyes and force myself not to look.

"Your room was dark, and I couldn't see where I was going," I blurt out, looking for a distraction from my thoughts.

"Is that why you jumped when I grabbed you?" he says, followed by the sound of a zipper.

I open my eyes. "Yes."

Rick pulls on a simple dark-gray shirt, leaving the front unbuttoned. He quickly pulls me into his arms and begins smoothing my hair. The heat and familiarity of Rick calms my storm.

He opens the bathroom door and the light spills into the dark space. He takes a few more steps and flips on the light — lighting every corner of the room.

I examine the space and see a suitcase lying open on top of his bed. I look up at him. "Are you leaving again?"

Shadows linger in his green eyes. "Yes, I was going to talk to you at supper tonight. I will be gone for three days this time." He gathers my left hand in his. "I regret having to leave you. I wish to have you by my side ... always," he says and raises my hand to his lips.

My heart melts with an emotion that causes whatever hatred left for Rick to dissolve. The emotion twists into something lighter, less heavy. I feel as if my heart isn't sinking at the bottom of the sea. *I'm not drowning.* But somewhere in the layers of my heart, a grain of sand rolls into the tiniest pearl.

My chest squeezes. *I know I have love for Rick ... but it's the first overwhelming emotion —*

His warm lips land on my finger where my ring is absent. "Where's your ring?"

I feel color drain from my face. "You told me to take it off... Lenny put it in my room —"

"Go get it," he demands, and I make a quick exit.

The last time he was mad at me in my room, I ended up with evidence of his anger, I think as I walk into my bedroom. My stomach squeezes.

I quickly open the nightstand drawer to retrieve my ring and slide it back on. Turning, I see that Rick followed me. *Oh, shit...* My body begins to shake in anticipation of his anger.

"Come," he orders.

I stand in front of him but don't meet his gaze.

He takes a deep breath. "This ring is important to me, Emma... You must never take it off — *ever.*"

"Yes, I'm sorry... I was just doing what you wanted last night."

"No, I never said for you to take it off."

"You didn't tell me to take it off? But —"

"No, I never said that," he says, taking a deeper breath. "I told you it was my mother's, and before she died, she told me ... whoever picks this ring will be the one she approves of... It's just..."

I look up at him; everything about the ring makes sense now and I meet his eyes, which are full of pain. The image of a scared little boy comes to my mind's eye. "Rick, you don't need to explain ... I promise, I will never take it off ... ever again..."

His eyes flame with life, and he leans down, softly landing his lips on mine — silently thanking me.

I feel the string tug on my heart and the tiny pearl grows. I open my lips — welcoming him. He wraps his arms around my body and pulls me against the length of him. *This Rick... I can love for life —*

A sound at my bedroom door brings me back to reality. *What are you doing, Emma?*

I push at his chest, breaking the kiss, and look to the doorway to see no one.

"One day, love... One day your heart will be all mine."

CHANCE

SITTING IN RICK'S office, all I can do is stare at the pen and paper in my hand. *Why did Emma not listen to me and go into Rick's room? She purposely ignored my request and now I can't stop wondering what in the hell happened in there.*

"Mr. Fletcher, are you paying attention?" I hear Rick say and force myself to remain in control.

"Sorry, long night."

"Yes, I wanted to talk to you about that," Rick says and leans back in his chair. "What do you remember about last night?"

I shrug my shoulders and act indifferent. "Not much... I got drunk. My girl left me for another man," I say with grit. *Fuck, it's half the truth...*

He stands and walks around the desk and claps me on the shoulder. "Sorry to hear that," he says with surprising empathy.

"Yeah, thanks…"

I watch him walk to the bar and pour out two whiskey neats. He hands one to me and sits back on the edge of the desk. *This is not like Rick…*

He tips the glass in a silent toast before downing it in one swallow. I follow suit and hand my glass back to him.

"This is why this is hard for me … the things we do for love," he says, returning the now empty glasses to the bar. "The love of a woman." He pauses and then takes a seat behind his desk. "The paper I have in front of you is a contract. In the contract, it states that you will be agreeing to protect Ms. Andrews for the remainder of her life. I have made compensation for you and it will make you a very wealthy man. There are plenty of little details in the contract, but the main points are stated on the front page."

Looking down to the paper, I try to wrap my mind around what this is about. *This isn't how I expected this meeting to go. I thought we'd talk about last night, but this… Emma for life…*

"Sir, I … I don't understand," I say, trying to make out one word on the front page.

"I trust you with her safety, Chance. And if something were to happen to me, I need to ensure she will always be safe," he says in a cool, controlled tone.

"Of course," I reply, connecting the dots. Whoever is making demands of Rick, Rick plans on refusing them. I know without a doubt I will do anything for Emma, even if she doesn't love me in the way I love her.

"Sir, what if she doesn't want me to?"

"She has no choice in the matter. She already signed her contract," he states matter-of-factly.

Without question … I sign.

I KNOCK ON Emma's door. *Emma signed to have me protect her for life…* A thousand questions flood my mind all at once but the minute her door opens, everything fades to the background.

"Oh… Hey, Chance." She smiles.

"We are starting training at the gym tonight. Are you in?" I blurt out.

She takes a step back. "Umm, yes … when?"

"Can you be ready in ten minutes?"

"Yes."

"Good." I turn toward my room as I try to convince myself everything will be fine.

FIFTEEN MINUTES LATER, Emma comes out of her room wearing the gear I provided her as a disguise. Her hair is pulled into a dark brown wig with a baseball hat to hide her face and she has on the gym clothes I picked out. She looks nothing like herself. *But God … she is still beautiful* –

"Well … how do I look?"

"It will do," I say and wave in the direction of the gym.

On the way, I answer question after question that she drills at me. From explaining how Rick is in a meeting with one of the men, to Brett running security cameras, and why we are using the disguise to make sure Rick's goon squad doesn't recognize her.

Walking into the gym, I hear her squeal in delight, causing my shaft to jump as I think of other ways to make her sound like that…

"Andy is not here; he is the one at the meeting. He will be here tomorrow, but James will be here helping tonight."

As if I summoned God himself, James strolls out, holding his arms wide. "It is I, James."

"Well. It is I, Emma," she laughs and plays along.

"Okay, that's enough, you two. Andy just texted and said we have roughly thirty minutes. So we better get started."

EMMA

Confusion of the yearning
Is equivalent to the burning.
It's all too concerning,
How one man is deserving,
And the other is disturbing.

Setting my pen down, I bury my face into the pillow. *What the hell, Emma?* I'm trying to rewrite the poem Chance confiscated, but now it's taken on a whole new meaning. *What am I going to do? How can I love two men ... and Mr. Ocean Eyes? No, Emma. He is not real. Chance and Rick, on the other hand, they ... they are very real.*

Chapter Thirty-Nine

EMMA

MY PHONE CHIMES, notifying me of Lenny's reminders for the day. I press the ignore button and take a seat at my desk, bringing my attention to the loose pages of my journal. *Shit, how am I ever going to get this organized again?*

My hairs stand on end and I feel as if someone is watching me. I quickly scan the room, seeing no one. *What the hell?*

My phone chimes again and I jump. I look down to see Chance's name.

"Hello."

"Hey, Rick called me into a meeting this morning. You need to take this time to go down to the gym. James will be there shortly to pick you up. So be ready."

"Okay, I thought Rick left—"

"He said he is leaving after the meeting."

"Okay, can you tell James to meet me in my study?"

"I will. Oh, and Emma, remember what I taught you."

"I will," I say and mentally prepare myself for training without Chance.

"It's important for you to learn strategy against other opponents."

"Of course."

"Okay, then ... I will see you later." He hangs up.

I set my phone down and look up to see James entering.

"Good morning, beautiful, you summoned me?" he says with a broad smile.

"Hi, that was quick. Chance just called. I can be ready in five."

"I was already on my way… I figured you would be hiding out in here. I couldn't wait to get my chance to pin you down," he says with a wink.

My cheeks heat and I look down to my feet. "I … umm —"

"Shit, Chance wasn't kidding about how shy you are. And damn, it's cute. If I didn't have a girl already, you would be in trouble —"

"I'm going now," I say and quickly head to the exit.

"Make it quick, girly," he says as he picks up an apple from my desk and takes a large bite.

CHANCE

I WALK INTO Rick's office and take a seat. *God, I hope Emma remembers her training.*

"Mr. Fletcher. I want you to meet Mr. Jarret Gage. Mr. Gage, this is one of my top men here," Rick says.

I turn in the direction Rick indicates. *Gage. Where have I heard that name?*

"Mr. Gage stopped by for a … surprise visit this morning. He is one of my most valuable … clients," says Rick.

I stand to address the man and stop as my eyes connect with The Lieutenant. *What the fuck? Client? The Lieutenant is a client of Rick's?*

The Lieutenant doesn't miss a beat and walks over to me, takes my hand, and shakes it.

"It's good to meet you, Mr. Fletcher, " he says with an overly firm handshake.

"Um, yeah … it's good to meet you, too, Mr. Gage," I say, taking a minute to gather myself.

"You see here, Mr. Fletcher ... Mr. Gage has requested to check in on our ... merchandise," Rick says, sounding uncharacteristically nervous. *Merchandise? Is he talking about his trafficking ring?*

I wait for The Lieutenant to respond. *What am I missing? How is The Lieutenant a client – ?*

"Yes, I just made a quick stop to check on how *business* is going for Mr. Stevens, but we can talk about that another time," The Lieutenant says, waving it off.

I watch as he shifts his stance, as if he is going it bolt for the door. My gut tells me he doesn't want me to know he is here – that he didn't intend to see me. *But why?*

"But I thought you wanted to talk about the merch –" Rick questions.

"No, that will be another day. I must be going now," The Lieutenant states as I watch him exit the room.

I look back to Rick and stand, but he holds his hands up, signaling for me to stay. "Chance, we need to talk."

Chapter Forty

EMMA

A PAIR OF perfect blue-green eyes look up to me and I stumble on the mat in the gym. *Holy, hell…I* think as Mr. Ocean Eyes walks in our direction. *He's … fucking… real!*

A tall man with short black hair walks up to James and I drink him in as his lips form inaudible words. *Oh shit … his mouth,* I think, remembering exactly what that mouth is capable of. Heat floods my cheeks.

Mr. Ocean Eyes stares at me as if he is awaiting a response. "I, umm… I … what…?" *Shit, what were they talking about?*

James's throaty chuckle catches my attention and I look to him as the heat in my cheeks begins to sting.

"Sorry —"

"I was just introducing you to Andy. But you must not have heard me," James says.

"Andy … umm … yes, sorry."

"James is going to work with you on the bags, teaching you technique. Then I will work with you on take-downs and defenses," Mr. Ocean Eyes, I mean, Andy says.

I shake my head to clear it. *Focus, Emma. Obviously, he doesn't recognize you.*

James claps his hands together, causing me to jump. "All right, girly, this way," James says and tugs on my arm.

"WHERE ARE YOU?" I hear James ask.

I wipe the sweat off my forehead and turn to face him. "What?"

"Your mind is not here," he says and points at the bag.

I can't stop myself from peeking over my shoulder; I can feel Andy watching me.

Embarrassed that I was caught, I look down at my feet. "Sorry, I'm just not used to training without Chance."

Andy's voice whispers low from behind me, causing a chill to run down my spine.

"Chance will not always be there to save you." Without warning, I feel my legs leave the mat and I land flat on my back.

Before I have time to react, a powerful body positions overtop me. He grabs my wrists in one large hand and straddles me, pinning my hips down with his thighs. With his free hand, he covers my mouth, silencing my scream before it escapes my lips. I buck my hips, trying to free myself, but I'm unable to move his solid frame. My eyes blur from the panic that starts to rise from my chest.

He leans down. "Always know your surroundings, analyze your attacker for any weakness," Andy whispers in my ear.

I take a slow, steady breath. *Think, Emma, what's his weakness?* Analyzing my position, I hear James cursing in the background. Andy shouts, "Go take a hike." I hear James's footsteps storm away. *Oh fuck ... think... What did Chance teach you? Breathe.*

I use every bit of my energy and buck my hips hard. *If I can just throw his weight off,* I think and buck harder. He releases his hold to catch himself before he falls flat on his face. I seize the opportunity and roll onto my side. I feel his weight shift and I bring my knee up—kneeing him in the balls and causing him to curl. I duck and slide out from under him. Jumping to my feet, I come to a defensive stance.

"Well done," he says with a grunt.

He makes his way up to a standing position. "I see Chance has been training you well, but for further demonstration, you don't have to kick us in the balls. You can just say it ... so we know you would be using it as a defense in that position."

"That is what you get for taking me by surprise," I say and wipe at my watery eyes.

"Attackers don't announce when they are going to attack," he says with his hands on his hips.

"So now you have all these rules. Like I can't fully defend myself and ... and you can just attack me ... whenever ... because 'no attacker' —"

"Did you not hear me before we started?" he says, irritated.

"No, I..."

"An attacker will take you out when you least expect it; when you are most vulnerable."

I open my mouth to respond, just as he advances on me and sweeps me to the floor. I quickly adjust my position; when he pins me, I have one of my legs free.

"That's better... Now get yourself free."

I turn and rock myself underneath him in an attempt to wiggle myself free. His hand lands on my hip, firmly holding me into place. The heat of his hand sends a tingle across my skin, stopping me. *Shit...* I think as the sensation drives to my center. He pins me deeper into the mat. Warmth radiating from him awakens all my senses. The smell of pure woodsy male assaults my nose, causing me to feel dizzy with need.

His weight shifts and he hovers over me. "Emma?"

I blink myself back to reality and nod my head.

"Are you okay? Did I hurt you?"

"Um... No..."

"You went limp, I thought you blacked out."

"Oh... I..." I stutter, watching his eyes question me.

He looks down my body and I begin to heat like a wildfire everywhere his eyes touch.

He stops and I watch his eyes flicker to life.

"You..." he says in a deep, low tone.

My chest squeezes and I lose all words as I dive into the depths of emotions that flash through his eyes. First, shock to disbelief, and then the green of his eyes flame with hot desire. *He knows it was me ... that I was the woman in the mask.*

I feel his hand cup the curve of my thigh and he runs his

thumb across my birthmark. His eyes lock onto mine. I watch as the blue depths of his eyes vibrate with longing. I'm completely powerless in stopping him as he lowers his lips to mine.

Do I even want him to stop?

He softly brushes his lips against mine, so light at first it feels dreamlike. Then his lips come crashing down, causing a thousand sensations to explode inside me. His lips part and he licks the outline of my bottom lip. A surge of desire slams hard to my core. *I… I have to have him…* My soul vibrates with need.

A loud crashing sound startles me, and I break the kiss.

"Fuck!" Chance's angry voice echoes off the gym walls.

No, no, no... my head screams and I push Andy off me with little effort. I look in the direction of the sound to see Chance storm into the men's locker room.

I stand and run to the locker room just as James exits.

"I don't know if I would go in there if I were you. My man is … well, he is pissed."

"I have to talk to him."

James steps in my path.

I glare up at him and give him my own silent warning. He holds up his hands. "I'm just saying. I have never seen him like that. Don't say I didn't warn you." He moves away from the door.

Before I can change my mind, I swing the door open and march in. I immediately find Chance pacing the tight space. "Chance, I can explain."

"Emma, not now."

"But I need you to understand—"

"I'm pretty sure I understand what I saw."

"No, you don't understand." I step in front of him. "It's not what you think—"

He stops. "What about the other night when you ran into Rick's room? What happened when you went in there?" His eyes cloud with pain.

"What? You know that I have no choice but to be with Rick."

"You're saying there are no feelings there for Rick," he says, pointing to my heart. "Nothing?"

No, he can't know. How can he know? I feel the color drain from my face.

"That's what I thought," he says and heads toward the door.

I run quickly to stop him, pressing my back against the frigid metal door. *He can't leave ... not like this.* "Fine, yes there is a stupid tiny part of me that cares for Rick, but it doesn't even measure to what I am feeling —"

"And what about Andy? Who else is there, Emma?"

"No one, Chance; there is no one, and Andy..." I look down as my cheeks burn. "You wouldn't understand."

"Understand what, Emma?"

"It happened before I understood it was real and how losing you could —"

It a low, barely audible tone, Chance whispers, "What happened?"

I hold my breath. *How do I tell him what happened with Andy and have him understand that I thought I was dreaming? God, it sounds pathetic just thinking about it...*

"What happened?"

My heart sinks and I avert my eyes. "Well, I met him a while ago... Brutus said that no one was in the penthouse ... then there were these recurring dreams that I kept having about him ... so I thought I made him up, you know, in my head, which wouldn't be the first time... So when I met him again at the masquerade party ... I thought I was —"

"Damn it, what happened?" he says, causing me to jump.

"We hooked up at the party. Well, I mean, I think that's what you would call it... We didn't have sex, but —"

"Move," he snaps.

"Chance, I didn't —"

He pulls at the door, causing my feet to slide against the slick floor, leaving me behind on shaking knees. I regain my control and make my way back to the main gym, just as I hear a loud crash.

"Fuck, man, bring it down," James shouts.

I look to see a stack of punching bags strewn about the mats. James is standing in between Chance and Andy with his arms up. I watch as Chance paces the floor and Andy sits at a bench with his arms crossed at his chest.

Chance says, "Fuck, James, you don't understand what he is doing."

"It wasn't like that. I wouldn't do that to her," Andy says and meets my eyes. I feel a pulse of energy course through me. *What are they talking about?*

"Wouldn't do what?" I ask and look to Chance.

His wild eyes lock on mine and I instantly burn in their depths. "Forget it," he says and storms out of the room.

I look to James, who raises his shoulders as if he is also at a loss. I turn to Andy, only to watch his back disappear in the opposite direction through a doorway.

"Wait ... Chance," I say and make my decision to chase after him.

I find him in the hallway waiting for the elevator. "Please, Chance... Wait..."

"What? Please tell me... What is it, Em?" he says sarcastically.

I focus on my hands in front of me. "Chance, I'm sorry I ... I didn't understand —"

"Didn't understand what, Emma, that it would hurt me? Do you have any clue as to what you are doing? Is this all just a game to you?"

"No, I never wanted to hurt anyone, especially you."

"Then maybe you should just leave me alone."

The elevator doors open, and he steps in. *Think, Emma, I need him to understand what he means to me. Tell him you love him...*

"Chance, wait..." I slide between the closing doors and step in. "I've been having these dreams about Andy and I know you don't want to hear that, but I was starting to think I made him up in my head. So when I saw him for real, everything was a little — blurred together."

"Stop, you're not helping."

"No, I need you to understand. What I mean is ... Chance, I'm falling — "

The elevator doors open, cutting me off. I start to turn my head to see who is entering the elevator but Chance spins me around and pushes my back against the wall, covering my body with his. Just as I start to open my mouth, his lips crush mine, silencing me.

Heat electrifies through me and I seize the moment to show him what I have been trying to tell him.

I match his fierce intensity with every ounce of me. My body shakes with need. I lift my arms to wrap them around his neck and he catches them in midair and pins them behind my back, deepening the contact of our bodies.

Oh my...

The elevator pulls to a stop. *Shit, I forgot... We are not alone...*

An all too familiar voice says, "I'm glad to see you working it out with your woman, Mr. Fletcher, but next time take it to your apartment," Rick says.

I freeze in fear. Chance lifts his head and tucks mine into his chest. "Yes, sir... Sorry — "

"Very well, good day," Rick says and exits the elevator, leaving us behind.

Chapter Forty-One

EMMA

I TURN TO Chance as I hear the sound of the deadbolt of his apartment door sliding into place. He pivots and gives me his full attention, causing a flutter in my chest. Everything fades away in that moment, leaving only Chance and me in his room.

My breath catches. Chance's chest labors for breath and his eyes demand my obedience. *Oh, shit...* My body quivers as his eyes run up the length of me. His smoldering gaze lingers on my breasts, making my nipples harden and rub against my lacy bra.

I watch as he strides on his long, lean legs in my direction. My body reacts, shaking me to my core. My heart squeezes in my chest.

My head spins as I think of the intensity of what he means to me. He feels like home, my safety, my heart.

He stops inches from me and peers down at me.

"Emma..." he says as his need rings through me.

I lunge at him and land my lips onto his. I pour my heart out to him. I am desperate to give him everything—my need, my longing, my fear, my pain, everything. I lay the broken pieces of my heart at his feet.

His strong arms cling around me like a lifeline, erasing it all and leaving behind just us. He lets out a growl and pushes my body flush to his long frame. My nipples ache as they tease against his powerful chest.

He breaks our lips and takes a deep labored breath and

leans his forehead to mine. "We have to stop, before I can't..."

I pull back and stare into the depths of his chestnut eyes. "I don't want to stop... I want you, now," I say, barely recognizing my own voice.

His eyes darken and he lets out a shaky breath as he lowers his lips to mine.

His slow kiss is not like the vigorous explosion from before; this ... this feels different. His hands cup my ass, squeezing as he picks me up. I gasp and part my legs as he positions me to straddle him. *Oh, shit...* He carries me the few feet to his bed and slowly lays me down as he makes his way over me.

I slide my hands under his shirt, wanting to feel more of him. I explore his body, slowly and hungrily. His thick muscles flex under my hands. *Oh, dear God...* His hands tease, making their own discoveries, leaving a burning fire in the wake of their path.

My breath hisses as he slides a finger lazily across my bare stomach. I fist the back of his shirt. He sits upright and positions his thigh against my sex as he pulls his shirt over his head with one arm and tosses it to the floor.

Heat burns my cheeks as my eyes look over his chiseled upper body. My eyes connect with his and I feel as if I am giving him a piece of my heart in that moment. I suck in my bottom lip.

I love you, Chance...

As if he's able to read my mind, he starts slowly kissing my body, unwrapping my clothing from my body like I'm a cherished gift.

Once I'm undressed, I watch as he removes the rest of his clothes. I quiver with unbridled need and he lowers his naked body down on top of mine. At every point of contact, electricity sparks, sending waves in a direct line to my sex, dousing me in wetness.

His large cock jumps against the tender of my inner thigh, causing me to moan. Closing my eyes, I feel his large finger trace the entrance of my mouth. I part my lips and begin sucking on his salty finger. I arch my back with the intimate sensation as he strokes his finger erotically against my tongue.

A low vibrating growl resonates from his chest. "Emma, I'm trying to take this slow for you but you're breaking whatever restraint I have."

I meet his eyes and push my hips up to match his need. He trails his wet finger down my body and holds on to my hip as he repositions himself between my thighs. I feel the thick head of his cock teasing against my clit. I moan again.

"Emma... I—"

"I NEED YOU," I pant breathlessly.

In one fluid motion, he enters me, and I feel a twinge as I stretch to adapt to his size. After the twinge subsides, a pulse of pleasure waves through me.

He props himself up on one elbow and encircles my hips with his other arm. He lifts me to deepen our connection as he slowly begins to thrust.

As perfect as it feels, I'm not entirely sure what to do. Again, he can read my mind. He says, "Glide your hips up, like this..."

Using his arm from behind me, he grinds my sex up to meet his. I moan and buckle my legs around his hips.

He picks up the tempo and thrusts deeper, faster. I match his strides, feverishly. I scream as I shatter into a thousand little pieces from my climax. Simultaneously, his body shudders with his own release.

"Emma, I love you."

Chapter Forty-Two

CHANCE

"HEY, MAN..." JAMES says before stepping in my path.

I don't meet his eyes; instead, I lock my blazing eyes on Andy. *What the fuck is he doing with Emma? Is he using her?*

"Buddy, we need to stay a team ... for her," James says and plants a firm hand on my chest, stopping me. *Fuck, he is right ... it's the only way to protect her.*

I look down to control my emotions. "Fine. Andy, we need to talk ... alone."

"I'm not going anywhere," James says.

I move my glare to James then and take a step back. *Fuck, he's not going anywhere and I need to talk about fucking Rick...*

"Yeah, we do ... need to talk," Andy says before standing. He walks in the direction of his kitchen, then stops just before the door and turns. "Well, you coming?"

Sitting around the table, I look to see James avoiding any type of eye contact. The animosity in the room is palpable.

James finally breaks the tension. "Where is Emma?"

I stare into Andy's eyes before saying, "She is sleeping in my apartment right now. But we have something more important to go over—Emma's safety. My lieutenant is involved."

James stiffens and looks back and forth between Andy and me. "What are you talking about? And who the fuck is—?"

Andy holds up his hand and stops James. "This is the first

time I'm hearing anything about a lieutenant. So give Chance the opportunity to explain why we haven't heard anything about him until now."

I sit back in my chair. "Okay, it wasn't until this morning's meeting when I put the pieces together. My lieutenant assigned me to investigate Rick. I wasn't understanding why I was assigned to this case, but at the meeting with Rick, The Lieutenant, a.k.a. Mr. Jarret Gage, was in Rick's office. Rick was acting unsteady and nervous, even The Lieutenant acted odd, as if he did not want me there. When Rick brought up 'the merchandise,' The Lieutenant made a hasty exit. After he left, Rick told me that The Lieutenant has been threatening him about a package... That was when I pieced it all together. The Lieutenant has been asking a lot of questions about Emma... Then I remembered I'd seen the name J. Gage somewhere. It's on Emma's contract with Rick. Not to mention, Rick also pushed for me to sign a contract—"

James interrupts, "Wait ... hold up. A contract? How far behind am I?"

"Just give Chance a minute... What are you talking about, what contract? What exactly did you get yourself into, Chance?" Andy asks.

I sigh. "My meeting yesterday was about a contract to protect Emma if something happened to Rick. To protect her for life ... then last minute this morning I get a text from Rick to come to his office. That's why I wasn't able to bring Emma down—"

"Did you sign it?" James asks.

"Fuck, yes! I signed it," I snap and direct my full attention to Andy. "Nothing is going to happen to her."

"We need to call Dean and Brett in," Andy says and stands up.

"That sounds good. There is more, but I will grab everything I have in my apartment," I say as I stand.

James also stands up. "I'll go grab the guys. That will give me a second to process what the fuck is going on."

"Okay. Hey, Chance, hold up a second," Andy says.

James puts his arms across his chest. "If you two are going to go at it when I'm gone, you better have killed each other by the time I get back."

I mentally size up Andy, then turn back to James and nod.

James doesn't move until Andy also nods in a silent agreement. "Good, I'm off... Behave," James says and exits the room.

"First, I don't know exactly what Emma has told you—" Andy says.

"She told me everything," I say and just the thought of him touching her causes anger to rise up, but I swallow it back down. *For Emma's safety...*

"I want you to understand, I don't agree with the two of you because of your past. You should keep your distance from Emma. I don't want to see you repeat history. Especially not with ... Emma."

"Why? So you can fuck her? Is that all she is, a fuck to you?" I snap and clench my fists.

"No, it wasn't like that, it was ... It doesn't matter now," he says, his eyes glazing over before he blinks and regains his composure. "Things are getting complicated enough... We should both take a step back."

"It's too late. She is my responsibility; I can't walk away."

"Chance, so was Libby... She was also your responsib—" Andy growls.

"Don't you dare say her name ... this is not the same."

"Libby was also your responsibility to protect and where is she now, Chance?"

"Shut the fuck up, Andy. I'm done here."

"NO! Chance ... you're not! Not until you get it through your thick head what is at stake here... Where is Libby now?" Andy walks to stand in between me and my only way out.

My eyes go blind to my surroundings and a bright smile appears in my mind's eye. *Libby's smile ... so full of life.*

"WHERE is she NOW?"

"Dead ... she's dead."

"She was your responsibility to protect and you led her to

her end, all because she loved you... She trusted you."

"Wait, how did you know—?"

"You don't remember me?"

I stare blankly at him.

"You met me once, before I was deployed, remember?"

"Deployed?" Suddenly everything becomes clear. "You're Libby's brother..."

"Was," he corrects me. "I *was* her brother."

EMMA

I BOLT UPRIGHT. *Shit, where in the hell am I?*

The tender throb between my legs comes rushing in and heat crawls up my cheeks. *Chance...*

I look around the tiny space. Chance is gone. I throw myself back into the bed that smells so much like him and I cover my mouth with my hand. *My mouth, Chance claimed as his...*

I roll to my side in an attempt to find a clock, with no such luck. I force myself to crawl out of the comfort of the bed. *Where could he have gone?*

I gather my garments and set them on the bed. *Where did my cell phone go?* I think after not finding it in the pocket of my shorts. *I know I had it.*

Dressing quickly, I scan the tiny space. I hear a chime from underneath the bed. *My phone...*

I kneel down to look under the bed. I reach to grab it and hit a button, causing my screen to light up—illuminating the dark space.

In black ink written across a box are the names *Rick/Emma*. *What the hell is this?*

I pull at the box and roll my eyes. "Didn't anyone tell you not to hide things under your bed? That's the first place people look."

I sit down and lift the lid. My eyes dart to the first

document with my name written on the top line followed by: Contract of Protection.

What in the actual fuck?

CHANCE

AFTER CATCHING UP the other men, I sit back and absorb the scrutiny the guys throw at me.

Dean says, "Why didn't you tell us about The Lieutenant before?"

"I thought we were a team," Brent snaps.

"You guys, The Lieutenant was supposed to be classified... I thought I was just watching Rick for embezzlement. But when I started thinking The Lieutenant had a hidden agenda, I wanted to be sure ... because it was to be *classified.*"

"James, I want you to go with Chance, I want all the information you have on Rick. So we can work as a *team*," Andy orders.

"Okay," James says and slaps my back. "The boss made his order; let's go."

We stand and turn to the exit.

"Bring Emma back with you," Andy says in a low tone.

I WALK INTO my apartment and stop mid-step, causing James to slam into me.

"What the hell, man?" James yips.

In the middle of the floor is my box with all the intel. The papers lay scattered in a circle. *Emma... Fuck, where is Emma?* My heart hammers.

"Emma!" I call out. *God, let her be in the bathroom.* I call her name out again. No response.

"Please tell me this is not your info and that she didn't find it and now she is gone."

I ignore him and pull out my phone. I call her cell and it

starts buzzing near one of the stacks of papers. "Shit…"

I rush over to see what she was looking at. "Shit … Shit! Fuck ME!" I say and kneel down in the middle of the circle.

"Let me guess … she figured…" James's voice murmurs into the background as my mind races and I try to connect the dots. *What am I missing?*

I lean in and pick up a pile. *Where is my contract?*

"Chance, don't touch a fucking thing," James demands.

Why would she take that one?

I hear James typing on his phone. "Do you know where she would have gone?"

"No."

My mind scans the papers once more as James talks on the phone in the background, "Yeah … she's not here… But she has to know something… See you in a minute."

His footsteps sound as he walks up behind me. "Andy and the others are on their way."

I am too distracted to answer.

"Chance."

"Yeah," I snap and look up to him staring at his phone, just as the rest of the group walks in.

Andy snaps out orders. "Put it down … this is her way of putting it together."

I scoff at him. "No shit, but I'm at least trying to find where she—"

"I'm already on it…" James says.

"James is hacking into the security cameras with his phone. Is this everything?" Andy asks, waving to the display on the floor.

"No. My contract is missing."

"What was in that contract?" Andy asks.

"Mainly it's about protecting Emma for her lifetime, even if something were to happen to Rick."

"We have a problem," James says as he pales. With shaky hands, he lifts his phone to us. A black-and-white image of Emma carrying her pocketknife appears as she enters the foyer of the penthouse.

Chapter Forty-Three

EMMA

I SHUFFLE THROUGH the folders on my desk. *There … there it is.* I open the folder to my contract with Rick. I set Chance's contract down next to mine and scan both as I flip through the pages for the fine print.

I scan mine again: *J. Gage no longer has possession of any property and is considered void of any future payments in regard to E. Andrews. Total debts paid.*

Who the fuck is J. Gage…? I flip a few more pages on Chance's contract.

Well, shit… I think, scanning the fine print on his contract.

J. Gage is void of any future payments in regard to E. Andrews. Rick Stevens is now the sole beneficiary in regard to E. Andrews's possessions. If Rick Stevens is not able to hold such responsibility, all possession and ownership transfers to Chance Fletcher. J. Gage has no right or ownership to such possessions.

I knew I heard that name before – Gage… I feel like a concrete block hit me in the head. I had a Jarret Gage as a sponsor in the foster care program. *But how is he connected to Rick, and how do I owe him a debt?*

"Ms. Andrews, are you feeling well? You're pale." I look up to see Brutus in the doorway of the study.

"Umm … yes. Brutus, is Rick still here?"

"Why, yes. I believe he is in his suite –"

273

"Thanks," I snap and march past Brutus. *I'm getting answers … now.*

I CLENCH THE cold handle of my dad's pocketknife. *He will answer me even if I have to force him to.* A shiver runs down my spine as I turn the handle to Rick's door and enter into blackness. Fear stabs at me. *No turning back!*

A sound resonates from the bathroom and I inch closer. Three steps in and I feel a breath against my neck. *No one is here, just Rick in the bathroom,* I reassure myself.

Grabbing the icy handle to the bathroom, I turn it slowly. The image of my mother's naked body lying on the floor as she gasps for air fills my head. My tears blur my surroundings and I narrow my eyes, only to see my mother's slit throat spilling out red liquid.

A sound echoes off the bathroom walls. *What is that? It sounds like someone gasping for air.*

My mother's gasps. No, not mother's. She's dead… Rick!

I step through the doorway to see the once white floors splattered with blood, red hot. *No, please, God, no…*

My eyes follow the sound to a figure lying in a pile of bloody flesh. Blinking to clear my vision, I see Rick's mangled body and I drop my knife.

His face turns to me and his breathing shallows. I look over his body; he lies halfway on his side with his leg twisted in wrong angles. His upper body is bare, and his once tanned skin is now colors of red from the blood gushing from multiple cuts in his chest.

I rush to him and drop to my knees. I run my hands over the hot sticky liquid to find the main source of the bleeding. *Stop the bleeding, Emma, or he will die…* I find a jagged hole in the center, letting out a river of red. Covering the hole with my hands, I lean up to stop it.

"Love … runn—" Rick says in an airy hiss. I look down at his tortured and twisted face. The green fire of his eyes now clouded as his skin starts turning gray.

"Rick—"

The air from my lungs squeezes out as someone pulls me to my feet. Rick's lifeless body blurs in my vision. A scream trembles out of my lips before a large gloved hand silences it, followed by the smell of chemicals, making everything go black.

CHANCE

WHEN WE ALL reach the penthouse, I immediately begin barking out orders.

"James, do you see her? Where is she now?"

"No, I don't see her. She has to be in one of the rooms. There are no cameras installed in them yet," James explains.

"Chance," Andy says in a whisper.

I ignore him. "Dean and Brent, check the office. James, check the kitchen. Andy, come with me."

They all take off in search for Emma—all but Andy. *If she attacks Rick and doesn't succeed, he will kill her.* My body buzzes with adrenaline.

Andy's firm hand lands on my shoulder. "Chance, if we don't stop her, she's not ready to kill—"

"Yeah, I know. Rick will kill her."

"Yes, he will."

A muffled scream bounces off the hallways that lead to the bedrooms. Andy and I make a run for it, taking the stairs two at a time. *Hold on, Emma... I'm coming.*

Reaching the top of the stairs, I run past the living room and round the corner of the hallway. A frame of a man stands at the entrance of Rick's room with Emma's limp body over his shoulder, causing me to halt. A shadow is cast across the man's face but even from this distance, I know it isn't Rick. This man is much taller and leaner. He turns to the right side of the wall and reaches out as he fumbles.

Andy darts around me. "Come on, Chance." Snapping me back to action. *Fuck...*

A panel slides apart, revealing a hidden door and causing light to spill into the hallway. Andy and I chase the man in an attempt to reach Emma.

Just before he enters the pathway, he faces us. I freeze. *What the fuck?*

A sick smile crosses the man's face and he waves a key. "Good luck getting through," he says and slams the door, leaving us behind.

"Fuck!" Andy slams his fist into the wall and turns to me. "What the fuck, why did you stop?!" He storms past me.

I turn and follow him to the others, who are now at the end of the hallway. I listen with half an ear as I rack my brain...

James snaps his fingers in my face. "Hey, snap out of it. Do you know who took her?"

"Yes ... it was The Lieutenant."

T. L. MAHRT

within the Shadows

Prologue

JARRET GAGE

I FIST MY dick in my hands and squeeze. *Fuck, she looks just like her mother,* I think as my eyes take in the sight of her long blond hair spilling across my lap. My eyes rake down her unconscious body sprawled along the black leather seat, causing my dick to stiffen harder. *Yes, she looks just like that fucking whore.*

A little girl's icy blue eyes, Emma's eyes, look wild as she weeps, shaking her mother's cold dead body…

Why would a child ever cry for their whore of a mother…?

I blink a few times, bringing me back to the present. I think of how those same icy blue eyes wept for that motherfucker Rick. I was messy with killing Rick, much like I was with her mother, Elaine. *Blood, there was so much blood —*

The sound of Emma shifting on the leather seat causes me to look down. She lets out a groan and I pluck a syringe out of my jacket pocket. *Shit, not yet,* I think as I stab the needle into her thigh. I look up to the driver from the rear seat of the blackout Mercedes.

"Lenny, how long until we get there?" I call out.

"Thirty more minutes, sir."

"Good, she keeps waking up."

"Sir, what are you going to do about Chance —"

"Shut up, Lenny, and let me worry about him."

"It's just, he knows your real name —" *No one knows my real name…*

279

"I said shut the fuck up!"

My chest aches. Why the hell did Rick introduce me to Chance? *Fuck, I didn't want to have to take Chance out… but now… I don't have a choice.* Rick had to fuck everything up by falling for Emma and refusing to hand her over… Did Rick ever make the connection between Emma and Elaine? Fuck him, he's disposed of now… *It's about time Rick paid his debts and Emma was the perfect price.*

I reach my hand up and finger a silky lock of her hair that lies across my crotch as the image of Elaine rolls into my subconscious. The same icy blue eyes sparkling up at me. *She was a manipulative little fucking whore,* I think as my stomach squeezes. I pet Emma's head absentmindedly and I think of all of the lies Elaine weaved to make me believe she loved me.

I trace the lines of Emma's full lips and my dick stiffens harder. Yes, I'm going to take her just like I took her mother.

And if she's a good girl, she will be paying her mother's debts with these fuckable lips.

With

Emma Series:

Follow us on Facebook or Instagram for upcoming
new releases on Emma Andrews's story.
Check out for more releases tlmahrt.com

About The Author

T. L. MAHRT is a former business owner, where she utilized her education in cosmetology, barbering, and massage therapy for several years. She was raised on and is currently living on a farm in Nebraska, where you can find her running barefoot in the countryside with her loving husband, inspiring children, and massive dogs.

After having her son, who was born with cerebral palsy and DYRK1A Syndrome, she made the life-altering decision to stay home to care for her two children and pursue her love of writing. She has a passion for romance and poetry, where her overactive imagination, along with her adventures and upbeat lifestyle, drives her motivation for her writing.

T. L. Mahrt has a thirst for knowledge and is currently working on her Bachelor of Applied Science in Communication Studies degree.

Made in the USA
Monee, IL
24 May 2020